I0578491

Fine Line

INKED DUET – BOOK ONE

PERSEPHONE AUTUMN

BETWEEN WORDS PUBLISHING LLC

Books by Persephone Autumn

Bay Area Duet Series

Click Duet

Through the Lens

Time Exposure

Inked Duet

Fine Line

Love Buzz

Insomniac Duet

Restless Night

A Love So Bright

Artist Duet

Blank Canvas

Abstract Passion

Devotion Series

Distorted Devotion

Undying Devotion

Beloved Devotion

Darkest Devotion

<u>Standalone Romance Novels</u>

Depths Awakened

Sweet Tooth

Transcendental

<u>Poetry Collections</u>

Ink Veins

Broken Metronome

Slipping From Existence

<u>Standalone Horror Novels</u>

By Dawn (published under P. Autumn)

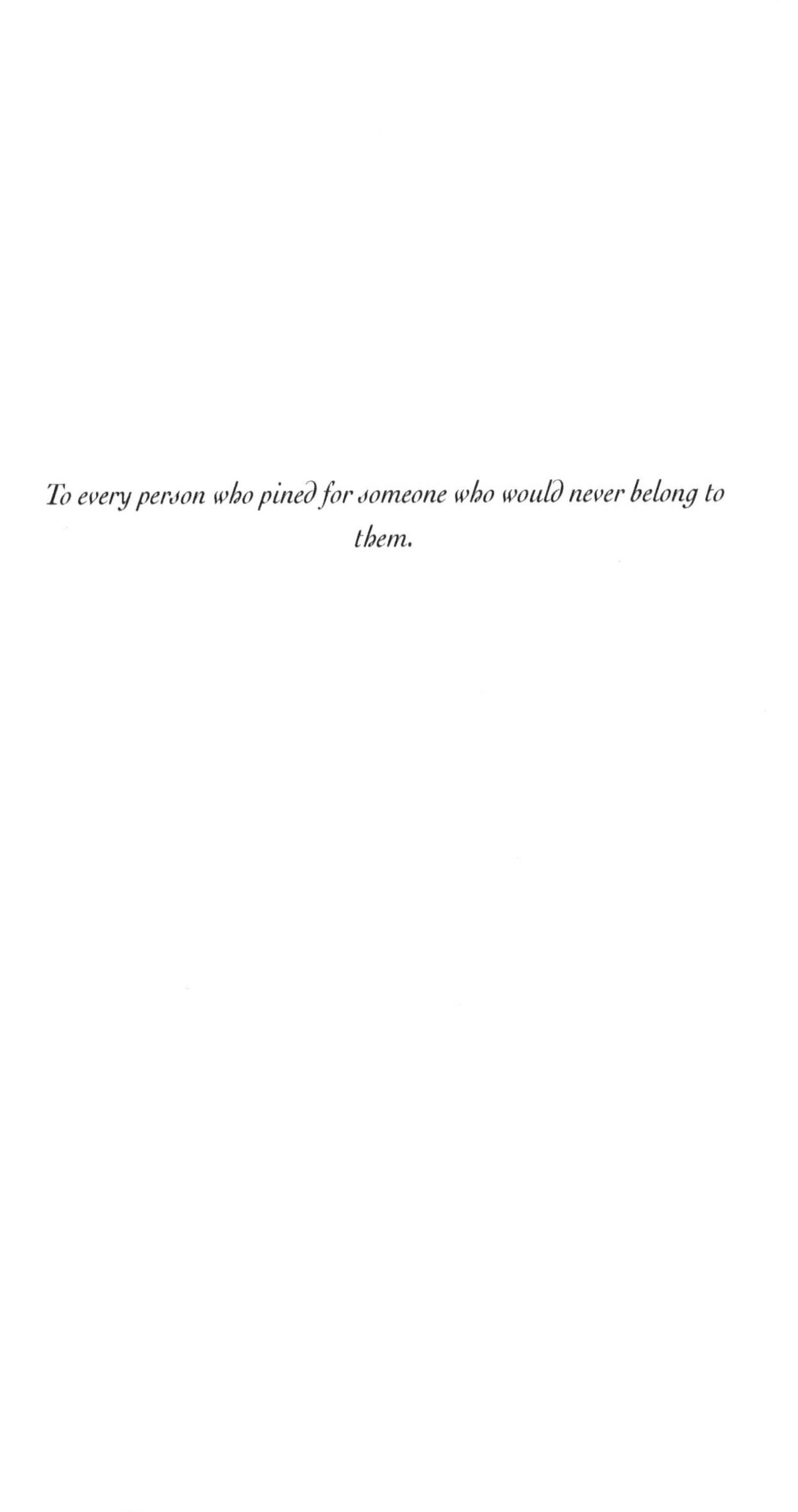

To every person who pined for someone who would never belong to them.

PROLOGUE

JONAS

Fuck, she is beautiful.

My best friend. The woman I have loved for years. The woman walking down a sandy aisle in a stunning black lace wedding dress. To another man. A man she has been in love with since high school. A man I will never compare to in her eyes.

And although he broke her heart at sixteen, she never fell out of love with him. Gavin Hunt. The luckiest fucking man on the planet. The man at the end of the aisle holding his breath as she steps closer.

I close my eyes and duck my head. "Can't watch this," I whisper to myself. Because watching the woman I have loved for nearly ten years marry the love of her life is… painful. No, not painful. Debilitating. Excruciating. Crushing.

Fuck, I can't breathe.

Don't get me wrong, my heart holds so much happiness for Cora. Glad she reconnected with the one person who puts a permanent smile on her face. The person who constantly sparks her laughter. Who fulfills her in a way no one else has been capable of for years. As gut wrenching as it is to admit, Gavin is Cora's soul mate. Her *person*.

Once upon a time, I filled the role. For a phase of her life, I was her person. Was the only guy she leaned on for comfort or support. The one person she laughed with and spilled her heart to.

Cora is my best friend.

But she isn't mine.

And as much as it hurts, she never was.

I dreamed of the possibility, but she always tossed out those "you really are a great friend" lines with such ease. Every time she did, it twisted the knife in my heart a little more. Tore away another piece of my soul that I willingly handed her.

The day I met Gavin, the day we all hung out and I witnessed their chemistry for the first time, I threw in the towel. The energy in the room shifted and I witnessed it ebb and flow and magnetize them closer to each other. Cora and I have an undeniable bond, but it paled in comparison to the connection she and Gavin share.

In her own way, Cora loves me. Just not the way I love her.

But now, I have to let her go. Finally let go of the daydream. Let go of the possibility I stood a chance.

Snapping my attention back to my best friend, I

memorize her happy, tear-stained face as she speaks her vows to Gavin. Tells him he was her first everything. *Twist.* Jokes how their middle names are similar—another sign they're meant to be. *Deeper. Twist.* Explains how life isn't worth living without him at her side. *Shattered. Split in two.*

I stop watching. Stop listening. My heart balls into a fist, clenches hard, and crumbles to ash beneath my ribcage.

Fuck, this hurts.

As badly as I want to rise from my seat and walk off, I won't. I will not ruin my best friend's wedding with my own selfishness. Won't squash her happiness with my sorrow. I am not that guy. Not an asshole. Or a prick.

Everyone laughs and cheers. I follow suit, not knowing the reason. My laugh floats off with the Gulf breeze, hollow and empty. Like my heart.

I chance a glimpse at my best friend. Bad timing. The moment I choose to look up, Gavin envelops her in his arms and kisses her the way I have always imagined doing. The way that haunts my dreams often.

The next hour trickles by in a fog. Shelly and Erin hang out with me. I remember to smile and laugh and joke at the right times. I hide the fact I am a withering mess inside. People scurry into the reception hall and tell everyone to prepare for the newlyweds. Reminding us to hoot and holler as they enter the room.

I clutch my stomach. *Think I am going to be sick.*

Cora and Gavin enter the room and everyone erupts in

cheers and wolf whistles. I mimic with an empty smile plastered on my face.

An emcee announces the newly married couple before soon inviting everyone to eat. I fall in line with Shelly and Erin. They must sense my mood. Neither of them has said a single word to me. Can't blame them, I am shit company right now.

Shortly after everyone eats, Cora and Gavin share their first dance as husband and wife. I struggle to keep my meal down, but I do. I refuse to make a scene. Refuse to ruin this for her.

Shelly elbows me and I peer over at her. "What's up, Shell?" But the moment I look up at her, I realize why she nudged me.

Cora.

The most stunning bride I have laid eyes on is standing beside me with a glowing smile. "Hey you," Cora says. She extends a hand out to me. "Will you dance with me?"

Fuck. *Fuck, fuck, fuck.*

I swallow and work to dislodge the lump in my throat. "Yeah," I choke out before coughing to clear my throat. "Yeah," I repeat.

She smiles as I take her hand and follow her to the dance floor. At the center of the room, she spins around and holds me like we are at senior prom. All too briefly, serenity blankets me. Cora in my arms has always felt *right.*

But she isn't mine. And I need to continue to remind myself of such facts.

"Are you okay?" she asks as we sway back and forth.

I won't lie to her, but the truth hurts like a motherfucker.

"Not so much." I lock eyes with her. "But I'm working on it. Promise."

"Jonas..." Cora smiles, but it doesn't touch her eyes. "Sorry. I wish..."

She doesn't continue. The way she holds my gaze tells me everything she wants to say, but can't articulate the words. How she wishes things could have been different. How she hopes I find happiness like she has. And how much she loves me. *Like family.*

I shake my head and close my eyes. "You have nothing to apologize for, Cora. Life has happened how it's meant to. You're my best friend," I whisper the last line and she lays her head on my shoulder. Closing my eyes, I soak up her warmth and relish the moment. "And no matter what, that will never change."

"Good." She laughs, but it isn't the unrestrained laughter I have heard countless times. "Because you're stuck with me, mister."

For the first time in months, a genuine smile stretches my cheeks and I chuckle. "Glad to hear it." I take a deep breath and swallow my pride. "Sorry if I haven't been the best party guest."

She lifts her head from my shoulder and I hide the disappointment threatening to flash across my face. "Jonas, you're here. That's all I care about. I don't give a damn what anyone else thinks. We've been through a lot over the years. If you're sad" —she studies my eyes for a minute— "you're entitled to feel how you feel. I'm sorry if this is hard for you. Being here."

The song changes and we continue to sway around the dance floor. Her sparkly green eyes stay on my hazels. The sweet, earthy floral notes of her perfume float in my nose. I will miss this. Miss the little pieces of her I have familiarized myself with over the years. But I need to do right by her. I need to remove the guilt she holds captive because of our bond.

I need to let her go.

For her. For me. For our future friendship.

Swallowing down the pain, I vow to myself to never let her feel guilt or sadness because of me. If I can't have her any way except for friendship, I need to accept it. Accept it and move on. Accept it and allow her to be happy.

"Cora..." I stroke my knuckles over her cheek and sigh when she closes her eyes. "It isn't easy." When I remove my hand, her eyes open and lock on mine again. "But I wouldn't miss this day for anything. The day you told the world you found love and grabbed it by the horns." She giggles and my pulse jump-starts. "Glad I could be here to witness this day. I will always be here. Even if we're just friends."

She lays her head on my shoulder again and snuggles closer to me. "My best friend," she whispers. "I love you, Jonas."

My eyes glaze over and I am damn glad she isn't

looking at me right now. Glad she won't witness the dam of tears threatening to unleash. I hug her tight. "I love you, too," I croak.

We dance for the rest of the song in silence. When it ends, Gavin walks over. "May I?" he asks. He fucking asks. If I were in his shoes, I would probably yank Cora out of my arms. But he doesn't because he knows her heart. More than anyone.

I step back and smile. "Yeah, man." I offer Cora's hand to him. As she breaks from my embrace and glides easily into his, I take a deep breath and release her. "Congratulations. Not gonna lie, I'm envious as hell. But I'm happy for you both."

Gavin glances down at Cora and the smile on his face tells me he knows he is a lucky son of a bitch. And he will never fuck this up with her. He faces me again. "Thanks, man. Means a lot. To me and Cora. Don't give up." I flinch for a second and he registers my confusion. "Hard as it is to believe right now, the right woman is out there waiting for you. You're a good guy. Fate won't fuck you over."

Okay. Wasn't expecting that. And I have no clue how to respond. So, I remain tight-lipped.

Cora lays her hand on my bicep. "How could no one love you." She meant it as a rhetorical, so I don't answer her. "I have a sneaking suspicion you'll meet her soon."

"Her?" I ask.

"Yeah. The one. The girl who will seal all the cracks and make you whole again."

This conversation is one of the most awkward of my life. The woman I have loved for almost a decade, the woman I am trying desperately to let go of, is telling me I will soon find the love of my life. Which is supposedly not her.

I nod. "Hope so. I'm gonna head out." I hug Cora and memorize her one last time. We will see each other again, but it won't be the same. Then I extend my hand to Gavin. He shakes it, then surprises me when he pulls me in for a hug.

"Thanks for taking care of my girl when I didn't," he whispers in my ear. "Don't give up, man. Your girl is out there, waiting."

We break apart and I smile softly. "Congrats again." I turn on my heel and head for the exit, keeping the torrent of emotions at bay.

Outside, I bend at the waist and slap my hands to my knees. *Your girl is out there, waiting.* Yeah, I don't see how that's possible. I hop in the Jeep, crank it to life, and let the tears fall.

I hope you're right.

ONE

AUTUMN

The flashing yellow arrow torments me as I patiently wait for a break in the oncoming traffic. With everyone and their mother out shopping, on the hunt for the deal of a lifetime, the roads are busier than usual.

Black Friday has never really been my thing. People swarming like agitated bees. Fighting over electronics and shoes and kitchen gadgets. Don't get me wrong, I love shopping. Love buying cute new dresses, fun graphic tees, and endless accessories. But you will never find me throwing punches for *things*.

"Caution" by The Killers spills out the speakers as the traffic breaks. I turn onto the side street and hook a sharp right into the tattoo shop parking lot. Driving to the far rear corner, I back into a space, hop out, and enter through the back door.

"Hey, chicky. Busy?" I ask Penny as I wander over to my booth.

She smacks her strawberry bubble gum and shakes her head. "Nah. But it'll pick up soon. You have a packed schedule today."

Mentally, I throw devil's horns with my hands. A busy schedule equals a kick-ass payday. "Awesome. Thanks, Pen."

"Just doing my part," she says as she ambles over to my booth. Penny gives me the rundown on my appointments as I resanitize my workspace. The distinct smell of disinfectant fills the air as I wipe everything down. For years now, this has been my favorite smell. Most of my appointments today are small jobs. A name here, a symbol there, and a couple photos to etch in ink.

"Well, I appreciate you."

Penny curtsies, tilts her head, and smiles wickedly. She is a freaking nut, which is why we are such great friends—and roommates.

"How was the wedding?" Penny asks.

She met the bride and groom months back when they came in to get tattoos. When they invited me to their wedding, she frowned. Think she was a little butt hurt, especially when I didn't RSVP with a plus-one. She will get over it.

"Gorgeous," I say with a green man on my shoulder. "Lots of black." I laugh. "But mostly beautiful. They're so sweet together. I envy their connection."

The green devil pops back up on my shoulder as I recall Cora dancing with a man other than Gavin. Remember the way he held her. The glints of his profile in the dim, shimmering lights. He held her closer than a typical friend. But the exchange didn't faze Gavin whatsoever.

A balloon swells in my chest as I reminisce over the way he held her. I ache to be wrapped in someone's arms like Cora was his. To feel wanted and loved without effort.

"Yeah, they seemed pretty inseparable when they came in. How does one nail down a guy like that?" Penny asks as she rests her thumb and forefinger against her chin, inquisitive.

"Not sure. If you figure it out, let me know."

I finish organizing my booth and Penny goes back to her seat at reception. Soon, the bell hanging over the door chimes and the bodies flood in. Reznor strolls in and starts cleaning his booth after he throws me a wave. I toss one back before Penny hands me my first client's paperwork.

Name—Sean. Age—eighteen. Tattoo—the name "Nina." Placement—over his heart.

I avert my eyes to the floor and roll them. *Kids*… will they ever learn to not tattoo names on themselves? No. Fingers crossed Nina is his mom. But, deep down, I know it isn't.

My guess? Nina is the bouncy girl on his right, gripping his hand like a vise. The girl smiles at Sean as if he is the reason she breathes. Hope she feels that way for many years to come. Him, too.

"Sean," I call out as I wander over to the couches in reception.

He kisses her knuckles and hops up. "That's me," he says. "Can she watch?"

I nod. "Sure. Come on over." I wave them over to my booth, then point at the chair. "Have a seat." Scanning over the paperwork one last time, I review his tattoo with him and verify the placement. After he agrees on a font, I print "Nina" on the transfer paper, moisturize his young, hair-free chest, and apply the stencil.

The next hour is full of minor flinches and loud hisses. When I set the tattoo gun down, he sucks in a lungful of air. I spray a paper towel and wipe it across the fresh ink as I explain tattoo care to him. He nods at all the right times and smiles feverishly when I hand him a mirror and he stares at the tattoo for the first time.

When he rises from the chair, he wobbles in place. "Be sure to grab a bite to eat when you leave here." I point to who I still assume is Nina. "Please don't let him drive until he eats." She nods and they head over to Penny to pay, leaving me a gracious tip.

The day trickles by much the same as usual.

My next appointment wants an old photo of her grandparents tattooed on her bicep with dates and the single word "forever" underneath. The memorialization is sweet, really. I press the pedal and the gun vibrates to life in my hand.

As I engrave her grandparents into her skin, the woman shares their story. How they met in a hospital during the Vietnam War and her grandmother nursed him back to life. How her grandfather could no longer fight on the front lines because he was too severely wounded to stand with his comrades. How pissed her grandfather was and how quickly he got over it because he saw a "pretty nurse lady" every day.

The way she conveys the love story of her grandparents, there was no doubt she heard their story firsthand hundreds of times.

Far too often, I dream of a love like theirs. One I hug close to my heart and brag to others about. *Maybe one day,* I mentally profess.

Halfway through, the woman closes her eyes with a smile on her face and remains silent for the rest of the session. While she zones out, so do I.

Every time a person sits in my chair or stretches out across my table, I mentally prepare for all or nothing. Clientele come in mixed bags. From nervous to somber to never-ending bursts of energy. Some talk your ear off for days. Others never speak a word. Then you get the ones who do a mix of both. Those who talk because they are nervous or shy, then quiet down once the initial buzz wears off.

I love it. Love my job. Love all the wonderful—and crazy—stories I hear. It's kind of like reading a new book every couple of hours. Living in someone else's shoes for a snippet of time.

When I finish up my second appointment, I clean and prep my station for the next—who Penny said is already here. After I wipe everything down, I pick up the clipboard with his paperwork and scan it.

Great. One of those. Lucky me (insert sarcasm anytime you would like).

My next client—male—wants the word "heaven" inked into his skin. No big deal, right? Sure, if he was getting it in any other location. I roll my eyes and lay out the narrow massage table in my booth. Because my next client is getting "heaven" tattooed an inch or two above the base of his penis.

Dumbass. Arrogant dumbass.

Penny waltzes over and sniggers as I lay paper gowns on the table. "Hope he's hung, otherwise a lot of people will be disappointed when they don't reach heaven as indicated."

I slap her arm and laugh. "Shut. Up." I shake my head. "How am I supposed to concentrate and act professional when you say shit like that?"

Penny shrugs, pops her pink bubblegum, and skips back to the reception area. Halfway across the store and I still hear her giggles.

Walking over to the waiting area, I retrieve Mr. Heaven and bring him to my booth. Without shame, I admit he is hot. Inches taller than me. Tan skin like he just left Clearwater Beach minutes ago. Bulky muscles showcasing his arms and legs.

But as I have learned, not all those qualities add up to "heaven" in the bedroom. I cough into my elbow to cover the laugh bubbling up my throat.

Get it together, Autumn.

"Any particular font you were looking for?" I ask.

He shakes his head. "Maybe old English. Something masculine."

I show him a few variations and he chooses one. Once I have the transfer paper ready, he shoves his sweatpants down until he exposes his hairless skin and I glimpse the base of his penis.

Ugh, this is going to be a long—ha ha—and awkward session.

Mr. Heaven raises his arms and tucks his hands under his head. He has the audacity to smirk at me. Cocky bastard. Can't wait to wipe the smirk from his face when the gun bites his skin.

An hour and a half and an H-E-A-V later, Mr. Heaven isn't as suave as he thought he was. *Ha! Take that!* A sick pleasure floats in my veins each time he jerks or flinches or hisses. *Hope it is worth it, buddy.*

As I am midway through the second E, the bell over the door jingles. When I lift the gun away from Mr. Heaven's skin and wipe the excess ink away, I glance up and spot Penny chatting with the guy who walked in.

I stop breathing. Stop thinking. Stop everything.

"You good?" Mr. Heaven asks.

Snap out of it Autumn. "Yeah, sorry." Mr. Heaven glances to the man up front. "Thought it was a friend of mine," I say to cover up my flounder.

"No worries," he says as I finish working on the end of his tattoo.

Every now and again, I peer up and see the man is still here. Currently, he sits on one of the couches as he flips through the artist's albums. He studies the photos with obvious interest. From my vantage point, I sporadically—and, fingers crossed, inconspicuously—survey him.

He hunches over an album as he flips the pages. His milk chocolate hair sticks out in different directions on top of his head—the underside buzzed short. When he swaps albums, I spot some of the ink between the bottom of his shirt sleeve and his elbow. Sacred geometry. Interesting.

I focus on Mr. Heaven as I finish the last of the N. As soon as I set the gun down and glance over at Penny, album-flipping guy waves at her and walks out the door. All I got was his backside.

But what a glorious backside it was.

Mr. Heaven rises from the table and hobbles over to the floor-to-ceiling mirror and inspects his fresh ink. He smiles like the cocky bastard he is. Penny cashes him out and he tips me well.

"At least Mr. Heaven was good for something," I say with a giggle as Penny heads my way.

"Yeah. But, girl, I'd climb that stairway to heaven." As if on cue, "Stairway to Heaven" by Led Zeppelin plays through the shop's speakers.

We both fall into a fit of laughter as I play slap her arm. "Shut up. You're sick." She shrugs without care. "Who was the guy?" I point to the door as if it explains who I am referencing.

When Penny deciphers who I am talking about, she smiles. "Your final on Wednesday. Hottie, huh?"

"Only saw the top of his head and a few inches of his bicep," I fib and pray she doesn't notice. Now is not the time for me to go into my starry-eyed moment. Fact is, I noticed so much more. But if Penny hears that, she will give me shit until Wednesday.

"Well, he'll be the cherry on your hot fudge sundae." Penny fans herself. "Let me just say it was hard not staring the entire time he was here."

Tell me about it.

"Stop," I tease. Couldn't place it, but something felt oddly familiar about him. "What's his name?"

Penny studies me a moment as I go through my usual sanitizing procedure. *Spray. Wipe. Repeat.* "Jonas. Why?"

I shake my head. "No reason. Just looked familiar. But I don't know a Jonas." I shrug and continue as if unfazed.

"You will," she teases and walks off.

I will. But something tells me I already do.

My last client is quick and easy. A young woman. I tattoo the kanji symbol for fierce on the back of her neck. The entire time I have the gun in my hand, my mind wanders to the tall, chocolate-haired man. His stature and sullen demeanor. Somehow, someway, I know him. Just can't place from where.

In my line of work, I see thousands of faces a year. Is there a possibility I inked his skin before? Maybe. But I would remember him. His broad shoulders and creamy brown locks. His long legs and strong hands. His stare-worthy ass as he strode out the door.

Jonas.

Don't remember a Jonas. And I would *definitely* remember him.

When I finish cleaning up my booth for the night, I walk over to Penny. "See you at home. Drive safe."

"You, too. Love you."

"Love ya, chicky."

I unlock my '57 Bel Air, slip inside, and spark the engine to life. Scanning my music, I tap on a rock playlist and sing along as I roll out of the parking lot. The entire drive home, I sing the songs I have heard hundreds of times, but don't hear now. Because my mind is stuck. Stuck on the future. On Wednesday, and a mysterious man named Jonas.

Consider me screwed.

TWO

JONAS

I pick up Spartan's leash and he yaps, running excitedly in circles around the living room. "Come here, nut. Have to put your leash on if you want to see Grandma and Grandpa."

Spartan drops his front legs to the floor—his hindquarters still up as his tail swats the air. I step closer to him and he pivots sideways. We do this a few times, mixed in with more barking. The same game happens every Wednesday when we head to my parents' house for dinner. I grab the leash and my goofy as hell, three-year-old fur-child loses his shit.

At least he brings a smile to my face.

"You want to see Grandma?"

Woof, woof, woof.

"Well, we have to put on your leash." I flick the clasp a few times and he jumps. "Get over here, dude."

Woof, woof, woof.

I rest my hands on my hips and give Spartan the look that says *we are not going anywhere until you put on your leash.* And just like that, he wags his tail, steps forward, and stands tall at my side.

Once I lock his leash in place, we head out the front door and hop in my Wrangler Sahara. When we are both in the cab, I connect his collar to a safety harness in the car. Last thing I need is my little man jumping out of a moving car because he spots a cat. His crazy ass would, too.

Windows down, I drive down the street and head toward my parents' house. Spartan hangs his head out the window with his mouth open as he squints at the oncoming wind. The temperature in our part of Florida is still warm—a toasty eighty-two degrees at four thirty—but you can feel a shift in the air. Not just the cooler days as we transition to Florida's version of winter.

Something else lingers in the air. A new beginning, maybe. Whatever it is, it terrifies and invigorates me.

I stick my arm out the window and shift it up and down in a wave motion. Glancing over at Spartan, I soak up a little of his boisterous energy. Smile at his silliness as he tries to bite the wind. Every time I peek over at him, I am grateful he is in my life. If not for this crazy as hell husky, I would be drowning in alcohol or in a hole some-where. He keeps me going.

Thirty minutes later, we park along the street at my parents' house in St. Petersburg. I jump out and Spartan barks at me as if I forgot him. Opening his door, I loop the leash around my wrist before unclipping his car harness. Once I do, he flies out of the car and yanks me toward the house. I barely get the car door closed.

"Who's excited to see Grandma?" I announce as Spartan drags me inside.

"Where's my good boy?" Mom calls back. "Where's my Sparty?"

I drop Spartan's leash and he scrambles across the floor in her direction. Mom has her arms open as she squats down and waits to hug Spartan. He bolts into her arms and it is a hugging and licking contest between the two of them. Spartan's the only one doing the licking, obviously.

Wandering into the kitchen, I step up behind my older sister, Jasmine, and peek over her shoulder. She is so focused on stirring the hamburger meat on the stove, she doesn't hear me come in. *Perfect.* Slowly, I bring my hands to her sides before going all in and tickling the hell out of her.

"Ah!" she screams, dropping the spatula. "Stop, stop, stop." I tickle her harder. "Jonas! Please…" She laughs so hard she snorts. "Please."

"Mommy, Mommy, Mommy!" My nephew, Lex, comes barreling around the corner. "I save you from Unkie Jonas." Lex is armed with his favorite stuffed animal and ready to whack me with it.

I drop my hands and step back. "Whoa, buddy." Scooping him off the floor, I twirl him in a circle. "I stopped. Please don't get me."

Lex stares over at Jasmine with the most serious expression I have ever seen on his face. "Okay, Mommy?" Such a protector at two years old.

She ruffles his hair and kisses his forehead. "I am now. Thanks for saving me from Uncle Jonas."

He nods with enthusiasm and I set him back on the tile. "Hey, buddy. Why don't you go play with Grandma and Spartan. I'll help Mommy in the kitchen." Without so much as another glance in my direction, he bolts from the kitchen and calls across the house for Spartan.

"We're making tacos tonight, if you want to dice onions and tomatoes and slice up some lettuce," Jasmine says.

I hug her from behind and kiss the top of her head. "On it." Grabbing the produce from the fridge, I step up to the counter beside the stove and get to work. "Anton here?" I ask.

Anton, my big sister's husband, doesn't always make it to Wednesday night dinners. Depending on his work schedule, sometimes he doesn't beat the Tampa traffic when he leaves work. If he runs too late on Wednesdays, he heads home and Jasmine brings him leftovers. Nine times out of ten, though, he makes it. For the most part, investment banking has a set schedule. Only time his schedule changes is when the firm gets a new client.

"Yeah, he's out back with Dad."

Garlic, peppers, and smoked paprika float in the air and my mouth waters. "Hey, we having grilled onions and peppers?"

"If you cut 'em, I'll cook 'em."

My sister and I work in the kitchen like a well-oiled machine. When we were growing up, oftentimes we cooked dinner for everyone. Dad sometimes got stuck at the shop late, while Mom was wrapping up her latest words of wisdom for the local newspaper's advice column. And sometimes our baby sister, Jillian, got hungry earlier than everyone else. Mom taught us early on how to fend for ourselves and help around the house. We didn't always have to, but we loved giving her a break from the kitchen after a really long day.

I chop up large chunks of onion and bell pepper for Jasmine. She rotates between all the burners on the stove, stirring the taco meat, a pot of beans, another with corn, and now the onions and peppers. On the fifth burner—whoever came up with that idea is brilliant—is Tex-Mex rice. Once I finish with the veggies, I shred a big bowl of cheddar cheese and lug out the other toppings. Just before everything is ready, I lay the taco shells on a tray and toast them in the oven for a minute.

A moment later, I wander to the sliding glass doors that lead to the back patio and pool and poke my head out. "Dinner's ready."

Dad and Anton pop their heads up simultaneously as Dad rubs his hands together. "Perfect timing. I'm famished."

Everyone piles up their plates—Anton helps Lex with his—and we all sit down at the table built for six, but extends out for ten. We all wait to start eating until

Jasmine has Lex situated in his booster chair. We have never been a religious family, but Mom always likes to say a few words of gratitude before we eat.

"I'm so glad everyone could be here tonight." Spartan barks in the living room and we all laugh. "You, too," Mom says. "Seriously, though. I'm grateful to have all three of my kids here, plus Anton and my baby boy, Lex. You all are the highlight of my week."

Smiles and *awes* spread throughout the room. Moments like these are my favorite. Of course, we banter. What family doesn't? But these moments are the ones I hold close when I have a bad day. Like watching my nephew make a hot mess of his tacos and hearing my Mom laugh when my dad leans in and whispers in her ear. Truly the best.

"So, what's new with you, oh quiet brother of mine?" Jillian teases.

Jillian was a surprise baby. But she is the best little sister anyone could ever ask for. She keeps me levelheaded with her jokes and nagging. Where Jasmine is two years older than me, Jillian is seven years younger. For a mature young woman, sometimes she still acts like a teenager. She gives me clarity when I am stressed and makes me laugh when I am down.

"Nothing exciting," I answer. "Same stuff, new day. What about you? How's the wild world of fashion?"

She rolls her eyes. "Nice avoidance tactic, big bro. The store is great. Just got a glimpse at the spring line. We're putting in out just before Christmas."

I cock my head and stare at her. "It's not even winter, technically. Why so early?"

"You have so much to learn, dear brother. It's kind of like when car dealers put the next year's model out months before the year begins. Sales tactic." Jillian taps the side of her head as if her brain holds all the secrets.

Jillian is smart. Not like Mensa-smart, but pretty damn close. Her IQ is stellar. She graduated Salutatorian of her class in high school and graduated two years early —with honors—from college where she studied business and marketing.

At least she went to college. My path has been carved in stone since I picked up a wrench in Dad's garage. You don't need college to be a mechanic, but I did attend a trade/vocational school. I wanted the merits under my belt. Plus, school taught me more of the computerized auto information Dad occasionally searched for online. This way, we both brought something to the table.

And one day, when Dad finally decides it is time to retire his coveralls, I will take over Thompson's Garage and Body Specialists. Dad put a lot of time and energy and grease into our shop. I want him to be proud when I take over.

"I will never understand fashion," I tell her.

"True. And you're still avoiding my question," she repeats and I hang my head. The table goes silent and Jillian leans in closer. "If you don't want to talk about it, just tell me to shut up."

I laugh and she backs away. "You're fine. Just been a

rough week. But I'll be okay. And if not, you can tease me more." Off in the living room, Spartan barks. "You, too, buddy," I shout.

The rest of dinner goes by a little quieter. Conversations and laughter still carry on around the table, but the mood has tapered. They all know about Cora. Hell, they have met her and invited her to dinner a few times. They knew we were just friends, but thank god they bit their tongues about more. It has been obvious for years I had feelings for Cora, but no one ever shed light on those feelings. Which makes this whole new awkwardness a little less weird. Only a little, though.

Once everyone finishes eating, I help clear the table. "Hey, Mom?"

"Yeah, honey." She sidles up next to me and wraps her arm around my waist.

"You mind if I head out? Know it's early, but I have an appointment at eight."

She squeezes me harder for a second, then releases me. "Sure thing. What's the appointment?"

"Time to brighten up the canvas," I say with a smile on my face.

It is no secret Mom isn't a fan of tattoos, but she never judges. "Just don't understand the desire to sit in a chair for hours, in pain, while someone paints lines on your skin."

I laugh. "Maybe one day I will better explain it to you, but I need to head out so I'm not late." I kiss her forehead and she hugs me as close as humanly possible.

"See you next week. Love you."

"Love you, too," I tell her.

After I make my rounds, I leash Spartan and drive home to drop him off. Thankfully, the tattoo shop is close to the house. I check the time on the dash as we drive away from Mom and Dad's. Spartan barks his goodbye before resuming his usual car window position.

I arrive at the tattoo shop with ten minutes to spare. Perfect amount of time to fill out paperwork and mentally prepare myself for being in the chair for more than an hour.

A bell chimes when I open the door and step inside. The same woman sits behind the counter. Her hot pink hair reminds me of the color candy companies give artificial watermelon. Nothing like the actual color of the fruit. She twirls a finger around the locks on her shoulders while she pops her bubble gum.

All I do is laugh internally. She is a strange mix of pinup girl and grunge princess. Hair to the nines. Clothes casual and baggy. I wonder if she dresses like this outside of the tattoo shop?

I step up to the counter. "Hey," I say, giving a small wave. "Jonas. I have an appointment."

Bubble gum princess peeks up at me and sits a little straighter. "Hey, Jonas." The way she says my name insinuates she holds secrets about me. She grabs a clipboard and hands it to me. "Fill this out and I need to make a copy of your ID."

Fishing my license out of my wallet, I hand it to her before sitting on one of the couches and filling out the standard paperwork. Once I finish, I hand it back to her and she hands me my license with a smirk.

"She'll be with you in a minute, sugar."

While I wait to be called back, I mindlessly stare at the funky art on the walls. Each drawing and painting has one of the shop's artist's name below with a price tag. Kind of cool the artists put work on display to show their individual talents.

"Jonas?" a soft, cheery voice calls out.

"That's…" I spin around and stop short at the petite brunette staring at me. Clearing my throat, I try again. "Sorry. I'm Jonas."

She smiles and the room brightens instantly. "Autumn. Follow me." I follow in her wake as she leads me to her booth.

Unabashedly, I check her out as she walks in front of me. Autumn is roughly six inches shorter than me, but leggy as hell. In a pair of black and white plaid-like skinny pants which hug every curve and a black top with straps looping around her neck and a dangerous dip at her cleavage. Her hips sway slightly when she walks, and I remind myself to keep my eyes at a gentleman's level — up. As we reach her booth, I notice the bandana in her hair. It matches her pants and is a simple accessory to her pinned-up locks.

"Have a seat," she says, gesturing to the chair in her booth. "Your paperwork says you're wanting to continue one of your half sleeves."

I nod and search for my voice. *Use your words, Thompson.* "Yeah. I brought the drawing with me." I hand over a folded paper.

Autumn takes the paper, unfolds it, and studies the intricate artwork. Artwork I spent weeks drawing. This piece is my right arm. The left is similar in design, but not the same. Only a true enthusiast would detect the dissimilarity.

She examines the lines, dots, and shading on the paper, then peers over at my arm. After several back and forth examinations, I wonder if it would be easier for me to take off my shirt. My shirt sleeves block at least half of the current art on my skin, and she is probably gauging where to start.

"Need me to take off my shirt?" I ask.

Her eyes lift from the paper and meet mine. *Fuck.* The most delectable glass of cognac stares back at me. Dark chocolate rims her irises, softening from brown to a golden, bold orange near her pupils. A light rouge pinks her pale cheeks.

"Um." She swallows. "Probably a good idea," she mumbles. "So I can see what's already done, of course."

Is she nervous? If so, it is adorable as fuck. Seriously,

she has to have seen hundreds of people in her line of work. Work in the oddest places and a plethora of designs. I cringe mentally at the idea of her tattooing some asshole in awkward places. But pricks like that exist.

"Of course." I smile and tug my shirt over my head. If possible, her cheeks darken from a gentle blush to the soft petals of a pink rose and a surge of excitement floats beneath my sternum.

She swallows again and blinks rapidly. Her eyes drop back to the paper as she tucks her cherry red lips in her mouth. Is she fighting off a smile? When she keeps her eyes downcast too long for my liking, I lay my shirt over my chest in the hopes she will look up again. I need another shot of her cognac irises.

As soon as my torso is covered, she sighs. *Sighs*. The sound a mix of disappointment and relief. Dear god. This is going to be one of the longest tat sessions in history. And she won't even finish the rest of the design tonight.

Studying the current ink on my skin against the drawing, she bites the corner of her lip. I avert my gaze to the ceiling and pray to someone holier than me.

Please let me get through tonight unscathed. Please let me get through this without the embarrassment of a hard-on. At this rate, there's a high likelihood. I beg you, please.

"Be right back," Autumn says as she rises from her stool and strolls out of the booth. Once again, my eyes wander to her backside until she is out of sight.

I slide my shirt down and expose my skin to the cooler

air. Let it temper my overheated skin as I take a few deep breaths.

But the fire Autumn created still burns hot. I love and hate how it simmers in my veins.

What the fuck is happening?

THREE

AUTUMN

Jonas's eyes scald me as I walk out of the booth. For the first time in years, I enjoy male attention. Jonas's attention. His eyes on me make my blood pump harder, faster.

As I make copies of his design to cut and put on transfer paper, Penny sneaks up from behind. "I was right, he is a hottie."

I jump and slap a hand to my chest. "Jesus, Pen. Don't do that."

"Do what?" She feigns innocence while smacking her bubble gum. Why didn't I hear the distinctive smack of her lips as she came up behind me?

"Scare the shit out of me."

She throws her head back and laughs. I glance over at Jonas—who seems oblivious to Penny's obnoxious chortle—then back at my friend. I narrow my eyes at her and she lifts her hands in surrender. "Sorry, not sorry. But I wasn't lying. He is hot."

I focus on my task—Jonas is a paying client, after all. "Yeah, I guess." A heatwave spreads across my skin.

Penny leans in closer and scrutinizes my every move. "You guess?" Keeping my head down, I peek up at her. She smiles at me with wicked intent. "Girly, you must be blind if you don't recognize a good-looking man when you see one."

The printer finishes and I grab the transfer paper. "I'm not blind. Okay? Just trying to breathe through the next two hours of my night. So" —I point to her chair— "go back to your desk and do what you do. And don't pester me. Last thing I need is to fuck up his tattoo."

She giggles, salutes me, and walks off. "Yes, dear."

I take a deep breath and gather my wits.

You can do this, Autumn. He is just another guy in your chair. A hot guy. Shut up!

When I turn the corner of my booth and glance over at Jonas, I stop breathing. Since I left, he has pushed his shirt down his chest and sits perfectly still with his eyes closed. Is he sleeping? Stepping over to my stool, I set the papers down on the counter. His eyes remain closed as I start prepping for our session.

Part of me wants his eyes open. A big part.

As if I professed it aloud, Jonas opens his eyes just as I glance up at him. My stomach flips and I swallow. I have never seen eyes like his. Such fascinating shades of blue with a burst of sunshine at the center. As if his DNA couldn't decide whether to make his eyes blue or hazel. I prefer the indecision.

"So, I printed off more than what I'll actually work on tonight. Some of what I printed, you already have done. But I did that so I could line it up."

Jonas nods. "No problem. You know what you're doing. I'm not concerned."

He closes his eyes and lays his head back again. My whole body sags at the loss. "I need to shave your forearm. Thankfully" —I trace the corded muscles in his forearms with my fingertips— "most people won't notice the difference." His eyes pop open and lock on mine. I try swallowing the lump in my throat. "Your arms aren't really hairy. It won't look weird when I shave it, is what I mean."

He smiles and a dimple accentuates his left cheek. A dimple I want to kiss.

Shut up, Autumn. He is your client.

"I don't care either way."

When I think he is going to close his eyes again, he surprises me. Instead, his eyes drop to where I lather soap on his arm. I dry off the gloves and pick up a disposable razor. Inch by inch, I swipe the razor over his skin. Finished, I wet a paper towel and wipe away any excess soap.

After I rub a thin layer of natural moisturizer on his skin, I line up the stencil on his forearm and press it in place. I peel back the paper and smile at the purple lines on his skin. On the small rolling table next to my stool, I set his original drawing next to the small ink caps filled with black ink.

Jonas closes his eyes again as I go through the process of opening the sterile needle pack and loading it on my gun. I run through my usual routine and make sure I have everything ready before I start. Once everything is set, I pick up the gun and press the pedal on the floor.

When the gun buzzes to life in my hand, the old familiar joy of why I do this kick-starts my adrenaline.

As a child, I always loved to color and draw. The older I became, the more I honed my craft. I took every possible elective art class in school. Somehow, I also managed to coerce the art teacher during my sophomore year to give me art lessons outside normal class hours. We worked at the school, of course, and she gave me extra credit—which I didn't mind, but also didn't ask for. Through Ms. Gibson's lessons, I learned to love art over everything. She taught me every medium and how to open my imagination beyond what the human eye sees.

I took those lessons and the skills I learned, and eventually discovered my preferred canvas. Skin.

Leaning forward, I stretch the skin near Jonas's elbow and press the buzzing needle forward. He startles, then relaxes. "Okay?" I ask, not looking up.

"Yeah," he answers, voice scratchy. "No matter how many times I've been under the needle, when it first hits my skin, I jump."

I nod but don't look up. "Me too."

For the first ten or fifteen minutes, I work in silence and locate my rhythm. Every person you work on is different. Depending on their age, how often they are in the sun, and how well they take care of themselves deter-mines how easy or difficult it is to work on them. Skin is skin. But at different stages of life, it has different density and elasticity. The older you are, the thinner your skin is. It is a natural progression. Also, the more exposed to the elements—sun, wind, level of humidity, and so on—you are, the more your skin is impacted.

Jonas has nice skin. Slightly tan. Not the type of tan you get from regular visits to the beach. Jonas's tanned skin is from everyday activity—mowing the yard, jogging outdoors, driving with his arm out the window or the top down. For a moment, I picture him in a lush, green yard. Black shirt stretched taut on his broad chest. Khaki cargo shorts hanging low on his hips. A bright smile and that adorable dimple on his face as he pushes a little girl on the swings.

I lift the gun from his skin, turn my face away from him, and cough into my elbow.

Stop it, Autumn.

"Grab some water," Jonas says as I spin back his way.

"I'm good. Just a tickle." I play off the softball-sized lump of emotion in my throat. What I need is a distrac-tion. "So, Jonas…" His eyes shift from my hand dipping the needle in the ink cap to my eyes. "Tell me about yourself."

His Adam's apple bobs in my periphery before he sits a little taller. "What would you like to know?"

I bring the gun back to his arm and spark it to life again. "Girlfriend? Wife? Kids? All the good stuff."

"The good stuff, huh?" He snorts and I peek up at him for a second before refocusing on my work. "I'd laugh, but I don't want to throw you off." Out of the corner of my eye, he points to where I am currently working on a flower of life pattern.

"I appreciate that. No way I'd be able to sleep if I jacked up your tat."

"Good stuff," he mumbles then goes silent for a moment. "No girlfriend or wife." And I can tell—without looking up—his face is turned away. It piques my curiosity. "No kids. Unless fur children count. If that's the case, then I have one. Spartan. He's three."

"Spartan. He a fighter?" I ask.

He laughs, but not enough to jostle his arm. "Nah. He's a big softy. Fifty-seven pounds of pure energy. Loves hugs and barking."

Now it is my turn to laugh. "What kind of dog is he?"

"Husky."

I pause and meet Jonas's eyes. "So, a fur baby. But no fur baby mama?" My retort is meant to be funny, but a gray cloud suddenly masks his joy.

"Nope. No fur baby mama."

I hate how sad he sounds right now. Hate that I wrecked his mood. "Want to talk about it?"

First and foremost, I am no therapist. But far too often, people sit in this chair and spill some of the craziest details of their life history. Some fascinate me. Others... not so much. But I have learned over the years to just go with the flow. If people need to get things off their chest, I let them. Not like I am the gossiping sort.

"Yes. No. I don't know." He looks away and I slump at the obvious discomfort I spurred.

Instead of pestering him, I continue working on his tat. If Jonas wants to divulge whatever is bothering him, he will. A few minutes pass and neither of us says a word. But I feel his eyes on me. Not on my hand as it holds the gun and carves intricate black lines into his skin. No, his eyes are on *me*. A buzz ripples through my body. A buzz that has absolutely nothing to do with the tattoo gun vibrating in my right hand.

"My best friend just got married," he whispers. Voice so soft I almost miss it.

I stop working and gauge his expression. Eyes sad. Smile absent. Shoulders low. Everything in his body language tells me he is upset or disappointed over this marriage. "Not my place to ask, but shouldn't you be happy for him?"

"Her," he corrects.

Ah. There it is. The fine line detail. His female best friend just got married. And he isn't too keen on the idea.

"Shouldn't you be happy for her?"

He nods. "As painful as it is, I am happy for her. She's with the one person she can't live without. They've known each other since high school, but his family moved away when he was in high school. They reunited this past spring."

There is a peculiar familiarity to the story he tells me.

Could be sheer coincidence. But it might not be. What are the odds?

"This might be weird." And suddenly, I have his full attention. "But is your best friend Cora?"

His eyes widen at the mention of her name and a ball of jealousy forms beneath my diaphragm. His expression tells me he considered her more than a friend, but she never did. Most women would cringe at the notion. Me? I bask in it.

Bask in the fact he never overstepped his bounds with her. As quickly as my jealousy formed, it melts away.

Over the last seven months, I got to know Cora. Mostly through text and the occasional girls' night, where we had dinner and a movie at her house. She is super sweet. Told me about this guy she had known for years—who she had given the same title. Best friend.

Don't know the dirty details of Jonas's life, but I do know Cora thinks highly of him.

"He just needs to find the right woman, you know. Someone who will make him smile and laugh. Someone who will hug him tight and make every day better than the last."

Her words come back to me from a couple weeks ago at her bachelorette party. I had no clue who she was talking about, but she wanted to make it her life's mission to see her best friend happy.

Now I know why.

He swallows. "Yeah. You know her?"

I lock eyes with him and nod. "Yep. Did her and Gavin's tattoos back in April. We've chatted and hung out here and there. Attended their wedding." His eyes sparkle at this fact. "She never mentioned your name. And, obviously, we never all hung out at the same times."

"Obviously." He averts his gaze and mumbles, "I would definitely remember you."

I smile at the words I am sure he didn't mean for me to hear. "Back atcha."

He faces me again with a soft smile on his lips. "It hasn't been easy seeing her with Gavin, but I keep telling myself everything happens for a reason. Keep reminding myself she was never mine to keep. Not in the way I originally intended."

I continue working on his tattoo. "Sometimes, people come into our life to teach us something. Not necessarily like an actual teacher. In your case, maybe Cora taught you how to open your heart. How to love someone in a nonfamilial way. She may not be the person you're meant to love, but she helped teach you what love *feels* like."

He sits quietly in the chair for a few minutes as I get closer to the center of the flower of life in the middle of his forearm.

Did I say too much? Go too far?

From what Cora told me, her "best friend"—aka Jonas—has crushed on her for years. Several years. Honestly, I lived vicariously through her. The fact she had one man pining over her while she was in love with another… color me jealous and envious and dark, dark green.

Just as I start to apologize for stepping over the line,

Jonas speaks up. "I never looked at it like that. Actually puts it in a whole new perspective." He hums. "Not as if it concerns you, but I've been slowly working on letting her go. Not fully. She is my best friend, after all. But I've been trying to disconnect myself from her romantically. See her more like a sister or one of the guys. Know what I mean?"

"I do," I tell him. "But it's easy to say 'you are my friend.' The difficult part is accepting it."

"Yeah. Weeks before the wedding—which I did not see you at, by the way—I repeatedly told myself she was never mine to have. That I needed to find a way to get over her. Move on." I feel his eyes on me again. "I'm getting there," he whispers.

"I'm getting there." What exactly does that mean?

"You think?" I glance at him as I dip the needle into the ink cap.

Eyes locked on mine, the corners of his mouth tip up the slightest bit. "Yes."

Dear God. Please forgive me. But I really want to sin with this man.

I am the last person in the world anyone would consider to be religious. My history could sway the decision either way. But this man makes me want to drop to my knees, hold his gaze, and pray for him to let me make his life better.

I may not be a miracle worker, but I could do many miraculous things to this man.

"W-well that's great," I say with a little too much enthusiasm.

In turn, he laughs. And since I don't have the tattoo gun anywhere near his skin, he laughs harder than earlier. Deeper. Throatier. Louder. So loud, Penny and Rex—another artist in the shop—glance our way. Penny's eyebrows waggle and I roll my eyes at her.

When I sleep tonight, I will dream of his laugh and the way my insides swirl at the sound. The way my body sparks to life.

"Glad you think so," he teases. "Your turn." I cock my head to the side and narrow my eyes. "Tell me about you," he clarifies.

"Ah. Tit for tat, huh?"

He smirks and I realize the innuendo he has created from my words. "If that's what you want to c-call it." I love his slight stutter at the end. His jitters as we tease.

"What would you like to know?" I prompt.

He taps his chin with his free hand. "Boyfriend? Husband? Kids?"

Keeping my face down as I work on him, I stop breathing for a minute.

You can do this, Autumn. Baby steps.

I smile at his arm, but, if he saw my face head-on, he would know the smile is forced. So, I keep my head down. "No boyfriend or husband. Most guys I've dated were grossly immature. Don't get me wrong, I love silliness every once in a while. But some guys don't know when to be serious."

"I hate how I'm automatically lumped into this category because of the extremity between my legs." For a moment, I glance at his groin. No doubt he notices. *Great.* "But I get where you're coming from. I know plenty of guys who act exactly how you're describing them."

"Not trying to harp on the male species. Just noting the history I've had with them. Hasn't really worked in my favor."

I sit up straighter as I wipe excess ink off his arm. When he remains silent for a minute, I meet his gaze. He just… looks at me. Looking at me like no one else has. As if trying to read more into what I say. Tapping into my brain and digging for unanswered questions. Answers I am not ready to divulge yet.

"Sorry to hear. But you shouldn't give up."

I cock a brow at him. "No?"

He shakes his head. "Definitely not."

His words are laced with more. Emotions left unsaid. The sentiment weighs heavy and I blink rapidly to snap myself back to reality.

Is he suggesting what I think he is? When he says I shouldn't give up, is he inviting me to give him a shot? *"Definitely not."* His answer repeats in my head over and over. Unsure how to process it, I change the subject.

"What do you think?" He scrunches his brow. "Your ink? It's done. Well, done for tonight. What do you think?"

I grab a fresh paper towel and the alcohol blend I use to clean it up. Squirting some on the paper towel, I swipe the damp cloth over his skin and clean up the fresh tattoo.

"Perfect," he whispers.

And for a moment, I wonder if he's only referring to the tattoo. When I peek up, his eyes aren't on his forearm. They are on me.

The intensity of his stare sends a shock wave of heat across my flesh. Under the thin material of my bra, my nipples harden. At the apex of my thighs, dampness slicks my skin. I press my legs closer together and pray he doesn't notice. Pray he doesn't call me out. Because if he studies my reaction hard enough—pun intended—he will know exactly where my head is at.

Why has it been so long? Why the hell have I denied myself for so many years? And why has it worked until now?

"Thanks," I whisper back.

The answer to all three questions is simple. Because I have been waiting. For the right guy. For a guy like Jonas.

FOUR

JONAS

I soak up every line and curve of Autumn's profile as she cleans the new addition to my sleeve. Never thought I would say this about another woman, but damn, she is beautiful.

Autumn has a classic beauty, not one born of facials and layers of makeup. A heart-shaped face with a slender button nose and full lips. Scarlet paints her lips while a thin black wingtip accentuates her eyes. The only additions I note. We may be surrounded by beaches, but her alabaster skin tells me it isn't a place she frequents. A full sleeve of flowers and vines is inked on her right arm. And the style of her clothes and how she has her hair pinned… she reminds me of a modern-day pinup girl.

My pinup girl.

The errant thought catches me off guard, but I don't dismiss it. Not yet.

Autumn is a breath of fresh air. The fresh air I didn't

think would filter through my lungs ever again. A new breath of life. Invigorating.

Beside me, she adheres a thin film to the new ink. Lifting her eyes to mine, I hold her swirly cognac gaze as she explains the new product. "Not sure if you've used this yet, but it's called Saniderm." I glance down at the clear film on my skin for a beat. When I shake my head, she continues. "It's a new, breathable way to protect your tattoo while it heals." She goes over the specifics and I get lost in the sound of her voice.

How have I not seen her until now?

The answer sits on the tip of my tongue. I won't say it. Not even in my thoughts. Let's just say I was otherwise distracted.

Now, though... I see clearly. The curtains over my eyes have been shoved to the wayside. The light of a new day shines bright. Has me seeing the world I have ignored for years.

When Autumn stops her spiel on tattoo care—which she knows I am obviously familiar with because of my previous tattoos—she stands and leads me back to the front desk. Call me a pig, but I eat up every inch of her as she walks in front of me. How can I not?

"Hey, Penny," she says, talking to the pink-haired woman behind the front desk. "Will you add Jonas on my schedule for next week. Wednesday or after." Autumn leans on the counter, pops her hip out, and faces me. *Someone rescue me from my depraved thoughts.* "If that works for you."

I nod, not trusting my voice yet. After I swallow a couple times, I pray to not sound like a prepubescent boy. "Yeah." *Thank fuck.* "Thursday might be easier, though."

"It's a date," she says as her face flushes rosy. She tucks both her lips in her mouth and clamps down before releasing them. "See you next week."

"Next week," I reply.

She scurries off to her booth and it's fucking adorable how flustered Autumn is. *Me too*, I want to tell her. Because this is the first time I have felt so immediately enamored by a woman. Although I undoubtedly loved—still love—Cora, my heart never hummed with her. Never galloped. Nor did I forget to breathe around her.

Maybe Autumn was right. Maybe Cora was a lesson. The lesson which taught me nonfamilial love.

Cora was never mine to love. I know this now. She was just a star in the constellation leading me to where I belong. And the constellation shines brighter than any other star in the galaxy now.

My constellation.

Penny cashes me out and I hand her a tip to give Autumn. "I'll make sure she gets it, sugar. What day works best for your next appointment?"

Getting here tonight after the weekly family dinner was cutting it close. I would rather get here a little earlier, so I am not here until ten at night. Although I don't need to be at the garage until eight each morning, I usually arrive between six and seven to help Dad catch up on invoices.

"Is Thursday at six available?"

Penny leans close to the computer monitor, rests her chin on her palm, and clicks the mouse a few times. Her eyes flick across the screen as she scrolls down. She pops her bubble gum once then looks up. "Six is all yours, sugar." Her fingers run across the keyboard. "Probably another two-hour appointment."

I nod. "Thanks. See you next week."

She leans back in her chair, pops her gum, and gives me a spirited wave goodbye.

As I reach the door to leave, I glance over my shoulder toward Autumn's booth. She stands frozen in place, eyes on me, with a new wave of crimson on her cheeks at being caught ogling. A wide smile tugs at my cheeks as I raise a hand and wave her direction. She timidly lifts her hand and returns my smile with one of her own.

I turn just in time to not smack into the door and make a fool out of myself.

Walking out of the shop, I head for the Jeep, hop in, and crank it to life. I sit in the lamplit parking lot for a few minutes and stare at the steering wheel in a fog. Although nothing extraordinary happened over the last two hours, the most mysterious and alluring woman blipped on my radar.

How the hell am I supposed to function for the next week? On a shitload of caffeine and daydreams, that is how.

Daydreams of an exquisite, petite pinup woman named Autumn.

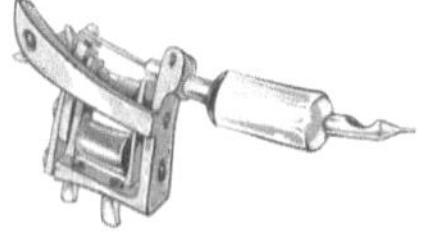

The alarm squawks on the bedside table. I roll over and slap the snooze bar as Spartan vaults onto the bed and licks my face.

Swinging my arms in the air, I jerk my face left and right. "Spartan." I laugh at his relentlessness. "Stop, stop, stop." I cover my face with my hands and he starts licking my ear. "Argh! Okay, I'm up."

I wrap my arms around Spartan's belly and wrestle him on the bed for a minute before I slip out of the covers and turn off the alarm clock. He jumps off the bed and bolts for the front door, barking. After a quick trip to the bathroom, I throw on a hoodie, sweatpants, and sneakers, then hook Spartan's leash to his collar.

Out the door, we wander in the dark around the neighborhood. Houses on the street only illuminated by porch lights. Most of the windows still dark as residents continue to sleep.

Spartan sniffs and marks as many patches of grass, bushes, and signposts as possible. Cool air whips through my hair and, for the first time ever, it invigorates me. For years, I gravitated toward all things sunny and warm. Now, I discover a new appreciation for the opposite.

The cool breeze reminds me of fresh starts and new beginnings. Something I am in desperate need of.

"Spartan," I call out. He glances back at me a second, but doesn't stop tugging me forward. "I met someone." Funny enough, he barks.

I laugh. "You'd like her, buddy. Real pretty." He stops, sniffs at something I can't see on the sidewalk, and I run into him. "Whatcha got there?" But before I get close enough to see what caught his attention, he drags me forward again. "Anyway. She's really pretty. Like the women in fashion magazines or something." He barks again and I shush him. Last thing I need is for an angry neighbor to complain my dog woke them up at five in the morning.

So, for the rest of our trip around the neighborhood, I stay quiet while Spartan takes me for a walk.

Once we get back home, I jump in the shower. The instructions for this new tattoo cover say I shower normally with it on, just not to scrub it. Tattoo innovations —gotta love 'em. Out of the shower, I scramble a couple eggs, fry up a few pieces of bacon, and butter some toast. In no time, breakfast fills my stomach.

I secure Spartan in his crate, turn on the radio to our favorite rock station, and head out the door.

It's no surprise Dad is already at the garage when I arrive. Parking my motorcycle behind the building, I stroll into the office and greet him with a thermos of coffee.

"Morning, Dad."

He pops his head up, checks the time on the clock over the door, and smiles at me. "Up early today?"

I set the thermos in front of him and grab his mug

from the small dish rack and hand it to him. When Dad bought this garage in 1980, he cleaned it up and changed a few things around before opening. Dad had worked in several mechanic and body shops prior to owning Thompson's Garage. He knew the ins and outs of daily activity. Knew what made a shop dysfunctional and what made it flow with ease. Taking bits and pieces of all the things he loved, he set up this garage.

Thompson's Garage and Body Specialists has four bays total. One bay is used for bodywork, unless we have no bodywork to work on. Each bay is only separated by the occasional pillar and larger machines. Along the back wall of the garage is section after section of chrome and black industrial automotive cabinetry. Every tool we possibly need inside. And if we don't have it, Dad orders it.

He also added a small kitchen dinette and a couch and small table in the office space of the garage. One thing he said bugged him at most shops he worked at was how they didn't have simple necessities—a sink for dishes, a fridge, and a small table for lunch (and breakfast for the early birds). Or a place to sleep on exhausting days. Dad made sure Thompson's had all of those, plus some counter space and a few cabinets.

Our garage was voted top family-owned mechanic of the Bay Area ten times. And we take pride in our work.

"Nah. Just moved faster than usual." I laugh and he joins in. "Best night of sleep in a while, I guess."

He fills his mug with coffee as I grab the creamer from

the fridge and sugar on the counter. Setting it down, I pour my own mugful. We both add cream and sugar, and sit in silence a moment as we take the first few sips. Something Dad and I have in common is our morning routine. Maybe it's because I am the only son and I wanted to be just like him growing up. Or I could chalk it up to the fact we both wake up crazy early Monday to Friday and share the same job.

"What changed?" he asks after sufficiently caffeinated. I furrow my brow. "What happened after dinner last night? Said you slept better."

I smile and bring the mug to my lips. He studies me when I don't answer and shakes his head, following it up with a smile that matches my own.

Dad and I, for as long as I can remember, share a secret language. As a child, I dubbed it the *Boys Only Club*. That's how I kept my older sister away. Jillian was a baby during the age of *Boys Only*, so I never worried about her. Over the years, it evolved and I learned Dad and I just shared the same mindset. He is simply an older version of me.

I lift my arm and show him the new addition to my sleeve. "Went to the tattoo shop last night."

"Son, tattoos don't make you smile." He points at me as he shakes his head. "Not like an idiot, anyway."

Slapping a hand to my chest, I gape at him. "You wound me."

"Dumbass." He laughs.

I finish off my mug and set it down. "Met someone. A woman," I clarify. "She works at the tattoo shop."

"And?" Dad drawls out the one-word question.

"And I don't know. Couldn't stop looking at her. Or thinking about her. We talked the two hours I was there. Not sure, but I don't think the feelings are one-sided."

He nods, drinks the last of his coffee, and looks me square in the eyes. "Well, it's nice to see you smile again." Rising from his chair, he goes to the sink and washes out his mug before setting it in the rack. "Time to get to work."

And just like that, the conversation ends. Another great thing about the relationship Dad and I share is how we don't need all the nitty-gritty details. If either of us wants to disclose something, we will.

One day, I hope to have more to share with him.

FIVE

AUTUMN

"Leaving the mall now."

I pin the phone between my shoulder and ear as I fumble through my purse for the keys. "Find anything good?" Penny asks on the other end. In the background, I hear my favorite sound ever. Little girl giggles.

"Show you when I get home. Just need to stop and pick up a few more ingredients for the lasagna. Anything else we need?"

I unlock the door, slide into the car, and toss my bags on the passenger seat. Cranking the ignition, I pull the phone away when the engine lags and rumbles rougher than usual. I shrug as the roar settles in its typical hum.

Bringing the phone back to my ear, Penny rambles on. Who knows what I missed. "And will you grab Twizzlers, popcorn, M&M's, Red Hots, and Mike and Ike's. Oh, and ice cream." God, she probably rattled off twenty other different forms of junk food before I paid attention. Oh well.

"Are we serving sugar comas for dessert," I joke. "We do not need all of that."

"Hey," Penny says in a stern motherly voice. "We *need* them for movie time. Don't be a Debbie Downer, Auti."

I laugh. "Alright, I'm hanging up now. Should only be another thirty minutes. You guys okay?"

More giggles. Tickle-fest giggles. "We're fine. Drive safe and see you soon."

Disconnecting the call, I toss my phone in my purse and back out of the space. Two miles down the road, the car idles high at a red light. I check the gauges and note nothing looks off. No warning lights light up the display. Giving the dash a gentle tap, I tell the car we are almost done for the day.

Inside the grocery store, I snatch up the final missing ingredients for our Sunday night lasagna. Reluctantly, I grab a handful of sugary snacks for movie night per Penny's request. After checking out, I head back to my car, slip inside, and go to start it.

But the engine doesn't turn over.

I crank the key again. Nothing. No ticking or whining. Not a single sound.

"Well shit," I say, slapping my hands against the steering wheel.

Digging my phone out of my purse, I call Penny. "Are they out of Cherry Garcia? Please tell me they aren't."

"Pen, my car won't start."

The television mutes in the background. "Won't start? Does it sound like it's trying?"

I shake my head, then remember she can't see me. "No. It sounded off when I left the mall, but nothing bad. Just louder."

"Need me to come get you?"

Giggles erupt in my ear. "No, stay with her. I'll call for a tow truck. Hopefully it won't take long."

"You at our usual store?"

"Yeah, why?"

When Penny doesn't answer right away, I pull the phone away from my ear to see if the call dropped. Nope, still connected. "Sorry," she says when I bring the phone back to my ear. "Was looking up tow places nearby. Looks like there's one a couple miles away. I'll text you the number."

A second later, my phone pings with an incoming text. "Got it, thanks."

"Sure thing. Keep me posted."

"I will."

After hanging up with Penny, I dial the number she sent to me. A gruff voice answers and I explain my situation and ask if he can tow my car. Thankfully, I am met with a resounding yes. The man tells me he should arrive within thirty minutes.

While waiting for him, I turn the key one click in the ignition and listen to the radio. *At least it's not the battery and I don't have to wait in silence.* Five songs and two commercials later, an older man pulls up behind me with a flatbed.

As I step out of the car, he strolls forward staring at my Betsy and whistles. "Where'd you get a beauty like this?" he asks.

"Long story short, it was my granddad's. He restored it and passed it on to me."

"Well she's a beaut." The man extends his hand my way. "Name's Aaron."

I shake his hand. "Autumn. Thanks for coming to my rescue."

"Tell me what seems to be the problem."

I explain to Aaron what happened earlier when I left the mall and at the traffic light. Then how it wouldn't start when I walked out of the store. Thank goodness I didn't buy any perishables.

"Mind if I give it a try right quick?" Aaron asks.

I shake my head and gesture to the driver's side door. He sits in the car a moment and turns the key a few times, leaning closer to the dash. He listens intently, trying to locate the source of the issue. A minute later, he hops out and closes the door.

"Not sure what's wrong with her, but I'll give it a full rundown at the shop in the morning. Anything you need to grab out of the car before I get it on the flatbed?"

"Just a few bags."

After I collect my bags and purse, Aaron loads Betsy up on the truck. Soon, we are driving down the road toward his shop. A mix of gasoline and pine-scented cardboard trees fills the cab. Aaron whistles along with a country music song on the radio as he taps his fingers on the steering wheel.

I glance over at his profile and can't help but think he looks familiar. Not sure how, but his profile gives me déjà vu. But I shake it off and stop scrutinizing him.

Just as another song starts on the radio, we pull into the parking lot of an auto repair shop. The exterior a bright and bold blue with an oval white sign in the center. Thompson's Garage is swirled in the same blue on the white sign. Several cars are parked on the side of the building, shaded from the afternoon sun by a handful of various trees.

As Aaron circles the lot and starts to back up to one of the white bay doors, it rolls up. I look in the side mirror, but don't see anyone and assume Aaron must have pressed a garage door opener.

When the truck stops fifteen feet from the bay, I glance over at him and he gives me a warm smile. "Time to get your girl inside. Then we'll do paperwork. Do you need a ride home?"

"No, I'll request an Uber. Thank you." We hop out and I hear him talking over the Diesel engine on the opposite side. I walk around the front of the truck, ready to ask him to repeat himself. "What was…"

Words fail me as I round the tow truck and none other than Jonas is eyeing my Betsy with a giddy expression. He says something to Aaron, and I can't quite make it out. He starts to say something else, turns his head to face Aaron, and spots me.

A brilliant smile lights up his face and Aaron notices. "Hey," Jonas says as he walks past Aaron, heading straight for me. "Is this you?" He points up at Betsy.

I nod. "Yeah. She won't start."

"Dad just told me." *Dad?* Now the déjà vu makes sense. Similar profiles because they are from the same gene pool. "Sorry she's being stubborn. We'll fix her up for you."

I smile. "Thanks, I appreciate it."

Aaron sidles up to us. "Jonas, you know this pretty lady?"

Before Jonas answers, I speak up. "We just met. I work at the tattoo shop a few miles down the street." I point to Jonas's forearm. "Worked on his newest addition."

A wide, toothy smile stretches from ear to ear on Aaron's face. "Huh." Aaron glances to Jonas then back to me. "Well you did a great job, sweetheart." He throws a wink my way. "Gonna unload your girl here. Shouldn't be long."

"Thank you." Once Aaron is out of earshot, I face Jonas again. "That's your dad?"

"Yep. And this is our shop."

Oh, wow. Suddenly, I am wondering if there were any photos online of the shop owners when Penny chose this place. Sneaky wench. Not sure if I should hit or thank her.

Not sure what to say, I glance up at the sign on the building. "So, has your dad owned it since eighty?"

Jonas follows my gaze. "Yeah. He'd been saving for years. Worked as many hours as he could to still pay the bills plus save. Lucky for Dad, the bank took over the place from the previous owner and he purchased it cheaper than expected. Kismet, I suppose."

"Kismet," I mumble.

I had never given much thought or energy to the term. Fate. Destiny. Devine providence. Fate had its place in the world, I suppose, but the idea of some outside force steering me this way or that way didn't sit right with me. I liked believing I was in control of my life. That I made the rules and held the power. The notion of being in control, I could apply it to so many scenarios from my past.

No one held power over me.

But the idea of kismet is starting to grow on me. How else could I explain meeting Cora and Gavin, and, by proxy, Jonas? Did they just stumble into a random tattoo shop? Or did some invisible force guide them my way? Not sure I will ever know the true answer. And the more I think about it, the more my head hurts.

What I did know for certain was Jonas walked in. He sat in my chair. And my heart somersaulted like a gymnast for hours. By the way he looks at me right now, I would venture to guess Jonas's heart is flipping and twirling too.

"While Dad unloads your car, we can step into the office and start the paperwork."

"Okay."

Jonas leads us into a spacious room on the south side of the building. As we step inside, I scan the room and see a couple rows of chairs next to a table with a Keurig and coffee fixings. A large window consumes half of the south wall and brightens the room naturally. A rack of magazines sits beside the coffee station and a small flat screen hangs near the ceiling. The large window is partially cut off by a wall, which looks to be an addition to the original structure. That specific wall is painted with a mural of the shop, I assume, when it first opened.

Jonas leads us through a door and into an office, where the large window continues. Two desks sit butted up against one another. There is a small kitchen/dinette area and a plush couch with a coffee table. The walls have a coat of beige paint with several framed photos—which I can't make out without closer inspection. Cozy—for an auto repair shop.

"Have a seat," Jonas says, gesturing to a chair near one of the desks. "Let me just grab the paperwork." He sits at one of the desks and rummages through a drawer. Retrieving a triplicate form, he puts it on a clipboard, grabs a pen, and leans back in his chair. "Just a few questions and then you can head out." Then he glances up from the form. "Do you need a ride? I can take you home, if you want."

I shake my head. "Nah. I'll grab an Uber. Only live a mile or two from here, so shouldn't cost much."

He nods, then prattles off a handful of questions. Name. Address. Phone number. When he asks for my number, I stumble for a moment. *Your phone number is for the paperwork, idiot.* At least that is what I tell myself. He continues the questionnaire as if he fills them out a thousand times a day. Most of it was simple maintenance history on the car.

After all the questions, I sign the bottom and he gives me a copy. "Once we get a look under the hood in the morning, we'll call you and let you know what we found."

"Sounds great." I rise from the chair, grab my purse and shopping bags. Retrieving my phone, I open up the Uber app and request a ride.

"Sure I can't give you a ride?"

I shake my phone in front of him and smile. "Already got one. Thanks, though."

"Mine is better," he teases.

No doubt about that. Heat crawls up my neck and blazes across my cheeks. "What if my Uber driver pulls up in a snappy sports car?" I joke.

He rolls his eyes and laughs. "Mine would still be better."

We wander out of the office and back into the sticky, Florida fall weather. Just outside the building, we pause under an awning. The sun still shines down from above, but is slowly fading as afternoon drifts closer to evening.

Beside me, I *feel* Jonas's eyes on my profile. Tracing the angle of my jaw to my chin with his hypnotic eyes. Skirting them up to my lips and honing in on them. I tuck my lips in my mouth for one, two, three before I pop them back out. And I don't miss the soft groan from him.

"Can I call you?" he asks.

I peek up at him and his eyes are exactly where I knew

them to be. "About the car?" I play innocent, but know his question has nothing to do with the car.

In slow motion, he shakes his head and meets my gaze. "You know I'll call about the car." His eyes drop to my lips for a split second before returning back north, and my heart skips. "What I mean is, can I call you" —he pauses and licks his lips— "and take you out sometime?"

Every atom inside my tiny five-foot-five frame jumps up and down like I just won a million dollar lottery. Because Jonas is definitely a prize. A prize any woman would be lucky to hold in her arms. So why am I hesitant? What is stopping me from blurting out *yes, yes, yes* at the top of my lungs. I know the answer to this question. It's a question I have had to answer several times over the years. But it's an answer I keep to myself.

"Jonas... I-I don't know..." His eyes wilt as his shoulders sag. *Damnit.* "It's not that I don't want to."

And just like that, hope glints anew in his eyes.

This is going to be so much harder than I imagined.

SIX

JONAS

She likes me. I see it in the upward curve of her lips. In the extra sparkle in her eyes. How her breathing changes. The way she automatically leans an inch closer. She likes me, but is afraid to admit it.

"What is it then?" I run my fingers through my hair. "Am I too pretty for you?" I tease.

Autumn throws her head back and laughs. The sound bubbly like a fountain-style cherry cola. "Maybe." She waves her hand up and down my body. "I mean, how's a girl going to compete with this?" Her words are meant as a joke, but they heat me from head to toe.

When I finally get my wits about me again, I say, "Swear I'm not always this pretty."

She laughs again and shakes her head. "You're persistent, aren't you?"

I shrug. "Only with people who count."

At this, her smile softens. Becomes more shy.

"Jonas…" She steps closer to me and I pick up hints of vanilla and something fruity—cherry, maybe. "I really would love to talk more and go out sometime, but…"

At the tattoo shop the other day, she said she wasn't seeing anyone. Right? "But?"

"I- I have other obligations."

What does *other obligations* mean?

Maybe she has a sick family member she helps when not at work. Or maybe she works more than one job. I never really took that into consideration. Could be something completely innocent. She could be a volunteer at a shelter or attend school during the day.

But does she have said obligations every day of the week? I wouldn't think so.

"Well, if you ever find yourself free of said obligations for a teeny, tiny minute, I would love to take you out. I'm willing to beg, if necessary." I glance over at Dad who continues to ogle Autumn's car. "Dad would never let me live it down if I got on my knees and groveled. But I'm willing to live with the incessant teasing."

She laughs again, and I press record in my mind. I love the carefree sound and want to play it on repeat. A white SUV pulls into the lot and Autumn glances down at her phone.

"My ride is here." She locks her phone and drops it in her black, white, and red purse which looks strikingly similar to a bowling bag, only smaller. "Let me see your phone."

I glance down at her outstretched palm. Without hesitation, I pull my phone from my back pocket, unlock it, and hand it over. Polished nails matching the rouge on her lips tap with efficiency over the screen. Seconds later, her phone pings in her bag and she hands me back my phone.

"Gotta go." She salutes me. "Talk to you later."

My head drifts in the clouds. I watch as she gets in the SUV and buckles up. I wave as the car drives off and just stand there like an idiot. Hand still up a minute later. Snapping out of my fog, I unlock my phone and stare down at the screen where she messaged herself from my phone.

Jonas: Can't wait for you to call.

A smile slowly creeps across my face as I fixate on the simple text. *Me either*.

"So, that's her, huh?"

I jump. "Argh! Dad, you scared the shit out of me."

He laughs. "Guess there's a first for everything. She must have you all kinds of twisted up if your old man scared ya."

"Guess so."

He points to my phone. "If my instincts are right—which let's get real, they always are—she's a keeper."

Yeah. But how do you keep something not yet yours? "Couldn't agree more."

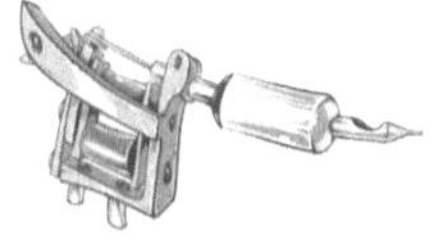

After parking my bike near the back of the lot, I enter the pub, wave to the hostess, and weave through the crowd to our usual table. Twenty feet away, I take a deep breath and throw on a smile as I approach Cora, Gavin, and Shelly.

More than a week has passed since Cora and Gavin's wedding. And so much has happened in that small blip of time.

Tonight will be the true test. To see whether or not the love I have had for Cora over the last ten years has changed. If it has really transitioned from romantic to friendship. Most people wouldn't be able to set aside such potent feelings. But when something else—someone else—clicks in place, you see the world a little different.

As I step up to the table, Cora laughs at something Shelly said and I absorb her laughter. Test how it makes me feel. See if it strikes me as it did weeks and months and years ago. It echoes across the table, has the corner of my mouth perking up for a beat, then settles.

The first thing I realize is it doesn't sink in. Her laughter doesn't seep into my pores, bleed through my veins, and root itself in my marrow. It just floats through the air and settles. The only reason I smile is because it's natural. Her happiness makes me happy.

"Hey, man," Gavin says as I settle on a stool next to Shelly.

"Hey." I raise a hand and nod at Chris, the bartender. He throws me a thumbs up. "Any good ones hit the stage yet?"

For years, Cora, Shelly, and I came to this bar at least once a week. The local bar and grill hosted karaoke several nights a week. If it was a slow night on non-karaoke days, the manager would let people go on stage and sing for the hell of it. The more drinks people consume, the more interesting the singing. Definitely some memorable performances.

Cora perks up. "You just missed the Momma Train Gang."

I glance over at her and *see* her for the first time. No doubt, Cora is a beautiful woman. But in a strange twist of events, I no longer see her how I once did. I don't study her eyes or lips or smile with too much depth. Don't feel the urge to stare at her for hours and pine over what I can't have.

The day I met Cora, I remember how her smile made me sweat a little. Made me a little fidgety.

Now when I look at her, a familiarity settles inside me. Still a form of love, but more comparable to what I feel when Jasmine or Jillian are around. Sibling love.

Maybe this is how close friendship should feel. Like family.

"Momma Train Gang? Dear lord, dare I ask?"

Shelly snort-laughs just as a beer is set in front of me

on a coaster. "Thought I'd seen it all." She slaps her hand on the table. "Boy, was I wrong."

I glance between the two women, both of which laugh uncontrollably, then to Gavin. "Care to fill me in since these two are obviously incapable."

Gavin tilts his head and eyes me for a beat. Once he satisfies the question in his head, he tells me what I missed. "Four women, probably in their mid-to-late forties, jumped on stage and mutilated 'My Humps' by Black Eyed Peas. Mix the singing with the way they shook their… assets, let's just say it was memorable."

We both take a sip of our beers and shake our heads. "You guys eat yet?" I ask him.

"Nah. Thank god. Might've come back up. Not sure how you guys have been doing this for years. Some of these people make me want to gouge my eyes out."

I throw my head back and laugh. Shelly and Cora join me. "Dude, the first time was a total accident. But it wiped the stress of the day away. So, we kept coming. Call it tradition. Need a good laugh? Come in for karaoke night." Scanning the bar for our server, I spot my oldest friend, Trevor. "Be back in a sec."

Slipping off my stool, I walk over to the bar and sidle up beside him.

"Hey," he says as soon as he notices me. "What're you doing here?"

I point over to the table I just abandoned. "Hanging out. Drinking beer. Listening to shit karaoke. Grabbing a bite. You?"

He stares down at his glass, rounds his shoulders, and sags. "Just broke it off with Christine."

Well, this throws me off. "Seriously, bro? What the hell happened?"

Trevor and Christine have been connected at the hip for the last three years. Went everywhere together. If we had a guy's night without her tagging along, we were lucky. So hearing that they are no longer together shocks the hell out of me.

"Got off work early on Friday. Thought I'd surprise her. Get home before her and make a nice dinner."

"Okay…" I drawl.

"When I parked at the complex and spotted her car home early, I was bummed I couldn't surprise her. But excited she was home early." Trevor pauses to down the last of his drink. Something tells me this tale is about to go south real fast. "I heard it before I unlocked the door." He cringes. "Her screams. The ones she only makes when…"

Fuck. His pain is so out of my element. But like a good friend, I listen and give him a shoulder.

"I walked into the bedroom. Saw *everything*." He taps the bar before peering up at me. "Dude, it's burned into my retinas. I can't unsee it and it pisses me off. So, I'm trying to forget," he says as the bartender sets another Jack and Coke in front of him.

What the hell do I say? How does a friend comfort another when something like this happens? Fuck if I know.

"Wish I could say or do something to make this better, man."

Trevor slaps the back of my shoulder. "You're a good friend, brother. Thanks for that."

I glance back at my friends across the bar and battle internally where I should be. With them? Or Trevor?

Why choose.

"Trev, come hang out with us." I point over to the high top. "We'll help take your mind off things for a bit."

He stares across the bar at the laughing trio and gauges what to do. "I don't know, brother. Not sure I'm in the mood."

"Exactly. Which is why you need to."

I grab hold of his arm and drag him off the stool. He stumbles beside me through the bar.

Fuck, he has had a lot to drink already.

When we reach the table, I plop his ass on a stool and sit next to him. Gavin scrutinizes every visible inch of Trevor then glances over to me with a silent question. Asking if Trevor is good. Subtly, I nod.

"Shelly, Cora, you remember Trevor?"

They chime in with a unified yes, followed by a bout of laughs.

"Trevor, this is Gavin. Cora's husband. Gavin, this is my oldest friend Trevor. We go back to the days of BMX bikes and when boys thought girls were gross."

Gavin laughs and it thins the bubble of intensity surrounding us. "Sometimes," Gavin says as he side-eyes Cora, "girls are still gross."

"Hey!" Cora play slaps him. "Take that back or you'll regret it."

For the next couple of hours, I sit in the middle of a bar surrounded by a group of people I care about. Smiles and laughs and banter bounce back and forth the entire time. Happiness hovers in the periphery when I catch Trevor smile for a moment. Because if anyone can come out on the other side stronger after something shitty like cheating happens, it is Trevor. And I will help him however possible. Maybe lug him to Wednesday night dinners for the foreseeable future.

Whatever it takes.

The only person missing from this semi-perfect moment is a petite brunette with stormy, cognac eyes and scarlet lips. Maybe I will get lucky. Maybe one day, she will sit on the stool beside me.

SEVEN

AUTUMN

Two days. Two days have passed since I pushed past my doubts and insecurities. When I, for the first time in years, handed out my phone number to a guy.

And he hasn't used it. Not once.

What the hell?

Jonas threw out every hint. Practically begged to call me. So why hasn't he?

And why the hell am I being such a *girl* about the fact he hasn't called or texted? This is one reason why I don't put myself out there. Why I haven't dated in years. Because I can't get my hopes up. Not when my heart isn't the only one on the line. Relationships—no matter the type—don't involve just me. Others have to be taken into consideration.

Penny plops down on the couch and lays her head on my shoulder as I sip my coffee. "Whatcha thinking about?" she asks.

I lean my cheek on her crown and shake my head. "Ridiculous nonsense."

Her body vibrates with laughter, but she contains the sound. "Just call him already. Pull a Sadie Hawkins and woman up."

I laugh at her reference. Penny is always so gung ho and dives in headfirst. Her energy and enthusiasm boost the parts of me I squander. Like reaching out to a guy who is seemingly interested in me, but has been radio silent since I gave him permission to call.

"But…"

"But what, Auti? From everything you told me, the guy is interested. So no buts."

I roll my eyes, sit taller, and spin to face her as she falls from my shoulder into the couch cushions. Drama queen. But I wouldn't want her any other way.

"What if I'm reading him wrong?"

"What if you're not?" Penny garbles into the couch cushion before sitting up and swiping her hair out of her face. "I saw the way he looked at you last Wednesday. Girl, you can't fake the way he reacted. He wants you. Probably more than either of you cares to admit."

"Say you're right." Penny waves her hand in the air and rolls her eyes. I ignore her antics and trudge on. "Why hasn't he called me yet? If he is as interested as you suggest, why am I sitting here questioning it?"

Penny crisscrosses her legs and lays her hands on my knees. "Because he's a guy." I shake my head as she continues. "And because he's probably working all day to fix your car."

I hadn't thought about Betsy or the fact Jonas has his hands all over her. Is it weird to suddenly be jealous of a car? That she's getting more action than I have in years. Hope she isn't too broken. Hope it won't cost a fortune either.

"Forgot about Betsy," I admit.

Penny lifts her hands to clutch my shoulders. "Then use Betsy as a reason to call. Ask how things are going with the repairs. Throw out a little charm. No way he'll resist."

I inhale a deep breath and tuck my hair behind my ear. "Say I call. Besides Betsy, what else do I talk about?" I drop my eyes to my lap. Study a nonexistent loose thread on my pants. "You know how long it's been."

"Yeah, I do. And I question your sanity." I go to interject and she holds her hand up to stop me. "Hear me out. I know *why* you haven't dated or gotten close to anyone in years. But it has been *years, Auti.* Enough time has passed. It's okay to do what makes *you* happy. No one will fault you for that." Penny picks up my hands and envelops them in hers. "Give yourself permission to live. To find happiness."

Although I hate to admit it, she is right. But owning the truth in your head is wholly different than speaking it aloud. Because once the truth leaves your lips, you can never rein it back in. The words can never be unsaid.

"How?" I whisper. "How do I *live* when..." I trail off

and she squeezes my hands.

"You let us help. Just as we always have. Me, Reznor, Iliana, Rex. We may not be conventional, we may not share the same genetics, but we're family. And family always sticks together. Through thick and thin."

I nod robotically. Times like this, I wish my actual family gave a damn. Wish they actually loved me for who I am, instead of hating me for the choices I made over the years. Choices I wouldn't change if given the opportunity. Because all my choices led me to where I am now. To Penny and my tat family. To happiness and potentially more. To so much love.

I reach for my phone and Penny claps like a lunatic. "You need to leave the room. I can't call him with you sitting in front of me, judging every word or gesture."

Penny sighs like the drama queen she is and rises from the couch. "Fine." She huffs and wanders down the hall. "If you need me, I'll be in the tub, reading and soaking up lavender bubbles. I expect a full rundown after."

"Yeah, yeah."

Once the bathtub faucet cranks on, I bite my lip and scroll through my text history. I tap on the message I sent myself from Jonas's phone and read it for the hundredth time. *Can't wait for you to call.* And it suddenly dawns on me. If I read this as the recipient, it sounds as if *he* is waiting for *me* to call.

Shit. Has he read this message over and over, wondering why *I* haven't called?

I tap the top of the message and stare at the different

options below his phone number and blank contact image. My finger hovers over the small phone icon as I suck in a deep breath.

Now or never, Autumn. Just tap the screen.

Swallowing, I press the phone icon and lift the phone to my ear. One ring. Two. Three. Just as I consider hanging up, the line connects.

"Hello?" Jonas's low, throaty voice floats through the line and settles deep in my bones. A flutter stirs in my belly. My tongue suddenly thick. "Hello? Autumn?"

Did he add my name to his contacts? A new wave of excitement washes over me as I clear my throat. "Yeah, sorry," I answer.

"Everything okay?"

No, because I am a complete moron. "Yes. Just calling to check on Betsy." And ask why you haven't called me yet.

"Betsy's doing just fine," he answers with jubilance in his voice and I picture a smile brightening his face. "Should be done with her in time for Thursday."

"Thursday?"

"My appointment." Right, he will be back in my chair in two days. My belly does another flip. "Thought I'd bring the car to you. If that's okay."

I nod, then remember he can't see me. "Yeah, that's fine."

The line goes silent for a moment as I pick at the chipping polish on my finger nails. *Need to repaint them later.*

The longer the silence stretches, the more I wonder

why I am so bad at this. Years ago, I never had issues talking to guys. Hell, most of my friends are men. Always have been.

So why am I struggling to find a single thing to say? Why is it so difficult to ask him how he is doing? Or if he would like to hang out sometime. Penny's words from minutes ago repeat in my head. *Give yourself permission to live. To find happiness.*

Is Jonas the happiness I have been missing all these years? Maybe. But I will never know until I put myself out there. Until I ask.

Just as I open my mouth to ask if he would like to get together sometime and get to know each other, a bang on the other end of the line breaks the silence.

"Shit," Jonas mutters. "Sorry, but I need to go. Some people can't be left unattended." He doesn't sound angry. Amused, maybe. "Glad you called."

"You are?" I slap my hand to my forehead and close my eyes.

"Definitely. But I really do need to go before *someone* breaks shit." I pick up on the humor in his voice. "See you on Thursday."

I nod. "See you Thursday."

"And Autumn?"

"Yeah."

He stays silent a moment. "Nothing." I hear his dimpled smile in the single word. "Bye."

"Bye," I whisper as the line disconnects.

I keep the phone at my ear long after Jonas hangs up.

What was he going to say? Doesn't he know my mind will spin with endless possibilities until I see him again? Until I ask him.

Holding on to the phone, I drop my hands to my lap and stare at the screen. Stare at the generic contact image and the number beneath it. Tapping the top of the screen, I click on the info icon and add Jonas's contact information. Somehow, I need to figure out a sneaky way to get a picture of him. I hate not having images to associate with my contacts. Just a weird preference.

"Why aren't you in here telling me all the juicy details?" Penny yells from the bathroom.

Rising from the couch, I head down the hall. When I reach the bathroom, I peek in and laugh at Penny as she bobs in the middle of a two-foot tower of bubbles. "You're a freaking nut," I tell her.

"And you're avoiding a conversation. Better luck next time."

I roll my eyes, walk into the bathroom, and plop down on the closed toilet lid. "There's not much to tell. I called him, he was busy at work, there was awkward chitchat about Betsy, then silence, and goodbye."

"You should've been in here with it on speakerphone. Then I could decipher all the things you're leaving out."

Forever wanting all the dirty details. "There was this one thing," I trail off.

She sits up taller in the tub, sloshing water over the sides and flashing me her boobs. I cover my eyes with a hand and she laughs.

"First, you've seen my boobs a million times. No need to be prude now."

"But we weren't talking about guys then."

Penny shrugs and scoops bubbles closer to her chest to appease me. "Anyway. Elaborate. What does *this one thing* mean?"

I huff and lean back on the toilet tank. "There was this one point when it sounded like he wanted to say something. Maybe ask me something. But then he just blew it off and said bye."

During the call with Jonas, that moment of silence dragged out for hours in my head. I filled it with daydreams of my hand cradled in his. Of his cheek pressed to mine as he whispered sweet words in my ear. Of his soft lips brushing mine while his stubble scraped my skin.

Did his mind wander much the same? Did he picture the possibility of us?

Penny shrugs and the bubbles flatten a little in the tub. "Maybe he was going to ask you something, but didn't want to over the phone. Have you ever considered the idea he may be just as nervous as you are?"

Have I given the idea consideration? No. I pictured most men as forward and cocky. Majority of the men I ink represent the notion well. Hundreds have asked for my number. When they do, I just hand over my business card for the shop.

Except for Jonas.

Granted, he has my phone number on an invoice in

Thompson's Garage. But I never picture him abusing the privilege. He asked for my number because he was raised to be a gentleman. He asked for my number because he wanted to give me the choice. To say yes or no. When I said yes, I assumed he would use my number sooner rather than later. Most men don't have the patience to sit idle and wait for the woman to make the first move. Obviously, Jonas has many redeeming qualities I have yet to learn.

"Actually, I haven't. Suppose you could be right."

"Could be? Girl, I'm right ninety-nine point nine percent of the time. And you know it."

"Alright, conversation is officially over," I tease as I stand up and head out of the bathroom. "Finish your bath and we'll head out."

"Yes, mother," she teases back. "Be out in a jiff."

I amble into my bedroom and sift through my closet. Tugging a shirt from the hanger, I toss it on the bed and grab a pair of jeans. Mindlessly, I dress and replay Penny's response to Jonas's silence.

Is Jonas nervous? If he is, I am curious as to why. He doesn't come off as timid. At least not to the degree where he would be nervous asking a woman out. In some respects, he already did. So why would he be nervous to ask again? Is it the simple notion of being rejected twice? I hope that is not the case. Because if Jonas asks me again, my answer will be different.

If he asks me again, I will say yes.

I crank the Bel Air to life and smile when it purrs like the beauty it is. Dad wanders over and I roll down the window.

"She sounds good as new." He wipes his hand with a red rag then stuffs it in his coveralls. "Tell Autumn I say hello."

I laugh under my breath. Since Autumn's car arrived at the garage and she went home, Dad has given me a ration of shit every single day. Teases me about wanting another grandchild. Asking me over and over if I called Autumn yet. If I asked her on a date. Sometimes, I swear he is worse than Mom.

And when she called on Tuesday, Dad knocked a fender off the workbench as he snuck closer to eavesdrop. Always lurking about. Hence why I ended the call abruptly with Autumn.

"Will do." Dad taps the roof before I throw the car in reverse.

Since the trip to the tattoo shop from the garage is short, I take the 'scenic' route to listen better to the car. Thankfully, nothing major was wrong with the engine. Just typical wear and tear on easy-to-replace parts. Cars like the Bel Air can be more challenging to repair if it's a major component. Engines just aren't made how they once were. When this car was manufactured, the engine didn't rely on hundreds of little computers and motherboards. They were solid and metal and everlasting. And their parts weren't easy to find nowadays.

Five miles later, I roll into the back parking lot of the tattoo shop. Shutting off the engine, I sit in the car another minute, study the silver and black upholstery, and inhale the peculiar Coke float scent.

Every inch of this car screams Autumn. Fits her personality and the way she carries herself.

Question is, do I? Do I fit into her lifestyle? Who she is and the life she leads.

Because I want to. Desperately.

Other than Cora, I never thought it possible to feel so intensely for a woman. And I never thought I would feel it so soon and easily.

Exiting the car, I lock it up and head for the front entrance. The bell jingles when I walk in and I love the smile on Autumn's face when she peeks up and notices my arrival. Her smile brightens the room instantly. *Hey* I mouth and her cheeks pink.

I wonder if she blushes this much with other men. Hopefully not. I would like to believe she reserves the crimson heat just for yours truly.

After I check in with the Bubble Yum queen, I pace the lobby and stare at the art on the walls. I scan each image but pay closer attention to the artist's names on the bottom. I stop at the third piece and study it intently. The eleven-by-fourteen heavy cream paper penned with millions of small dots. Up close, I spot each pinpointed speck of ink on its own. Stepping back, the dots form the image of two people holding hands and strolling down the sidewalk. Of the two people, you only see their hands and half their forearms. When I glance down at the artist's name, it doesn't shock me when I see Autumn's next to a hefty price tag.

But the art is worth every penny.

A finger tap on my shoulder interrupts my fascination with the art. I spin around to find Autumn. Her smile bright and shy. One-hundred-percent adorable and addicting.

"Nice piece," I say, pointing over my shoulder.

Autumn glances around me and eyes the art. "Thank you. Took months to finish." A fresh blush paints her cheeks and I love her bashful nature more.

"No doubt. Wish I had the patience to create something so priceless."

She tucks her lips in her mouth and bites down to fight against her smile. Then she pops them and I can't look away. Don't want to look away. Her crimson lips an invitation I want to answer with a resounding yes.

"You ready?" she asks.

I nod. "Yeah."

Autumn leads us to her booth, and I don't miss the way Bubble Yum winks and smiles as we pass. Interesting.

I sit in the chair while Autumn preps everything. In no time, she places the stencil on my forearm. After it's in place, I remember I still have her keys and pull them from my pocket. I set them on my lap and chance a look at her. She has been quiet. Too quiet.

"Sorry I didn't hand over the keys before you gloved up."

"No biggie," she says and shrugs. "Why was Betsy being temperamental?"

I love how she refers to her car as a person with an ill temper. Yet another quality to add under the adorable category. An ever-growing list.

"Just needed to replace the starter and a couple other small parts."

Autumn slumps and sighs before meeting my eyes. Her brows pinch slightly and accentuate her swirly cognacs. "Sounds pricey."

General automotive repair racks up over time. Certain parts and repairs costing more. But repairing Autumn's car was simple. Easier than most newer cars. The beauty of older cars is how spread out the engines are. How you don't have to remove half or more of the engine to get to one part. Whenever Dad and I get to work on older vehicles, we savor it. Drool like idiots. Take our time to have it around longer.

"Not at all, actually."

She perks up at that. "Great. Let me know how much I owe you, and we can settle up when we're done."

After Dad and I finished up Autumn's car earlier, he followed me into the office and closed the door. As I finalized the paperwork for Autumn's car, jotting down what repairs we had done, Dad walked over and slapped his hand on top of the invoice. *"No charge,"* he'd said. He looked me in the eyes and shook his head. His decision was final and not up for debate.

Honestly, I was happy to not charge Autumn. But I didn't have the final say in waiving payment. Dad still holds the power where Thompson's Garage finances are concerned.

"Not a dime," I tell her. "Dad insists. He says hello, by the way."

Autumn slouches and pouts.

Fuck me running. If I don't look away now, I will embarrass the hell out of myself. Nothing like sitting in a chair next to a beautiful woman with a hard-on while her eyes focus less than six inches away.

Think, think, think.

Images of my sisters pop in my head and is exactly what I need. Nothing like siblings to kill any sort of mood.

"Well, I'll have to repay him. Bake him a cake or brownies or cookies. Does he like any of those?" she asks.

"All of the above. He's not picky and will love whatever you make. Thanks."

"For what?"

For existing, I want to say, but bite my tongue. "It's a generous thing to do. Most wouldn't."

She nods. "Well, I'm not most people."

This much I have figured out.

For the next twenty minutes, I close my eyes and lay back while she starts on my tattoo. For the first time, I don't enjoy the silence. I want to talk to Autumn. Ask about her life. What she does for fun. What she does when she isn't working. Ask her to have dinner with me. Or do something she enjoys.

For obvious reasons, I haven't had an actual girlfriend in years. I tried. Tried to date other women while I pined over Cora. But it never worked out. Never got past the first kiss on the doorstep after our date. Because I never wanted it to.

But now... I want it more than anything.

Want to take her out and share a meal together. The food or restaurant doesn't have to be fancy as long as Autumn is there. I want to hang out with friends and have her hooked on my arm. Feel her warmth against my skin and bask in her sweet perfume and infectious laughter.

I peel my eyes open, lift my head, and glance down at her. Hunched over my forearm, she shifts my skin and runs the gun over the purple lines. I study her every move. The way she cocks her head when she scrutinizes her own work. How she leans back to see the tattoo from farther away. The way she tucks her lips in her mouth when hesitant—like she is right now.

"What are you thinking about?" I croak.

She sits up straighter and meets my gaze. Her eyes tell the tale of struggle. Struggle to do one thing versus another. A battle of wills.

Her lips pop out and I swallow. "What were you going to ask me the other day?"

I furrow my brow and tilt my head to the side. "When?"

"On the phone. Sounded like you were going to ask me something, and you didn't."

Ah, yes. Because I did have a question on the tip of my tongue. Until I caught Dad snooping. The plan was to ask if I could take her to dinner. But I chickened out when I spotted Dad ten feet away with his head leaning in close as he picked up the fender.

"Um." I rub the back of my neck with my free hand. "Was going to ask if you wanted to maybe grab dinner sometime."

I get drunk on her cognac irises as she doesn't blink or look away. Sweat a little from the intensity of her gaze. Stop breathing when she doesn't utter a single word in response.

A guy such as myself would strike gold if Autumn agreed to go on a date. I still have so much to learn about her, but from what I have seen so far, she is a rare gem. Sparkling in the sunlight and stealing your breath.

She parts her lips to respond, but snaps them shut a

moment later. When she does it again—and again—I perk up at her speechlessness. Before I have the chance to tell her to not worry about it, she dips the gun in the ink cap and works on my arm again.

Rejection washes over me—for a second time—as I slump in the chair.

What exactly stops her from saying yes? This is the single, most important—and frustrating—question rattling inside my brain right now. The one that makes me question her bashfulness and blushing and frequent eye contact. The reason must be huge. Has to be. Because the chemistry between us is off the charts. At least it feels off the charts from where I sit. And there is no way this attraction is one-sided. Can't be.

As I lean back and rest my head against the chair, I get a quick glimpse of her smile and a blush smattering her cheeks. I close my eyes and smile like a fool—not giving a damn who sees. She may not respond verbally, but her body language gives so much away.

The next hour breezes by as I daydream of taking Autumn on a date. Where we would go. What we would do afterward. Her warm, slender fingers woven with mine. My arms holding her close as I hug her good night. Her sweet perfume swathing me in a cocoon as I lean in to press my lips to hers.

A chill snaps me out of my daydream as Autumn cleans my finished tattoo.

"So jumpy," she teases. "Might start to think you're a virgin." Autumn laughs, then stops once she realizes what she said. "Sorry," she mutters. "That was inappropriate."

Tattoo virgin is what she meant. Not a virgin in the sex department. My virginity had been surrendered long ago in both areas. For obvious reasons, she knew I wasn't a tattoo virgin. But Autumn had no clue about my sexual history—which isn't extensive, but exists.

Which is the exact reason her cheeks are currently one shade lighter than her rouge-painted lips. And I love how the intimacy of this conversation makes her squirm. Her semi-shy nature is not something often seen nowadays.

"Would that be a bad thing?" I mean the question as a joke. But a joke she isn't privy to yet.

She tucks her lips in her mouth and clamps down. I want to reach forward and release her lips from their prison. But I stop myself. We don't know each other well enough for me to do such things.

"Um, no," she answers softly.

Although my tattoo is as clean as it will get right now, she continues wiping it to avert her eyes. "Autumn…"

"Yeah?" she says, eyes still laser focused on my distal forearm.

"Look at me," I whisper.

She licks her lips. "Mmhm?" Slowly, she lifts her gaze and locks it with mine.

"There's no need to be embarrassed." The desire to touch her expands like a hot air balloon in my chest. And I don't want to deny myself any longer. I reach forward with my free hand and graze the skin of her forearm near the black glove edge. Her momentary gasp trips my heart. I swallow and say, "Was only kidding." The corner of my mouth kicks up as I draw circles over her skin with my thumb.

"You were?" she asks, voice cracking.

I nod and she exhales. Her bashful nature continually takes me by surprise, but I love how flustered she gets when we are near. Because she has my stomach flipping on a trampoline nonstop. "About being a virgin, yes." She snorts quietly. "But not about wanting to ask you out."

Autumn peels off her gloves and tosses them in the trash. She rises from the stool and stretches. I study her a beat before standing up on stiff legs. Taking a moment, I stretch my limbs and arch my back, working out the kinks.

Please tell me I didn't scare her away.

She steps in front of me and moves to exit the booth, then stops and spins to face me. Tipping her head back slightly, she homes in on my lips. When I lick them, her lips quirk up at the corners as she nods.

"Yes," she whispers. "I would love to."

What? I stop myself from sticking my fingers in my ears and wiggling them. "Yes?"

She nods slowly as her nervous smile grows bolder and brighter. "I need to check my schedule, but yes. Can I call or text you later?"

I want to jump on the chair and scream *hell yes you can.* But like the proper gentleman my parents raised me to be, I keep my feet planted firmly on the floor and answer her as levelheaded as possible. "Of course. Wednesday is family dinner night, just so you know."

"Cool."

"Cool," I repeat and suddenly feel as if I am fifteen all over again. "Talk to you later."

She bites the inside of her cheek and nods. "Later." After a cute wave, she spins on her heel and wanders back into her booth with a little extra sway in her hips.

After I pay at the desk, I walk out the door and smile when the bell jingles. Who cares if I need to walk two-plus miles back to the garage to get my bike. Who cares if I forgot to bring a hoodie to the shop. Winter is still a few weeks away—not that the first official day of winter equals cool weather in Florida.

The only thing I *do* care about is the fact Autumn said yes to a date. And the promise of a date with Autumn is enough to keep me warm and has me walking faster. Has me smiling like an imbecile. Makes my heart beat faster and my breath stutter.

Today marks one of the happiest days of my life. A day I will never forget.

NINE

AUTUMN

Jonas leaves the shop and I stand like a fool staring at the door for who knows how long. Staring at the place he last stood. Imagining him walking back in for no other reason than to see me.

I agreed to go on a date with Jonas. Me. A date. An actual doll-yourself-up-for-a-guy date.

Oh my fucking god.

I want to cheer and scream and jump and puke all at once.

When was the last time I was on an actual date? I would have to consult a 2013 calendar to determine the answer. And that little fact makes my stomach ball into a fist and squeeze tight. I may have sequestered myself for all the right reasons, but in doing so, I lost part of who I am. A spontaneous and vivacious woman.

Not as if those elements aren't still inside me. But now

they have been tamped down by other qualities. Traits which currently reside in the spotlight for good reason.

"What just happened?" Penny asks as she skips into my booth.

I snap out of my daze and start cleaning my workstation. "Not sure what you're talking about," I reply, working hard to hide the smile painfully stretching my cheeks.

"Don't toy with my emotions, Auti. Spill. I know something happened."

After I drop the needles in the red bin, I peer up at her and shrug my shoulders. She widens her eyes when I hesitate and torture her a little longer. When she grunts, I decide to alleviate the torment. Because if I don't, Penny will make a scene.

"Jonas asked me on a date."

"And?" Penny steps closer, claps her hands in prayer position, and bats her eyelashes. Utterly ridiculous.

"And..." I drag the word out and count to five before continuing. Last thing I need is Penny strangling me because I am not forthcoming. "I said yes."

She gasps and leans back. Slaps a hand over her heart. "You said yes," she says in disbelief, voice decibels higher than normal. "Did I hear you correctly?"

I ball up the paper towel in my hand and toss it at her face. "Shut up." I laugh. "You heard what I said. Don't be a doofus."

"A doofus? Really? You sound like a five-year-old." Penny puckers her lips and cocks a brow. "Whatever."

She blows a bubble and pops the pink gum with a loud smack. "So, where's he taking you?"

Her question has reality setting in a little more and a buzz hums low in my belly. *Jonas is taking me on a date.* A real date. Out in the world. Where other people exist. Where other people sit together and eat meals and laugh.

Holy shit.

"Not sure," I whisper before clearing my throat and finding my voice. "Told him I needed to check my schedule and I'd call or text him."

Penny rolls her eyes. "Check your schedule? Girl, you make your own schedule."

"True. But I'd be an asshole if I told him a day and someone was booked on my schedule already. Not cool. Someone would end up disappointed, and you know how I feel about that."

She nods. "Guess you're right. So..." She drags the single syllable into a ten-letter word. "What are you going to wear?"

Her question stops me in my tracks. For the first time in almost a decade, restlessness blankets me. Any other day of the week, this question wouldn't bother me. Could prattle off my ensemble in the blink of an eye. But something about dressing myself when I know it's for a set purpose—what I imagine will be the most amazing date of my life—has me stumbling in my tracks.

Jonas makes me stammer. For all the right reasons.

"I have no clue." I stare at Penny dumbstruck.

Stepping closer, she lays her hands on my shoulders

and shakes me. "Snap out of it. That's what you have me for." I nod. "Okay, you finish cleaning up. I'll check your schedule for the next week and then we can game plan. Sound good?"

"Yes." I still can't believe this is real.

"Auti, I'm so excited for you."

I glance up at her and soak up her sunshine of a smile. Her enthusiasm has me smiling back. "Thanks. Pen?" She lifts her brows in question. "I'm going on a date," I squeal.

Reznor pops his head up from his client and smiles. "You know we all need to approve of him. Right?"

Stepping up to the wall between our booths, I prop my elbows on the ledge. "Yes, big brother. But let me have a date or two first. Before you and Rex scare him away."

Reznor dips the needle in an ink cap and leans back over his client's posterior ribcage. "Sure, little sis." He smiles and returns his focus to his work.

Once my booth is sanitized, I sidle up next to Penny. It surprises me when she tells me my Saturday night is free. Saturday is generally a busy day at the shop. Although not everyone works Monday to Friday, nine to five, majority of our clientele comes in on Friday and Saturday nights. So it blows my mind when she says my Saturday is bare.

When I question it, she winks conspiratorially and tells me all my other days are jam-packed. I narrow my eyes, but don't push the topic. Penny has been dying for me to get out in the world for years. She accepts why I haven't, but reminds me to live my life. *"How can you ever be happy if you never live outside the same four walls?"* Her words from over the years float through my thoughts.

Penny and I get home an hour later. Iliana is stretched out on the couch, asleep. *Gilmore Girls* plays quietly on the television. When there is nothing new to watch, we watch *Gilmore Girls*. Might be up to our seventh visit to Stars Hollow now. Never gets old.

I pick up the remote and press mute before sitting down next to her. Laying a hand on her forearm, I gently jostle her. "Ili. Wake up," I mumble.

She groans and squints. "What time is it?"

"Little after ten. Everything go okay tonight?" I ask.

"An angel, as always." Iliana scoots herself upright. "You guys finish up early?"

"Yeah. Rez still had someone in his chair, but said he'd be cool if we headed out."

Penny comes up behind me and rests her chin on my shoulder. "Auti has a date."

Iliana's jaw drops. "I'm sorry, but did you just say she has a date?"

Dear, god. Will I ever hear the end of their mockery? In short, no. No, I won't. My two closest friends will surely poke fun at me for quite some time. But I don't care. Wouldn't want them any other way.

"Well, more like the promise of a date. The actual day hasn't been determined yet. Although" —I turn and face Penny for a second— "my Saturday schedule is magically vacant."

"People must be out holiday shopping," Penny tosses out. "Can't help where people go to spend their money."

"Whatever." I roll my eyes, then refocus on Iliana. "I have to reach out to him and let him know what days I don't work."

Iliana leans forward, wraps her arms around me, and surprises me with a hug. "So happy for you," she whispers in my ear. Before I can squeeze her back, she releases me and rises from the couch. "I'm gonna head out."

"You're welcome to crash on the couch if you're still tired."

She smiles. "Thanks, but I'll make it home okay. Rather sleep in my bed, no offense."

After we exchange hugs and goodbyes, Iliana heads home. A second after the lock clicks in place, Penny hauls me to the couch and plops us down. She stares at me, expressionless, until I squirm under her scrutiny.

Why is she looking at me like that? Like a stern mother. Or a perturbed friend. She almost looks… bored. God, she confuses the hell out of me.

"What?"

"Auti," she says, more earnest than ever. "This is very serious."

My brows bunch together and I try to decode what the hell she is talking about. "What is, Pen?"

"Him. Jonas."

I nod. "Yeah," I whisper.

"I can't begin to tell you how excited I am for you."

She glances at the hallway, down toward our bedrooms. "But this is big. Not just for you."

"Why do you think I haven't dated in years? Not like I've never wanted to. Believe me, I *miss* it. But, over the years, I made the right choice."

She nods. "You did."

Solemnity settles between us for a few minutes as we sit quietly on the couch. It isn't just the fact I haven't sat across from a good-looking man and shared a meal in several years that weighs heavy. But also the emotions and expectations which usually come with said scenarios. Emotions and expectations I have no idea if I am ready to handle.

The occasional blip on my radar isn't love. Love takes time. Is substantial and messy. Swallows you whole and never lets you leave.

Thirst is what currently consumes me. Thirst and hunger. My years without companionship have left me starved. Practically emaciated. But my attraction to Jonas isn't some attempt to fatten the ravenous fiend living inside me. My attraction to him is pure and mystical. Makes the organ beneath my breastbone swell and gallop wildly. Has my lungs burning for breath and my stomach topsy-turvy.

Never have I experienced the sensations Jonas induces. Emotions and energy and a gravity that hauls me into his atmosphere.

"Enough with the heavy," Penny announces quietly. "We have more important things to discuss."

"We do?"

She nods. "Like what you'll wear. How you'll fix your hair. What color you plan to paint your nails. The important stuff."

Eyes meeting hers, I pucker my lips and wiggle them side to side. "Oh my god, Pen," I whisper-scream. "Oh. My. God. I have a date."

"What about…?" Penny glances down the hall.

I peek over my shoulder and follow her gaze. "Can you? Please?"

A smile kicks up the corners of her mouth. "I got you covered."

"Thanks, Pen."

Penny and I gossip and giggle on the couch for another half hour before she heads to bed. She mothers me and suggests which top I should pair with which bottoms. What shoes I should wear. How to pin up my hair. I cut her off when she tells me to paint my nails a different color besides my typical cherry red. Polish and lip colors don't get messed with. Ever.

When I hear her bedroom door click shut, I dig my phone out of my purse. Opening up the text history between Jonas and I—where I texted myself from his phone—my fingers hover over the keyboard. Where to begin?

I check the time on the top of the screen and realize how late it is. Almost midnight. He is probably in bed already. No doubt the garage opens early.

I will send a quick message. If he doesn't answer, we

can talk tomorrow. If he does answer, well… we shall see where it leads.

Autumn: Hey. You still up?

My finger hovers over the arrow to the right of my message. *Press send, Autumn. Just. Press. Send.*

I drop my finger and slump into the couch when the blue bubble populates the screen and it says *delivered* beneath. To my surprise, a small bubble hovers on the lower left side of the screen. Three tiny dots dancing as he types a response. My stomach dances alongside the dots.

Jonas: Still up. Too wired to sleep.

Is he ramped up from the adrenaline of getting new ink? Most people find it difficult to sleep shortly after getting a new tattoo. The adrenaline keeps them buzzed for hours afterward. Or is he riled up because I agreed to go on a date with him?

Hopefully it's the latter.

Autumn: Me too.

Jonas: You just finish work?

I smile. Why does him asking about work make me smile?

Autumn: No. You were my last victim. Pen and I got home an hour ago.

Jonas: You guys live together? Must be interesting.

This makes me laugh, and I slap a hand over my mouth. He barely knows Penny, yet has already deemed her a fascinating creature. Which is more than true. Penny is a sassy diamond in the rough.

Autumn: She keeps life interesting.

Jonas: I bet. You get to check your schedule?

Eager. I love it. More than I thought possible.

Autumn: I did. Somehow, the gods have shined down on me and I have Saturday free.

Jonas: Perfect. Would it be okay if I pick you up?
Autumn: Yes.

My cheeks sting from the broad, permanent smile plastered on my face. Why can I not stop smiling?

Jonas: Six?

Autumn: Can't wait.

Although he could dig it up from my paperwork at the garage, Jonas asks for my address. I give it without hesitation. He bids me good night with the promise of picking me up at six on Saturday. Less than two days from now.

I hug my phone to my chest like a preteen. After I swim in the sea of serenity a moment, I rise from the couch, flick off the light, and head down the hall.

Slipping into my bedroom, I quietly change into a tank top and boy shorts. I peel back the covers and ease into bed. Head on the pillow, I follow the moonlight as it dances on the wall and ceiling through the blinds.

I fall asleep with a smile on my face and gentle, sweet snores beside me.

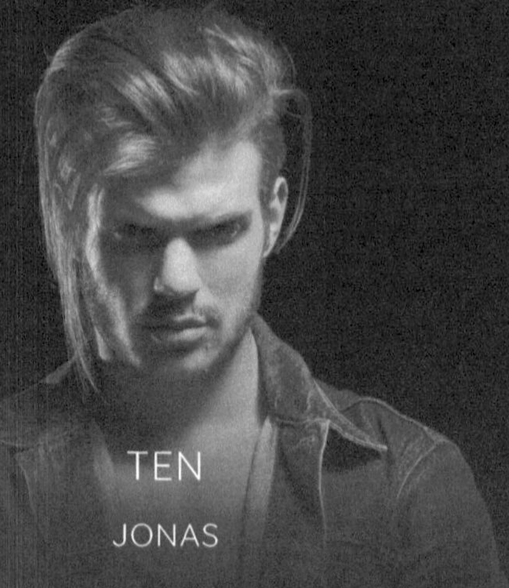

TEN

JONAS

I change my shirt for the seventh time.

Somehow, going on a date with Autumn has turned me prepubescent again. I have never cared so much about my clothes or hair a day in my life. Never lifted my arms so many times to check if I put on deodorant. In the last thirty minutes, I have probably sniffed my pits more times than in the last three months.

Someone send help.

I decide on a long-sleeve, black Henley, jeans, and my leather boots. Staring at my reflection in the bathroom mirror, I brush my hair left, then back again. Regardless of my efforts, the few inches of hair atop my head stays a mess. So I give up, comb my fingers through it, and abandon my reflection.

Spartan barks and zooms around the kitchen island like a bewildered maniac.

"Come on, nut. Let's get you dinner before I leave."

He barks in approval and drops on his haunches in front of his bowl. I scoop a cup of food into his bowl and make him wait with a hand signal. For a spaz, he obeys every command I give without hesitancy. Thank you obedience classes for all you do.

While Spartan vacuums down his dinner, I fetch my keys, wallet, phone, a couple blankets and my leather jacket.

Done with his dinner, Spartan runs up to me and barks. I shuffle my hand back and forth over his head, roughing up his fur. "Good boy. Let's go outside really quick. Then Dad has to go."

I open up the door to the back yard and let him loose. He runs the perimeter, finds several patches of grass he hasn't marked as his, then runs back into the house. I secure him in his kennel, turn on the radio, and head out the front door.

After stowing the blankets in the back, I crank the Jeep's engine and set the heat to low. Yesterday's cold front finally brought cooler temps to our part of the state. The air isn't frigid, but for us natives, it is on the cooler side. Especially once the sun goes down.

A second after I park the Wrangler in front of Autumn's apartment, her front door opens and she steps out. I swallow and all but choke on my own saliva.

How the hell am I supposed to focus all night?

Autumn stands in front of her door in a dress hugging every curve beneath her bust to her knees. The dress bolsters a snug but loose red top and a slim-fit black skirt.

The sweetheart neckline accentuated with a small black bow. Her dark, rich locks frame her face in soft waves.

I swallow again and remind myself to breathe. Remind myself to not be an idiot or say the wrong thing.

Cutting the headlights, I step out of the Jeep and we meet in the middle. A jacket drapes over one of her arms while a small black purse hangs on the other.

"Hi," I rasp. "You look… wow."

She giggles. "Hi. And thank you." Reaching forward, she traces her fingers over my bicep. "You look great too."

The corner of my mouth kicks up. "No one will give me the time of day with you in the room." She peeks up at me from beneath her lashes. "Shall we?" I gesture toward the Jeep and resist the urge to lay my hand on her lower back.

Not yet. Soon, but not yet.

Both of us buckled in, I flip the headlights back on and drive. We sit in the dark cab with only the low volume of my rock playlist floating around us. The air weighted with thrill and anxiety as neither of us speak. And for once, the silence kills me.

"Are you warm enough?" I ask to break the constant quiet.

Out of the corner of my eye, she swivels to face me slightly. "Yes, thank you. Where are we going?"

"Well…" I glance at her a second before returning my eyes to the road. Damn, she robs my every thought. "Wasn't quite sure what you liked to eat, so I aimed for variety. Hope that's okay."

"For future reference, I eat just about everything. Well, at least everything I've tried."

I don't miss the start of her words. *"For future reference."* Three simple words have me soaring high as a kite on a summer day.

"Good to know." I tuck away the new information for safekeeping. "Hope you're hungry. You'll want one of everything. Guaranteed."

"Now I'm intrigued." I hear the smile in her voice and wish I could take my eyes off the road.

Minutes later, I park and help Autumn out. This time I don't resist the urge to rest my hand on her lower back as I steer us to the front door of the restaurant. We may be at the start, but the simple touch feels more than natural. Right. The second we step inside; it feels as if we stepped back in time. Back to the 1950s.

Black-and-white tiles checker the floor. Pops of red and chrome accent backless stools and the lengthy diner counter. Fountains line the counter like keg taps in a bar. The back wall loaded with vintage metal signs for cola and floats and items more popular during a different era. Shelves packed with glassware for milkshakes and sundaes and banana splits. Red and black vinyl booths line the windowed walls, while small two-seater tables sit nestled between the booths and fountain counter. Each booth has its own jukebox. A handful rest on the counter for patrons who sit near the fountains.

A young woman seats us at a booth, hands us menus,

prattles off the evening specials and reminds us breakfast is served all day.

"How did I not know this place existed?" Autumn asks and I shrug. Her eyes float around the room. Awe and delight twinkle in her eyes as she takes it all in. "I think I'm in love."

When her eyes circle back and land on me, she tucks her lips in that cute way she does. A flush paints her cheeks. And I bite back the urge to say what is on my mind.

Me too.

"Wait until you taste the food. This is nothing," I say as I wave around the bustling mom-and-pop diner.

Silence falls over us as we study the menu. After a beat, the server returns to take our order. Autumn orders first and I bite the inside of my cheek at the amount of food she orders. She is either really hungry or had difficulty deciding. Either way, the notion is adorable.

Once both of us order and the server leaves, I laugh.

"What's so funny?" Eyes trained on my face, her brows lift incrementally.

"Hungry?"

My new favorite shade of red tints her cheeks. "There were a hundred different things on the menu I wanted. You're lucky I only ordered what I did."

"Autumn, if you wanted to order the whole menu, I wouldn't care."

And I didn't. As long as I get to sit with her, talk with her, have her in my presence, consider me a happy man. I believe in the simple things. That life doesn't need to be full of miracles, money, and endless *stuff* to discover true happiness. Moments matter more than material possessions. Moments can't be taken away.

"Well, damn. I should've ordered more." She laughs and I join in. "So, Jonas…"

"So, Autumn…"

"Tell me all there is to know about you." She leans forward, sets her elbows on the table, and rests her chin in her palms.

Damn, she is lovable. I mentally shake my head. Shake off the ease at which I fall so easily for a woman I barely know. Am I fortunate or cursed? Fate has yet to decide.

"All of it?" I tease.

"Don't leave anything out."

If possible, I would share my entire life with her in a split second. But light speeds aren't possible when it comes to relationships. The good ones built over time—marinate. Any great relationship starts with friendship. And friendships start with details and trust.

"Alright. Let's see how much I can spew before our food arrives." Just as the words leave my lips, the server drops off my cherry cola—a newfound favorite—and Autumn's vanilla milkshake. She plucks the cherry off the whipped cream and pops it in her mouth. "Uh, where to start…"

Her lips wrap around the cherry as she pops the stem off. Liquid cognac and red lips swirl my vision. The bright lights, bopping music, and bustle of the restaurant fade in the background as I stare at her mouth. How the hell am I supposed to speak basic vocabulary when she inadvertently teases me.

As if unaware of her influence, she suggests, "Tell me about your family. I already met your dad."

Family. A safe place to start, I suppose. I sip my soda to wet my throat and start somewhere near the beginning.

"Dad and I are a lot alike. I don't know if it's because I inherited more from him than Mom. Or if it's because I'm the only male child."

Autumn sits up straighter and sips on her milkshake. "So you have sisters?"

I nod. "Yep. Two. Jasmine and Jillian." She giggles and the sound spreads warmth in my chest. "What?"

"Do your parents have a thing for the letter J?"

"Never asked, but often wondered myself. Maybe it's because of Grandpa and Uncle John on Mom's side. Not sure."

She leans forward and resumes her position with her chin on her hands. "Continue, please."

"Jasmine and I are two years apart—she's older. But Jillian is seven years younger than me. And because Jasmine and I had more years together before Jillian was born, we're closer. We're all close, though. Mom made sure of it. Hence our weekly family dinners."

Across from me, Autumn sits back against the booth and sighs. Her bright spirit from seconds ago fades as she speaks. "Wish my family mirrored yours. I'd give anything for a close-knit, kind family."

Something in her tone stings when matched with her words. At times, my family annoys the heck out of me. Always in my business or making suggestions on how I handle this or that. As if they know what is best for my life. But I wouldn't trade them for anything in the world. And honestly, I might be lost without them.

"Want to talk about it?" I ask. Because I don't want to pry something out of her that she isn't ready to share.

She shakes her head. "Not tonight. Too heavy for a first date." A smile curves the corners of her mouth, but it doesn't reach her eyes. This moment is the most solemn I have seen her.

And I don't like it. One bit.

"Well, maybe sometime you can meet the rest of my family." Her eyes widen and I fear I have just sunk the evening deep at sea. "If that's something you'd like. Eventually."

The more I correct myself, the bigger her smile gets. "I'd like that."

The server stops in front of our table and sets the tray on a stand. Plate after plate, I laugh as the server keeps setting dishes on our table. When finished, she glances between the both of us and winces. "Anything else I can get you right now?"

I want to laugh because I know she is just doing her job. After looking at Autumn, I shake my head and relieve the poor girl. "Nah, we're good." When she walks off, I stare at the five plates in front of Autumn and laugh. "This will be interesting."

"Don't worry, I plan to have leftovers."

"Good to know. Because I don't imagine *I* could even scarf down mozzarella sticks, a plate of onion rings, potato skins, a double cheeseburger with all the fixings, fries, and coleslaw. Plus a milkshake."

She giggles and it vibrates across my skin and warms me more than the summer sun. "I plan to sample it all. But I have to save room for dessert, too."

"Dessert? Dear god, woman. How can you even think about dessert already?"

With a shake of her head, she says, "Dessert is the first thing I think about."

Something about the way she eyes me as she says the word dessert has me wanting to box everything up and leave. But Mom would smack me across the back of my head if I did. Lecture me until her voice scratched and my ears fell off.

I eat my BBQ-style double cheeseburger and fries while watching Autumn in awe. Surprisingly, she demolishes a third of the food without breaking a sweat. We ask the server for a couple to-go boxes before Autumn orders a banana split made with toasted marshmallow and Smurf-flavored ice creams.

When her dessert arrives, I gape at the heaping mound of sugary cream and fruit. Blue and white ice cream sits sandwiched at the base between a split banana and under a mountain of whipped cream, sliced strawberries, pineapple nibs, chocolate syrup, colorful jimmies, and three maraschino cherries.

"Holy shit," I spit out. "Are you going to eat all that?" Jesus. What is that, a thousand calories?

"Nope." I blink away from the mammoth-sized dessert to catch her expression. "You're going to help."

"I am?"

She slowly nods. Picking up one of the spoons, she scoops some of the confection up and brings it to her lips. I follow the spoon with my eyes and swallow when it disappears between her lips. She closes her eyes and hums. The sounds go straight to my groin.

"Here," she says as her eyes pop back open and she scoops more on the spoon. "You need to taste this."

My gaze locks on to her lips and I imagine better ways to taste dessert. More intimate ways. She holds the spoon inches from my mouth. The whipped cream and blue ice cream melt together as a piece of strawberry dips slowly in the middle. I lean forward, lift my eyes to hers, and open my mouth as she feeds me dessert. I haven't even tasted it yet, but know it is—and forever will be—the best damn dessert to hit my tongue.

The sweet confection melts over my tastebuds and I moan. As messy and funky as it seemed, it tastes damn good.

"Was I right?" she asks. All I do is nod.

We take turns feeding each other until we have scraped every last bit of dessert out of the small glass boat. It is the most innocent and provocative meal I have eaten. A meal I won't soon forget. After I pay the check, we walk out to the Jeep and I start it up.

"Is it okay if we are doing something else, too?" I ask.

As much as I don't want the evening to be over, I don't know how she feels after eating half her weight in food. Not that I could tell when she stood from the table.

"I'd love to. What'd you have in mind?"

I tap my temple and smile. "Top secret."

"Fine," she huffs out and rolls her eyes. "Take me on your top secret adventure."

I laugh and put the Jeep in gear. Music floats in the cab and Autumn asks if she can change it. I hand her my phone and tell her the code to unlock it. "Sure. The app should be open already."

Out of the corner of my eye, I see her gawking in my direction. I want to ask why, but I think it's because I just gave her the code to my phone. If something so simple surprises her, it breaks my heart. But I have nothing to hide. Hell, I already told her about Cora the first day we met. The only skeleton I had in my closet has come out.

Trust is a big deal in every relationship. As of now, I have absolutely no reason to not trust her. I don't know much about her, but I hope to change that. Hope whatever keeps her from opening up—her avoidance on discussing her past—can be ripped to shreds. But everyone exposes themselves in their own time, and I need to give her the space to do it at her own pace.

She scrolls through the app and selects a song. An upbeat rock tune spills from the speakers and I can't help but bop to the sound. After the next song, I pull into a parking lot and weave through the rows until I locate a spot.

"The park?" she asks.

I cut the engine and glance over at her in the dark. "Yep. Tonight is *Movies In The Park* night." She bites her lip and shrugs. "Every two weeks, the park hosts a movie night after the park closes to foot traffic. You bring your own blanket or chair and they supply the movie."

"Really?" There is a lightness to her voice. A level of wonderment. And I love that I put it there.

"Really."

I slip out of the Jeep, open the back door to grab the blankets and my jacket, and round the back to help her out. A man in a bright orange vest wielding a flashlight approaches and directs us down the path for the movie. We walk across the lawn in silence, weaving between the people already set up and waiting for the movie to begin. Twenty feet on the lawn, my knuckles graze hers and a jolt of energy zings me head to boot. My pulse whooshes behind my ears and I remind myself to breathe.

If she affects me this easily from a single graze of the hand, it's unimaginable how I will feel when we kiss.

"How about there?" Autumn points to an open spot on the lawn since I have obviously stopped focusing.

"Perfect."

We weave between more blankets and finally reach the vacancy. I ask her to hold the extra blanket and my jacket while I spread the one for us to sit on. Once set up, we plop down and kick off our shoes.

"What movie are we seeing?"

"Not sure. I didn't look up the schedule. Mom and Dad have come to a few of these. That's how I knew about them."

"Fun. I like surprises."

You are the best surprise of them all.

A few minutes later, the movie flickers on the temporary screen. One I haven't seen.

"Oh god."

"What?" I ask.

"I'm going to cry."

Shit. Is this bad? Should we leave? "We don't have to stay," I suggest. Although every atom in my body screams to stay put.

"No." She presses her hand to my chest and I stop breathing. "It's a good movie."

About five minutes in, the title *A Star Is Born* pops up in red on the screen. Now I understand why she said she will cry. Jasmine told me she and Anton saw this in the theater and she bawled like a baby, but it was worth every tear.

We slip on our jackets as the movie rolls on. I lay back on my forearms while Autumn sits up, leaning back on her hands. My attention shifts between Bradley Cooper and Lady Gaga to Autumn. I follow the lines of her profile as her eyes remain glued to the screen. The slim line of her nose. The voluptuous curves of her lips. Down to the slight dip in her chin. I would rather watch her for two hours than this movie, but I force myself to alternate between the two.

Halfway through the movie, she shivers beside me. "Cold?" She nods. "Here." I unfold the second blanket and go to wrap it around her.

"What about you?" she asks as she mimics my position.

"I'll be fine."

She shakes her head and sits back up. "Sit up."

"What? Why?" She gives me a pointed look. "Fine."

When I sit up, she cocoons us both with the wool blanket. My mind thinks a hundred different ungentlemanly thoughts and I tell myself to shut up. Slowly, she starts to lie down and I get the hint.

We lay on the blanket—my front to her back—and I stop watching the movie altogether. All I can focus on is the way her body molds to mine. How she pulled my upper arm down and wrapped it around her waist and laid hers over top. How her fruity, vanilla scent wafts from her hair into my nose. And how perfect she feels in my arms. Like she belongs there. Like she has always belonged there.

With Autumn in my arms, I close my eyes and get lost in my imagination. Lost in the fantasy of what kissing her will be like when it finally happens. Because it will happen.

I keep my eyes closed as I splay my fingers on her belly and she weaves hers between mine. Everything about this moment, about us, continually comes together with comfort and ease. Without difficulty, I envision Autumn in my arms often. Imagine her lips pressed to mine daily. Believe this rhythmic rush beneath my sternum will only get stronger the more I see her. Spend time with her. Hold her.

Hopefully, she believes and feels the same. That she reciprocates this unfamiliar rush of emotions.

Before long, the movie ends. I mentally whine at the fact I have to unravel her from my arms. But I do. We fold up the blankets, hop in the Jeep, and head back to her apartment. The entire ride back, neither of us says a word. The silence isn't uncomfortable, but seems like a missed opportunity to learn more about each other. Soon, too soon, I park in front of her apartment and cut the engine.

We sit in the dark a moment before I finally open the door and walk around to her side. Out of the Jeep, we take slow, measured steps to her front door. Not that I have a professional dating degree, but if I am reading the signs correctly, neither of us wants tonight to be over.

When we reach her front door, she spins to face me. But she doesn't look up. Not yet.

"I had a really nice time," she whispers into the darkness.

Lightly, I brush my knuckles from her temple down to the angle of her jaw. "Me too," I whisper. Her gaze lifts to meet mine. "Can I kiss you?" Her eyes dart between mine for a moment before she subtly nods.

Thank fuck.

I lift my other hand and frame her face with my palms.

She sucks in a breath as I lean down, but doesn't exhale. The red cotton covering her breasts brushes against my chest and my heart bangs its fists against my ribcage. Less than an inch from her lips, she closes her eyes just before I do the same.

And then my lips press to hers and nothing else exists.

The faint porch light fades away. The occasional roar of a car engine or pitter-patter of an animal scurrying across the grass in the dark disappears. I lick her lower lip and she opens up like a flower blooms. Every sense I own homes in on her.

The residual taste of ice cream on her tongue. Her sweet perfume in my nose. How warm her body is as it presses flush with mine. The small whimper from her lips when I break the kiss. How her cognac eyes slowly open and beg for more. And how I *know* this will not be the last time our lips meet.

I lean in for one last peck and love how she whimpers again when our lips separate.

"Thank you," she whispers. "Best date ever."

I hold her gaze. "Hopefully I can top it next time."

"No doubt about it." I step back from her and a slight frown mars her face. I brush my thumb over her cheek. "Good night, Jonas."

"'Night, Autumn."

ELEVEN
AUTUMN

Jonas walks back to his Jeep, and I want to run after him. I press my fingers to my lips and reminisce in the fire he set moments ago. A fire I don't want extinguishing.

"Wait," I holler then jog out and meet him by his car door. "Please don't think I don't want you to come inside."

Although he never made such a suggestion, part of me feels the need to confess this aloud. To share what I desire, but am not ready to explore. For him to hear it from my lips—not only the words, but the subtle message behind my tone.

"Autumn, I would never assume anything." He caresses my cheek with his knuckles again and I melt into his touch as emotion dances like carbonation in my chest. "Much as I would love for you to invite me in, I don't think either of us is ready for that step. Not yet." He inches forward, the proximity of him hot on my skin. "I will wait until you're ready."

I peek up at Jonas from under my lashes and wonder where the hell he has been all my life. Why I hadn't met him sooner. A man with endless patience and unshakable kindness. A man that looks at me with gentleness and ardor.

"Jonas..."

Another shuffle forward, his lips now a breath away from grazing my own. Oh, how I want to taste him again.

"Please don't feel like you owe me an explanation. Because you don't."

Our eyes meet and my throat goes dry as I soak up the intensity of his gaze. The magnificent swirl of blue and green and gold, but a hint darker. They remind me of an incoming rainstorm at sunset. Not a storm worthy of fear, but one that lures you outdoors and begs you to get lost in it. To dance in the rain rather than try to escape the waterfall.

God, how I want to kiss him again. More than I want to breathe.

"Thank you. For telling me I don't owe you anything." My eyes drop to his lips and I tell myself to look back up. To focus on what I should say. To use my words. "There is so much I want to tell you. So much. But I need things between us to go slow. Not because I don't want you. I do, believe me." *You're rambling, Autumn.* Rambling aside, Jonas gives me his smile. One full of contentment with a dash of humor. "But my past has roots. Roots I need time to dig up. And it may take time."

He frames my face in his hands. "Hey." When he

knows my attention is solely on him, he continues. "Like I said, we go at your pace. I'm not in any rush. I'm not going anywhere."

I really hope his words hold truth. Because what I haven't told him could be the one thing which scares him away. Jonas doesn't seem the type to scare easily, but it is best not to assume. Some people surprise you.

"You're the first person I've dated in a really long time," I confess. He cocks his head, toys with a strand of hair, and waits for me to continue. "Years ago, I dated this guy who swore he'd always be there for me. But" —I swallow and hang my head— "when things got more serious than he wanted, he bailed. It threw a wrench in everything. With my parents and my sister, and other parts of my personal life." I glance over my shoulder at the front door. Picture who is on the other side. "If it weren't for Penny and everyone else at the shop, I would've stayed on the street."

Jonas drops his hands from my face and the immediate loss sends a chill across my cheeks. But before I dwell on the absence of his touch, he slips his arms around my waist and envelops me in a hug so potent, emotion stings the back of my eyes. He holds me close to his chest, shushes the tears threatening to fall, and whispers how everything is fine now because he is here.

And I believe him. Right here, right now, I believe him. Regardless of how little I know Jonas, some facts are undeniable. Jonas is a good man. A good man raised by another good man.

I sense it when he hesitates to do things other men would assume is normal and acceptable. Like resting his hand on my back or taking my hand in his. Like asking for my phone number or address when he had the means to get it without my consent. Or when he asked, only minutes ago, permission to kiss me. Most men don't ask, they just take.

Jonas isn't like most men. He is levels above.

Not sure which of us initiates, but we slowly pull back from each other. Jonas lifts his hands back to my face and swipes his thumbs over my cheeks before leaning in and pressing a sweet, chaste kiss to my lips. "Although I don't like why you were crying, you look more beautiful than ever."

I close my eyes and get lost in the gyroscope of emotion spinning in my chest. Before Jonas, no man ever had me so tongue-tied and wobbly. Although I have walked on my own two feet for years, with Jonas I feel as if I am truly learning how they work. How they will carry me where I need to go. Toward him.

"Only you would think I look beautiful with mascara staining my cheeks."

He shakes his head. "You don't get it." No, I don't. Though, I won't admit such things aloud. "It's not that you have tear-stained makeup. It's the reason why. That you're exposing a piece of yourself and letting me see the parts no one else gets to."

When he explains it like this, I understand better. Little did I realize, I unintentionally opened myself up to him. I let him in when I never let anyone else in. With the exception of Penny. Reznor, Rex, and Iliana know minor, rough-around-the-edges details, but they don't know anything with depth. Penny, on the other hand, knows everything. Not because I favor her over the rest of my tattoo family, but because we live together and there is no possible way around it.

I drop my gaze from his eyes to his lips again. He won't make me ask permission, but I want to taste him one more time before we say good night again. Taste the sweetness of our shared dessert mixed with a flavor I define as distinctly Jonas. When my eyes remain on his lips, he makes my wish come true.

He leans forward and the space between us disappears. I close my eyes and fist his shirt as his lips press mine with unprecedented tenderness. He kisses me once. Twice. On the third kiss, I sweep the tip of my tongue along the seam of his lips. A low groan rumbles in his chest. I tighten my grip on the cotton as he slips his fingers into my hair and opens up to let me in.

Then I taste him again. Hot and sweet and addictive on my taste buds. The heat of his tongue tangling with mine is a shock wave throughout my body, waking all the parts once dormant. Loosening my hold, my hands trail up his chest, cup his cheeks and revel in the gruff grain against my soft palms.

He groans at my touch, drops his hands to my hips, and draws me impossibly closer. Close enough for the bulge beneath his zipper to brush my abdomen. The temptation to invite him in multiplies tenfold seconds before he breaks the kiss.

"You might be the death of me. But it'd be a good way to go," he says, gasping.

"Back atcha."

"As much as I don't want to leave, I should go."

I fight the urge to disagree, and nod. "Yeah," I whisper. "Will you call or text me?"

"Better believe it."

I smile and peek up at him. "Good night, Jonas."

He sweeps a stray hair out of my face, tucking it behind my ear. "Good night, Autumn."

As I walk back to the front door, he gets in the Jeep and starts it. We keep our eyes on each other until he backs out and drives away. For a moment, I stare at the space where I last saw his taillights. Absorb every moment of the evening, now that I am alone. Well, alone for a minute longer.

I take a deep breath and dig for the house key in my purse. Just as I go to insert the key in the lock, the door swings open and an overzealous Penny yanks me inside.

"I want details. Now."

I stumble over my own two feet as she closes the door and drags me over to the couch. "Pen." I laugh and plop down on the middle cushion.

"Don't you *Pen* me. And don't pretend like you weren't just outside kissing a hot-as-fuck man. Twice."

Biting the inside of my cheek, I fight the smile and laughter dying to burst free. But I lose the battle.

"Do you want a complete rundown of the evening? Cause I promise the entire date wasn't like what you witnessed out front, Peeping Tom."

"Girl, you better tell me everything. Beginning to end. And don't you dare leave a single detail out."

I kick off my shoes and tuck my feet beneath my butt. Penny draws her legs to her chest, rests her chin on her knees, and listens to every intricate detail about my date with Jonas. From the cutest retro diner I ever set foot in to the movie in the park where he held me close and I stopped paying attention to the screen and focused solely on his warm body curled behind mine. How his fingers splayed my belly and held me close. How I never wanted to miss a single moment of his breath on the back of my neck. She already witnessed the two separate kisses out front.

As I tell Penny how I broke the barrier and told Jonas a little about my past, she slaps a hand over her mouth. Me explaining an ounce of my past to anyone—no matter how big or small the detail—is a huge step. Penny knows I wouldn't tell just anyone. Which means I believe Jonas and I could become far more than just two people dating for the sake of dating.

"Auti, I'm so happy for you." I give her a half smile. "Seriously. It is way past time you did something for yourself. Be a little selfish for a change. Be happy. It looks good on you."

"Thanks, Pen." I yawn.

Although I have been awake much later than this

countless times, the exhilaration from the evening is slowly fading and exhaustion is taking over.

"Go." Penny throws a thumb over her shoulder toward the hall. "Wash up and go to bed. We'll go out for breakfast in the morning. My treat."

I squint at her and she shakes her head. Rising up from the couch, I snatch my shoes off the floor and kiss the crown of Penny's head. "Thanks for always being the best. Don't know where I'd be without you."

"Love you too, Auti. Sleep tight."

After stowing the leftovers in the fridge, I go about my normal nightly routine before bed. As I brush my teeth, I zone out and replay my evening with Jonas. Recall the buzz zapping every inch of my skin and the hum deep in my belly as he laid behind me and pressed his palm to my lower abdomen. Jonas encasing me in his arms… I never felt more at home.

Flipping off the bathroom light, I tiptoe into the bedroom, change into my pajamas, and quietly slip between the sheets. I curl onto my side and face the opposite side of the bed. Face the angelic form beside me. Chest steadily rising and falling in the darkened room.

"I'm not going anywhere." Jonas's words creep back in from earlier. And as I take in the most important person in my world, the little girl less than a foot away, I pray his words stick when I tell him.

I lay awake in bed, eyes on the ceiling but not really seeing it. Spartan twitches and dream barks at the foot of the bed. For once, it doesn't bother me. Nothing could right now.

When was the last time I felt like this? Lighter. Carefree. Happy. Like the future has a million possibilities and I can't wait to explore them all.

Easy. I haven't.

Date night with Autumn was literally one of the best in my life. Hell, I spent all day yesterday smiling like a goddamn idiot. I never enjoyed doing housework so much. Never enjoyed tearing up the back yard to landscape it like I did yesterday. Spartan ran around the yard, barking incessantly at squirrels and hunting for lizards. But it didn't irritate me as per usual.

The alarm blares on the bedside table and I slap the

snooze button to shut it up. Spartan pops his head up from the mattress and yips.

"'Morning, buddy."

He yips again. I like to call it his quiet voice. As if he knows it's too early to use his full bark yet. Either way, it's adorable how quiet he is until I get out of bed. Then his typical, boisterous bark commences.

We get out of bed and ready for our morning walk. Once we step out the door, Spartan leads us down the street and along our usual morning path. Glad he can focus and lead the way because mentally I am still standing in front of Autumn's apartment, kissing her.

Lost in my daydream, it seems as if only a few minutes pass before we arrive back home. After filling Spartan's bowl with kibble, I go about my morning routine. I slip on a Thompson's Garage shirt and a pair of jeans before heading into the kitchen to make breakfast. Belly full, I slip on boots, secure Spartan in his kennel, and head out the door. A moment later, I zip through Clearwater on my bike, relishing the sharp sting of wind on my cheeks, and arrive at the garage early again.

When I walk into the office, Dad glances up from the stack of papers in front of him to the clock and shakes his head. "You keep this up and I might start setting your schedule earlier."

"Ha ha, old man." I brew a fresh pot of coffee before sifting through the invoices on my desk. "Looks like a busy day."

Dad doesn't say anything for a moment and I wonder

if he didn't hear what I said. When I glance over at his desk, he stares at me with the biggest shit-eating grin on his face. The type you see when people know something you don't. I cock a brow and he shakes his head.

"Interesting," he says, cryptically.

"What?" I drop my head and scan my shirt to see if my breakfast is still hanging around. Nope.

"How was your weekend, son?"

My weekend? Why the hell would Dad ask about my weekend. Not that we never chat about how we spend our time apart, but it isn't an automatic Monday question. I think back and try to remember if I told him I was going on a date with Autumn.

Think, think, think.

No, don't think it ever came up. Especially after his snooping while I was on the phone. He means well, has a good heart, but it suddenly feels as if I'm a teenager all over again.

"Great. Why?"

His grin widens further. "Great, huh? What'd ya do?"

What the hell is this? Twenty questions of obscurity? Dad isn't the type to be evasive. At least, not from past experiences. Then again, I have never openly discussed my interest in someone. Does he know what I did this weekend? I mentally shake my head. Not possible.

"Went out. Did stuff around the house. Why?"

"Where'd you go?"

Okay, game over. Between him skirting around what he wants to say and the devious smile on his lips, I am about to explode from curiosity. "Why don't you just spit it out, old man."

He tips his head back and laughs. A full belly laugh. Similar to the thousands I have heard over the years. He's yanking my chain and he full well knows it. Even enjoys the slow torment with a wicked gleam in his eye.

"Back at ya, son." He points to my face. "Only reason I'm giving you a hard time is that."

"What?" I swipe my palms over my face and feel for the evidence he refers to. But I don't find it.

"Your permanent smile." My cheeks heat. "Don't be embarrassed, son. The smile suits you." He gets up, walks to the coffee pot, and pours us each a cup. "Plus, a smile like that could be good for business."

"Alright." I laugh. "That's enough from you, old man."

He hands me a mug while he fishes the creamer out of the fridge. After he pours some in his coffee, he passes it my way.

"In all seriousness, it's really great to see you happy, son. And if a certain female car owner has anything to do with it, then I approve."

I pour cream in my cup then spoon in a little sugar. "Thanks, Dad. Means a lot."

We drink our coffee and work for the next hour in silence. But it isn't awkward or filled with the expectation to spill more details. Although, if I keep dating Autumn—which I have every intention of doing—Dad will dig for more. And I won't hold back.

The Thompson family is an open family. We don't hide

anything from each other. We were all raised—Mom and Dad included—with the belief it is better to be open and honest from the get-go. Just saves from stirring up future problems.

After I finish paperwork in the office, I head to the garage bays and start on the first clients of the day. As of now, most of the morning is filled with appointments for routine maintenance. I step up to an SUV and match the vehicle to the invoice then get started on the oil change.

As I wipe my hands clean after finishing, my phone pings in my pocket. Pulling it out of my coveralls, I smile down at the screen. Two bays down, Dad laughs and points between my face and my phone. *Yeah, yeah, old man.*

Autumn: Morning. Hope the rest of your weekend was good.

Her text has me smiling for two reasons. One—she sent me a text. How can I not be happy over that small fact? Getting a text means the other person was thinking of you. Two—her actual text. The message is sweet, but also makes me think she had no idea what to say. She simply wanted to text me, but didn't know how to initiate conversation. It reminds me how she said she hadn't dated in years. She didn't go into great detail, but someone probably didn't treat her right.

Jonas: Good morning. Best weekend in years.

Autumn: Yeah. What made it so great?

Is this Autumn subtly flirting? And why does every single word from her lips — and her fingers, I guess — make my cheeks sting? Heat me head to toe. Make my mind wander to places it never has. Places which include her in every facet.

Jonas: Oh, you know. A night on the town with a beautiful woman. Being domestic at home.

Autumn: Domestic, huh? *screenshots for future reference*

And there it is again. *Future reference.* The term sinks deeper into my marrow every time I hear — see — it. I love how she sees us beyond a single date or moment in time. How she wants more between us, even if she doesn't openly say it. Little indicators such as saving something I say for *future reference* means more to me than imaginable.

Jonas: What can I say... My parents raised me to be self-sufficient. Want to know a secret?

Autumn: *steeple fingers and leans in close* Dish it out already.

I laugh as my fingers fly over the screen.

Jonas: Mom taught me how to sew buttons when I was 5. Said every man should know how.

Autumn: And now I'm in love with your mom.

A small tornado swirls in my chest—flipping things upside down and causing my heart to beat violently. *Don't take it out of context.* Her text is meant to be funny or cute. That she loves my mom because she taught me things the general populous deems a female activity. But Dad taught my sisters how to change their own oil and swap out a flat tire. It's just how the Thompson family rolled. Being self-sufficient is a life skill, not a gender skill.

Jonas: Is it too soon for me to tell her that? She might replace me with you. The third daughter she never had.

Did that come out wrong? I reread my text and mentally wipe my brow with the back of my hand. *Whew.* For a second there, I thought maybe I insinuated something else. That our relationship would lead her to becoming my mother's daughter—in a sense.

Autumn: Aaron already know me. Wouldn't bother me if you told your parents.

Dating. Not "went on a date." I glance up and across the garage. Dad leans against a silver pickup with a knowing smile on his face as he watches me text Autumn.

Time to wrap this up, otherwise Dad will tease me until the end of time.

Jonas: Hate to cut this short. Dad's giving me the side-eye.

Autumn: Sorry 🙁 I'll bring him cookies later.

Jonas: No need to apologize. And sprinkles are his favorite.

Autumn: Sprinkles. Check. See you in a bit?

Jonas: I'll be here.

I tuck my phone back in my pocket and look over at Dad. "What're you smiling at, old man?"

"Ah, to be young and in love again," he says and I stop breathing.

Autumn is gorgeous and funny and downright lovable, but I never indicated I was *in love* with her. Did I? I mean, Jesus, I have only known her just shy of two weeks.

"Dad…" I warn. But he just waves me off. "By the way, since you wouldn't let Autumn pay for the repairs, she's bringing you cookies later."

"Really?" I nod and his grin brightens. "Well, son, I approve."

An hour later, I hear the telltale sounds of a classic car. Rolling out from under the sedan I currently work on, I sit up and swallow at the woman walking toward the bays with a bag in her hand.

Autumn strolls up in an off-the-shoulder, black-and-white striped top under dark denim overalls folded up to land just below the knee. Her black-brown locks are pinned up high on the back of her head while a folded bandana loops from the base of her skull up into a bow at her crown. Lips painted scarlet, as are her nails. And today she wears dark-tinted, black-framed, wingtip sunglasses.

I swallow harder with each step she takes in my direction. This woman will be the death of me. No doubt about it. Dad steps out of the bay next to me and meets Autumn five feet away from where I still sit on the ground.

"Hey there, sweetie. My son tells me I get cookies for being a nice guy."

Autumn slides her sunglasses up to rest on top of her head. "And I hear you love sprinkles."

Dad smiles down at me before meeting Autumn's gaze again. "You hear correct. Honestly, haven't met a cookie I don't love. Sprinkles just make them fun."

She laughs and hands Dad the bag. "Well, I didn't have time to bake. But there's lots of sprinkles plus some other flavors, in case anyone else wants cookies."

Without asking permission, Dad leans forward and side hugs Autumn. Doesn't seem to bother her one bit. "Very generous of you." Dad hands me the bag and I rise from the ground. "Son, why don't you take lunch and put these cookies in the office."

It's a suggestion, and one I appreciate. "Yeah, sure."

Walking over to a shelf, I set the cookies down and slip out of my coveralls. And I don't miss, in my periphery, the way Autumn ogles me as I disrobe. Although I am fully clothed beneath, she looks me up and down as if I stripped bare.

"Hungry," I croak out as I lead us into the office and set the bag of cookies on my desk.

"Starved," she whispers. But her response seems weighed down with so much more.

A foot between us, I keep my arms tucked at my sides and hold her fiery, cognac gaze. "Wish I had more than an hour for lunch."

Autumn steps closer, leaving a breath between us. "Any amount of time is better than none at all."

I nod and take a deep breath. My time with her now is limited. Lunch dates are not the same as dinner and a movie and her lips pressed to mine. Lunch dates are time crunched and light conversation and hugs until next time.

"C'mon. There's a sub shop up the street. My treat."

We walk out of the office and into the lot. "Well, if you're buying, I'm driving."

"I have no qualms about riding shotgun. Besides, I rode my bike to work."

"You own a motorcycle?" I nod as I slip inside the car and she cranks the engine. "Never been on a motorcycle before. Maybe sometime soon."

What is it about Autumn that lights my soul on fire? With a simple suggestion, my chest swells and my stomach ties knots faster than a sailor. Hell yes, she turns heads everywhere she goes. But her heart-shaped face and curvy body are just the tip of the iceberg. Autumn is so much more than the physical sum of her parts. All her remarks about the future, I ink them into my memory for later reference.

"I'd love to take you for a ride. Early morning works best on the weekends. Less traffic."

A couple miles down the road, I point out the sub shop and she pulls in. We head inside, order, and sit at a table while we wait for our sandwiches. I tell Autumn about some of my favorite places to ride during the early hours of the day. On a few occasions, I left town earlier than I leave the house for work and drove north. An hour or two north, the roads have fewer commuters and there are several small towns with attractive scenery. If the opportunity ever presents itself, I would love to take Autumn on one of those day trips.

"It'd be nice to visit these places you're telling me about."

"Well, if you're ever up for it, let me know."

A man deposits lunch on the table and walks off with the numbered plastic tent. We dig into our sandwiches and eat in silence for a minute. For some reason, a weird vibe bounces off Autumn. Not sure if it is because I mentioned going out of town on the bike or if it's something else altogether. She never mentioned how the rest of her weekend went.

"Sorry I didn't get to ask earlier, but how was the rest of your weekend?"

She finishes chewing the bite in her mouth, but still covers her mouth with her hand when she speaks. "Good. Went out for breakfast yesterday. Then binged on snacks and Netflix. I was definitely not productive." She laughs and it is music to my ears.

"Love those kinds of days. I try to have one at least once a month. Spartan and I spent most of the day digging up old flower beds in the back yard. Previous owners had a thing for cementing pavers together. Was probably a great idea thirty-plus years ago, but now it's just horrible."

The rest of lunch goes by way too fast, and before I know it, we have to head back to the garage.

At the traffic light two blocks before the garage, I lean my back against the passenger window and soak up every inch of Autumn. I want to kiss her again. Soon.

"Are you busy tomorrow night?" I ask.

She peeks up at the red light then over to me. "Haven't checked my schedule for work yet. Why?"

"I'm meeting friends at the bowling alley. Cora should be there. We get together at least once a week. Tomorrow, we're bowling. Wanted to know if you'd care to join."

She tucks her lips between her teeth and I want to reach over and pop them out. But I don't.

"When I get to work, I'll check my schedule. What time is everyone meeting up?"

"Seven. We usually bowl a couple games and call it a night."

"I'll tentatively say yes, but let you know if there's a schedule conflict."

She steers the car into the garage lot and stops parallel to the storefront. I unbuckle my belt and lean toward her. Her eyes drop to my lips and I take it as a sign of permission to kiss her.

The moment my lips graze hers, the cooler December temperatures vanish. Our slow and sweet kiss ends far too soon. "I'll text you the details for tomorrow night when I'm off work."

Our lips a breath apart, her eyes shift back and forth between mine. "Look forward to it," she says, voice drug laced and lips parted.

One last chaste kiss and I force myself to exit the car. "See you tomorrow." She nods, and I love how I struck her speechless.

I turn on my heel and walk back to the garage bay with an ear-to-ear smile. Dad spots me. "Good lunch?"

Best damn lunch in the history of lunches.

THIRTEEN

AUTUMN

Is this a mistake?

I turn into the parking lot of the bowling alley. Since when are bowling alleys this busy on a Tuesday night? Sure, it has been forever and a day since I have set foot in one, but it was always a weekend day. And every place is busy on the weekend.

Winding through the lot, I park Betsy and cut the engine. Facing the entrance of the bowling alley, I scan the sea of faces standing outside. Among them is Jonas. With his messy chocolate strands, broad shoulders, and booming laughter, I will always be able to pinpoint him in a crowd.

He stands with two other women—a dirty-blonde nearly as tall as him and a curly redhead closer to my height. For a moment, I observe how he interacts with them. By the ease at which they interact, it's evident they all know one another. They smile and laugh and look completely comfortable with one another. When the blonde pushes at Jonas's chest and the trio laughs in unison, the little green monster perks up on my shoulder as a rush of jealousy spikes my bloodstream.

"Get it together," I chide myself. "Men and women have non-romantic relationships all the time."

Nothing but truth. After all, the same can be said about some of my male friends. Then why does seeing Jonas so casual and relaxed with two other women make my jaw clench? More than likely, it is the result of not dating or being in a committed relationship for years.

Taking a deep breath, I open the door and exit the car. Seven steps forward and Jonas homes in on my presence. Locks eyes with me. Stops listening to the two women at his side. Smiles so wide, the dimple I love makes an appearance. Pushes off the wall and walks my direction. Meets me a few feet from the paved walkway around the building.

"Hey," he says as he steps into my space.

"Hi."

When he drops his lips to mine, I don't stop him. If anything, I encourage him to give me more. His tongue sweeps over mine and I moan. He tastes of cherry cola and desire. Far too soon, he breaks the kiss and chuckles under his breath as I lean into him.

"If we keep this up, we'll never see the inside of the bowling alley." *Sounds good to me.* He laces his fingers with mine. "C'mon. Let me introduce you to Shelly and Erin."

Hand in hand, we walk back to where he stood earlier.

Where the two women he chatted with stand. "'Kay," I whisper.

A few strides forward, he pauses. "Everything alright?"

I nod and tighten my hold on his hand. "Yeah. Just nervous. Don't hang with new people often."

He drops my hand and I pout until he frames my face with his palms. "It'll be okay. Promise. Everyone is pretty chill. Plus, Cora and Gavin will be here too." He plants a chaste kiss on my lips and I silently beg for another.

We step up to the two women and I paste on a polite smile. If I thought they were attractive from a distance, I was sorely mistaken. Attractive isn't the proper term. Because up close, they captivate and hold my attention more. And the wicked green monster pops up on my shoulder again, swinging its legs and whistling. *Shut up.*

"Shelly" —Jonas gestures to the blonde, then the redhead— "Erin, this is Autumn. Autumn, this is Shelly and Erin. Shelly and Cora have been friends since boys were gross. And Erin works with Cora."

I extend my hand to each of them. "Nice to meet you both."

Shelly performs a quick scan. "You are fucking cute." I laugh and peek up at Jonas who chuckles under his breath. "Really dig your vibe."

"Thanks." Although we just met, it's easy to see Shelly is a hoot.

Jonas wraps his arm around my shoulders. "Ladies,

let's head inside and grab lanes. Everyone else should be here soon."

We stroll through the automatic doors and are immediately hit with the cacophony of Tuesday nights at the bowling alley. Colorful globes of resin clash against wooden pins. Upbeat dance music booms from the overhead speakers. Patrons hoot and holler and cheer each other on. Claps and whistles. Middle-age adults jumping off the floor when they manage to knock all the pins down.

The energy is boisterous and infectious.

We pay for shoes and get assigned two lanes. On our way to the lane, we pass the bowling alley's food bar. Melted cheese and baked bread and cinnamon sugar waft up my nose. My stride falters and Jonas pauses beside me.

"You okay?"

I point over at the neon lights highlighting every party food known to man. "Yep. Just swallowing down my hunger."

He laughs. "After we get everything set up, we'll order food."

After swapping out our shoes, Shelly, Erin, and I venture off to find a ball. Can't remember the last time I bowled, let alone what weight ball I used when I played. Once I decide on a lime green, eight-pound ball, I head back to the lane where more bodies have congregated.

Cora and Gavin stand near the seats of the left lane we rented. Arms wrapped around each other; she looks up at him as if no one else is here. Maybe it holds true for them.

Their happiness makes me smile and spreads warmth in my chest.

I set my ball down and sidle up to Jonas. He curls his arm around my waist. "Everyone else is here. Let me introduce you." I nod and bite the inside of my cheek. "Hey guys." Six sets of eyes glance over at us. "This is Autumn." Although I have met four of the six, the attention from all of them makes me wilt into Jonas's side. "Autumn, this is Cora, Gavin, Shelly, Erin, Micah, and Trevor." With each name Jonas prattles off, he points to each person.

Lifting a hand, I wave to the obviously tight-knit group as heat crawls up my neck and lands on my cheeks. "Hey everyone. Nice to meet you." I am not necessarily a shy person. Hell, sometimes I am pretty outgoing. Just don't prefer the spotlight. Especially around new faces.

"Let's order food while everyone finishes getting ready," Jonas suggests.

Three pizzas, two pretzels, a basket of loaded fries, and two churros ordered later, we head back to the lanes with two pitchers of beer and glasses. The young girl at the counter told us they would bring the food to our lane soon.

We settle in the chairs at the lane. Jonas places an arm around my shoulder and inches closer to me while I snack on the churros. As we wait for Trevor and Gavin to come back with a ball, I people watch the group Jonas calls family.

The dynamic between all of them is fascinating. If I

had to guess—strictly by appearances and the way they interact—Shelly and Micah must be siblings. Same dark blonde hair. Same dark blue eyes. And they tease each other in a way only brothers and sisters do. When Gavin winds his way back over to us, I follow his every move until he sits down next to Cora. Who is staring at me. With piqued intensity.

Nothing in the way she watches me feels malicious or worrisome. If anything, she studies me with intrigue. Beside me, Jonas talks to Trevor—who I hadn't realized returned—with his arm still around my shoulders. A small smile perks up the corners of Cora's mouth. But her smile amplifies when Jonas stops talking to Trevor and he presses his lips to my temple.

Cora is happy for me. For Jonas. And her silent interest says more than any words could express.

Jonas drops his lips lower and his breath heats the shell of my ear. "Ready to bowl?"

You have no idea. "Yes."

One by one, we roll our ball down the oil-slicked lane and occasionally knock down pins. Early on, I learn Jonas, Shelly, and Trevor play a decent game. The rest of us are mediocre. The first game ends and I land a whopping seventy-eight points. Thankfully, I don't stand alone in my meh score. And I didn't score the lowest.

I snag a third slice of pizza and laugh when Jonas catches me scarfing it down. "What?" I ask around a mouthful of dough, cheese, ham, and pineapple.

He steps up to me, rests his hands on my hips, and

draws me close. "Nothing. You're just so damn cute." I swallow my bite just before he leans down and kisses me.

Not sure if it's because we are surrounded by hundreds of people—and a handful of Jonas's close friends—but this kiss feels different. Loaded. Intense. Powerful.

Jonas brings both his hands to my cheeks and holds me reverently as our lips move in time and his tongue dips inside my mouth. I reach forward and grip the hem of his shirt, bringing him closer. Warmth radiates off his chest and seeps into every one of my pores. Heats every molecule in my body and fevers my skin. The cacophony surrounding us vanishes. Bursts of red and orange splash the backs of my eyelids like fireworks in the night sky. The pericardium encasing my heart swells and constricts with each frenzied swipe of his tongue against mine.

I drag him impossibly closer. Deepen the kiss. Sink my nails in his hips. Moan against his lips.

Until someone coughs behind Jonas and dumps a bucket of ice water over us.

"Sorry to interrupt, man. You're up," an embarrassed Gavin says.

If anyone should be embarrassed, it sure as hell shouldn't be him. It should be me. He wasn't making out in the middle of the bowling alley like a hormonal teenager. Nope, that was most definitely me.

Jonas inches back and meets my eyes. His palms still pressed to my cheeks; I swelter beneath the swirl of his irises. Like two thermal hot springs, they smolder as the blue and gold and orange devour me. I can't look away. Won't look away.

He places one last, all too brief kiss on my lips. I visibly pout when he retreats and he chuckles. "Be right back."

Stepping up to the ball return, he picks up his ball, positions himself, and follows through. The ball whirls down the lane and knocks all the pins down with a loud *whack*. He returns to my side and kisses my temple.

"You're up," he whispers against my skin.

I bowl my turn and knock down nine—which is better than most of the frames in the first game—and slap a few high fives on my way back to Jonas. A few more frames pass with *ooh*s and *aw man*s. The laughter is nonstop and I quickly love this group of people. They remind me of my tat family. Not conventional by any means, but everyone cares about each other. How real family should be.

As Jonas refills his beer, my phone vibrates in my pocket. I tug it out, glance at the screen, and let Jonas know I will be right back.

Stepping away from the lane, I head near the entrance where it is somewhat quieter. Covering my left ear with my palm, I lift the phone to my right. "Hello?"

"Hey, someone wants to say good night," Penny says.

I step a little farther from the noise. On the other end, the phone changes hands and a sweet voice filters through the speaker. "Hi, Mama. Are you having fun?"

"Hey, pumpkin. I am. Are you and Auntie Penny having fun?"

"Yep. We watched *The Nightmare Before Christmas* again."

I laugh internally. Penny groans every time Clementine wants to watch it. Probably because she has seen it a hundred times. "Was it good?"

"Better than last time," she announces. "What time will you be home?"

"In a little bit. My friends and I are almost done playing our game. Then I'll be home."

"Okay, Mama. I love you."

I smile into the phone. "Love you too. I'll kiss you when I get home."

"M'kay. Night night."

"Good night."

As I disconnect the call, I look up and spot a confused Jonas a few feet away. *Shit.*

Is there ever a good time to tell someone you're dating you have a seven-year-old daughter? Nope. Because no matter the reason, Jonas will be upset I haven't told him about her. Which will end in one of two results. One—he will drop me faster than a hot pan. Or two—we will stay together, but his trust in me will diminish for a bit until I can prove myself again.

Either way, it sucks.

"Who was that?" Jonas asks, pointing to my phone.

I want to tell him. Want to let him in on this part of my life. But it's too soon. We still have so much to learn about each other before I let him know this other part of my world exists. And I don't let many people know Clementine exists for one reason. Hurt.

If Jonas decides to stop seeing me because I have a daughter, I can suck up the pain that will undoubtedly consume me with his absence. But my daughter, she doesn't need to feel hurt or pain or sadness. It's horrible enough her own father has never been around. Never seen her face or heard her precious laughter. I don't need Clementine to suffer the loss of a pseudo-father.

"Penny called," I say.

He purses his lips and breaks eye contact. "Does she often call for a *love you* and *good night*?" His tone isn't angry or spiteful. But he knows I am not telling him the whole truth. And this is not the right time or place.

But before the end of the night, I will have to tell Jonas about Clementine. Hopefully afterward, he won't hate me for keeping the biggest secret from him.

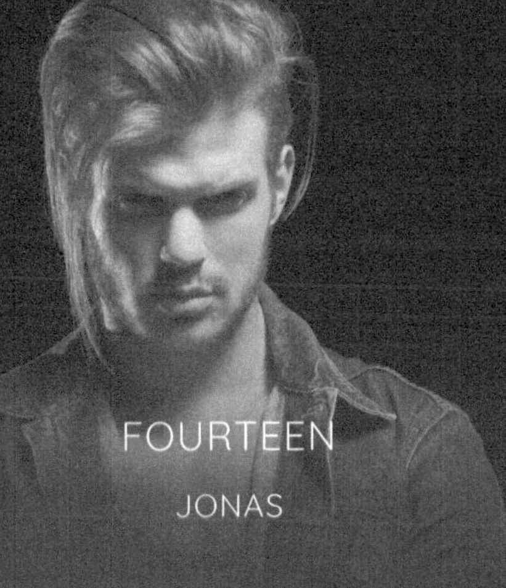

FOURTEEN

JONAS

Am I an asshole? Because right now it is difficult to tell.

A minute ago, I heard Autumn tell whoever she was talking to that she loved them, would kiss them when she got home, and wished them a good night. When I asked her who she was talking to, she said Penny called. Is her relationship with Penny more than friends? Because I didn't sign up for that.

But here I am, lipping off like a douchebag. Throwing accusations at my girlfriend when I haven't given her the chance to explain anything. Going against everything my parents taught me—which is to never assume. All assumptions do is cause harm and way too much stress.

Yep. Official asshole.

We walk back to the lane in silence. Usually, silence with Autumn is easy. Comfortable. Pleasant.

This new version of silence sucks.

Every few steps, I peek over at her out of the corner of my eye and berate myself mentally. Autumn hangs her head—not sure if she is embarrassed, angry or upset. Regardless, I hate how I put her in a foul mood. How I am the reason she went from enjoying a night out with me and my friends to probably wishing she wasn't here.

Before I buck up the courage to apologize, we reach the lane. She lifts her head, smiles, and pretends like the last few minutes never happened.

For the next five frames, neither of us speaks. We don't whisper to each other, kiss or remotely touch. And I hate every single second. It sears my heart like a branding iron. Except this brand doesn't mark me as hers, it just keeps pressing on and scalds until I black out from the pain.

When the game ends, Cora sidles up beside me as Autumn puts her ball back on the rack.

"Everything okay?" she asks.

This is beyond awkward. The woman I thought was the only person I wanted, who recently married the love of her life, is asking me about the woman I have been dating for almost no time at all. Funny thing is, it feels as if I have known Autumn for years. As if she has always been mine. What Cora and Gavin have, I get it now.

"Not sure." I glance toward the wall with the ball racks and spot Autumn chatting with Shelly. A smile sits on her face, but it isn't genuine. I have seen the genuine smile. "She was on the phone earlier and I overheard part of the call. Then I said something dickish."

Cora smiles subtly. "Your relationship with her is still very new, Jonas. But the way you both look at each other... it's deep. You guys need time. Don't rush it. Get to know each other. Autumn is a sweet woman. But we all have history and baggage. The older we get, the more we have."

I stare at my best friend straight-faced. "When did you become so wise?"

She slaps my arm and laughs. "Jerk. I've always been wise." Another laugh. "It just takes everyone else way too long to realize it and catch up."

"Ouch," I say, and it has nothing to do with the playful smack a moment ago.

Autumn walks up to us with a shy smile on her face. Without permission or announcement, Cora hugs Autumn. Cora squeezes her tight and whispers something in Autumn's ear. Too quiet for me to hear. When Cora lets her go, she braces her hands on Autumn's shoulders and gives her a pointed look. Autumn's lips curve up and she nods.

"Have a good night. See you next time," Cora says to Autumn before turning to me. She gives me a hug and whispers in my ear next. "Assumptions are the death of relationships. Ask, but be patient. Because I love the way she makes you come to life."

Before Cora pulls away, I whisper *thank you* in her ear.

Everyone else leaves before me and Autumn. As if they wanted to give us privacy to talk. To hash out whatever changed both our temperaments three-quarters of the way through our night out.

On the way out of the bowling alley, I desperately want to wrap Autumn's hand in mine. But I don't. I feel as if I don't deserve her hand right now. Not after how I behaved earlier. How I accused her of being dishonest.

It was super shitty and I wish there was a way I could take it all back. Take it back and say something different. Or not say anything at all.

But instead of giving her time to slowly divulge her past to me, I ripped the proverbial bandage off and basically forced her to explain herself. My parents would be pissed with my juvenile behavior. I am.

Her conversation could have been completely innocent. But instead of allowing her the opportunity to tell me in her own time, I snooped and jumped to conclusions. Mom always taught my sisters and I that snooping never accomplished anything except for causing more problems. And I have learned, over the years, Mom always steered me down the correct path.

A couple cars from Autumn's, I reach for her hand and she lets me take it. *Thank goodness.*

"Hey" —I halt us at the back of her car— "I'm really sorry about earlier. I shouldn't have been such an ass."

Autumn closes her eyes and essentially cuts me off from her sweet, addictive cognac irises. And the loss of her eyes on me sends a sharp pain through my chest. Slow, yet steady and debilitating. I don't like it.

"Jonas..." She says my name as if it causes her pain.

The ice pick in my heart twists and deepens. "Please don't make me choose."

I shake my head, confused. "Choose?"

She opens her eyes and my pulse silences for one, two, three beats. "Jonas, I…" She swallows and peeks up at me. Tears stand on the ledge of her eyes, thinking of jumping. And I hate how I have put her in this place.

"What is it, Autumn? Please tell me. I… I hate that I did this. I hate that I upset you." I wipe away a tear that escapes and rolls down her cheek. "That I made you cry. I will never forgive myself."

She leans into my touch and I take it as a good sign. "Thank you. But, Jonas…" Autumn kisses my palm, then stands straighter. "I need to tell you something."

I bend at the knees and lower myself to her height so we stand eye to eye. "You can tell me anything," I say.

Her eyes dart between mine. She swallows and nods. "Jonas, I have a daughter." Her confession comes out barely audible.

What did she just say? Did I hear her correctly? Did Autumn just tell me she has a daughter?

Dumbstruck, I have no clue how to respond to her confession. Does it bother me that she has a daughter? A child? No. But the only thing I know about kids I have learned from being around my nephew. Which isn't often enough to say I have knowledge. He is cute and fun and says the craziest shit sometimes, but I don't spend long periods of time with him.

"Jonas?" Autumn asks after I don't say anything for far too long.

"Sorry. I'm just…"

"Terrified?"

I shake my head at her. "No. But I don't know what to say or do next." Her phone call earlier makes perfect sense now. And I hate how I reacted. Ugh, I am such a prick.

"There's nothing to do," she says. And the way she says the words adds a new wound. But this one feels different. Deeper. Harsher. One which will leave a vicious scar. "I think we should take a break."

Shaking my head and pinching my brow, I stumble back from her. "Wait, what? Why?"

Is she really doing this? Breaking up with me before we even begin. I can't fucking breathe. Can't hear anything except buzzing white noise. Can't see anything except Autumn's face slowly fading in the darkness.

Please tell me I misheard her. Please tell me this is all a farce.

"This is why I never dated, Jonas. Because it just gets in the way."

Seriously? How on earth is this reality? Two hours ago—hell, even an hour ago—everything was perfect. We were perfect. And now…

"Is that what I am, Autumn? In the way?" Anger seeps into my veins and coats the hurt residing there. Because anger is easier to manage than heartache. Heartache and I seem to be besties nowadays.

"Jonas, that didn't come out right."

I throw my hands in the air, ready to go to battle. Hours ago, I would fight to the death for Autumn's happiness. But this stubborn rejection she tosses at me for shits and giggles… it's bullshit.

"Then please, clear it up for me. Explain it so I understand."

She rolls her eyes. "Please don't make this harder than it is."

I laugh without humor. "Why? Because you like me? Because I like you? Breaking up a relationship shouldn't be easy, Autumn. Not when both parties feel the way we do." Part of me wants to drop to my knees and grovel. But I won't. Not here. Not tonight.

"It's just easier this way."

"For who? You? Me?" I step within an inch of her face and lock eyes with her. "Losing you will never be easy," I whisper. "Never."

Autumn closes her eyes as if it pains her to look into mine. Good. It should hurt. Breaking off what we have, what we could have, should hurt. Nothing has ever crippled me like hearing Autumn tell me she no longer wants me.

A tear rolls down her cheek and, this time, I don't reach for it. Don't swipe it away with my thumb while muttering sweet reassurances. Words which tell her everything will work out. That we will be okay. That we will survive this.

Because I don't believe it myself. How can I?

"As great as we are... were..." Tears spill from her eyes more easily now. Pain floods every line and curve and dimple of her face, but she won't admit the pain this causes her. Not aloud. Not when she believes being alone for her daughter is the right thing to do. "I can't do this, Jonas. It wasn't a good idea."

I bite the inside of my cheek to prevent myself from saying something I will later regret. As determined as Autumn is, I will find a way to make this better. I have to.

"If that's how you feel," I say before swallowing down the wad of cotton in my throat. "If this is what you want, I guess there's nothing I can do to change your mind."

I take a step backward. Then another. And another.

With each falter back, the pain on her face intensifies. Each move away from her, she flinches. But I refuse to be a punching bag for someone. Refuse to stand on the side-lines while she lives her life as if I don't matter to her. Because I do. I do fucking matter.

She won't admit it to herself, but she cares. Maybe a little too much. And perhaps therein lies the problem.

"Jonas," she mumbles.

I take another step away from her. And another. Then I spin around and stride toward my bike. After I slip on my helmet, I rev the engine louder than appropriate. I am in no condition to ride, but I can't be here any longer. Not after everything that has happened here tonight.

How do I go from being on the cusp of slipping the

infamous *L*-word to breaking up with the one woman I can't imagine life without?

Fuck.

I smack the handlebar as I fly down the highway. As I ugly cry for a woman for the first time in my life. As I feel my life crumbling into a pile of ash.

Jonas revs his motorcycle louder than polite several spaces down from me. Still standing at the back of my car, I stare glassy-eyed at him as he backs the bike out of the space then zips out of the parking lot and onto the highway faster than safe.

And the moment I no longer see him, when I no longer hear the angry growls of the bike engine, I start shaking head to toe. My heart hammers in my ribcage. My breath coming in short bursts.

What have I done?

I reach behind me and brace myself on the car. Slowly, I guide myself to the driver's side door as a torrent of tears spills down my cheeks. I fumble through my purse—frustrated as hell with my oversized bag—until I locate my keys. Drop the keys from my trembling fingers as I try to unlock the door.

Once I finally get the door unlocked, I fall into the seat and slam the door shut. Tossing my purse on the passenger seat, I white-knuckle the steering wheel as I rest my forehead on top.

My chest wrenches violently as the sobs continue to come. I can't catch my breath. Can't think clearly. And there is an ever-expanding hollowness beneath my breastbone.

It fucking hurts. Hurts more than anything I have ever known. The exponential pain unbearable.

I lean back into the seat with my grip still firmly on the wheel and scream at the top of my lungs. Slightly cathartic, it only serves to exacerbate the emptiness taking over my heart.

"Why," I scream at the windshield. "Why did I do this to myself? Why did I do this when I knew it would be a bad idea? When I knew it would end badly."

Simple. When your heart is involved, your brain no longer makes rational decisions.

And Jonas was definitely in my heart. Still is.

But doing this, breaking things off, before either of us becomes too heavily invested, is for the best. At least that is what I keep telling myself.

How could it be for the best if it hurts this much?

Shouldn't I be relieved? Now I don't have to worry about the awkwardness of being a single parent and trying to fit another person into my life. Don't have to worry about my daughter becoming attached to a man who won't stick around. Don't have to worry about her little heart being crushed by losing another person in her life.

I should be relieved, but I am far from it.

Minutes tick by as I work to cease the dam of tears spilling from my eyes. Once they subside enough for me to see clearly, I pop the key in the ignition and start the car. I ease out of the space and exit the lot.

The drive home is a blur. Not because I can't see, but because I go from point A to point B on autopilot. No music to distract me. No visual stimulation to spark my brain back to life. And somehow, I make it home safely.

After I cut the engine, I sit in the dark for a moment and try to compose myself. Surely, I look like shit. There will be no hiding what happened tonight from Penny. Nothing except time will erase the pain on my face and in my heart. Quite a bit of time.

I suck in a deep breath and tug the handle to open the door. Each step toward the front door feels like a step closer to my demise. Where I will have to relive every-thing all over again. A vicious cycle of hurt on repeat.

As I unlock the front door, the television mutes inside. When I swing the door wide and Penny sees my face, her smile vanishes as she bolts from the couch.

"Oh my god, Auti. What's wrong?"

And I lose it. Again.

Penny wraps her arms around me and holds me in a death grip hug. I cry into her neck. On her shoulder. And she gently strokes my hair and shushes me, telling me everything will be okay.

Before I realize it, Penny has walked us to the couch and is sitting us down. She lets me cry until I am ready to stop. Doesn't ask any questions and just lets me sob uncontrollably.

When I finally compose myself enough to speak, everything comes out broken and stilted. "I broke up with Jonas." A new torrent floods my eyes. Penny rises from the couch, disappears down the hall, and returns with a box of tissues. She pops one from the box and hands it to me before settling the box on the couch in front of me.

Penny brushes fallen strands of my hair out of my face as I swipe my eyes dry. "Want to talk about it?" she asks, her tone soft and cajoling.

I blow my nose and try to rein in my sobs so I can explain how everything unfolded at the bowling alley. When the tears settle to a lesser flow and the sobs quit wracking my body so heavily, I dive headfirst into how everything went from fantastic to shit in the blink of an eye.

"Let me start by saying, the night had been perfect up until your phone call."

Penny scrunches her brow. "My call?"

Nodding, I continue. "We bowled. Ate all the junk food from the food bar. Had some beer. Shared smiles and laughs with his friends." I suck in a breath. Futz with tissue between my fingers. "He kissed me in front of everyone like no one else existed. It was perfect," I whisper. "And then a couple of frames later, you called and I stepped away."

She reaches forward, takes my hands in hers, and gives them a little squeeze. Encouragement to continue, but also to remind me she is here. That no matter what she says, she has my back.

"I guess he saw me walk off and followed. But I had no idea. He overheard part of my conversation with Clementine. After I hung up and saw him watching me… Pen, you should've seen the look on his face. It's like he didn't trust me. He asked who I was talking to and I told him you had called."

Penny snorts and shakes her head. "Truth and not."

I nod. "Yeah. Well, I guess he heard me tell Clementine I love her and that I'd kiss her when I got home. I never said her name. And when I told him you'd called, he flipped on me. Got upset and thought I was lying. Asked if you called for a good night often. I'd backed myself into a corner and had no idea how to get out."

"You should've told him about her then."

"I know," I say as I hang my head. "But he was acting like such a jerk. And I didn't have the energy to go into explanation right then. Plus, his friends were all waiting on us to return. When we did, they all knew something was off."

I go on to tell Penny how we finished the rest of the game in the thickest cloud of tension. How I got more and more frustrated with each passing moment. How I decided, when the night was over, that I would break things off with Jonas because it seemed like the right thing to do. To just cut out the heartache now. To eliminate the need to skirt around the truth. That I had a daughter and she was my world. Clementine would always stand front and center in my life, no matter how much I cared for someone else.

"When we got ready to leave, Cora came over to me and gave me a hug."

"Cora? As in Gavin and Cora, Cora?"

"Yep. She and Jonas have been friends for years. He supposedly had the hots for her."

"Had?"

"Until he met me," I whisper.

Penny stares at me wide-eyed. "Wow."

"Yeah. Well, when Cora hugged me, she whispered something to me."

"What?" Penny asks, leaning in closer, hungry for all the details.

"She told me she'd never seen Jonas so happy. And she hoped he made me happy too. When she pulled out of the hug, all I could do was nod. Because I knew I was about to rip it all away."

A new onslaught of tears pours down my cheeks as Penny tugs me forward into her arms. God, I have never cried this much in my life. And it fucking sucks.

I thought getting this all off my chest, spilling all my pain out, would help. That talking with Penny would alleviate some of the devastation coursing through my veins. Bring a sense of comfort and slowly wash away the heartache I know will reside in me for days or weeks or months to come. But it isn't. If anything, it only serves to amplify it. Spark it with new life.

Penny eases her embrace and leans back to swipe at my tears. "Auti, do you really think what you did was the right thing?"

What? Why is she asking me this? Of all the people who I assumed would be Team Autumn, I pegged Penny at the top of the list.

"What kind of question is that?"

She shakes her head as she cups both my cheeks and locks eyes with me. "Don't be upset. It's a fair question. If you thought breaking up with Jonas was the right thing to do, you wouldn't be crying like this. Not after dating for such a short period of time. Neither of you knows much about the other. Your relationship is, was, still in the beginning stages. You're getting to know one another. Finding the quirks and kinks. Learning about pasts as well as likes and dislikes." She drops her hands from my face and leans back slightly. "Please don't take this the wrong way, Auti, but you didn't even give him a chance."

I narrow my eyes at her. Did she really just say that? Or did I mishear her?

"Let me clarify," she says.

"Please do."

"Auti, you left him high and dry not explaining the phone call. Then, when you finally do go into explanation, when you finally tell him about Clementine, you break it off with him. You never gave him a chance to register any of what you told him. You never gave him a minute to comprehend what you'd just told him. To grasp the fact you are a mom. It's a lot to process. I hate to say it, but it isn't fair to him. It isn't fair for you to have dropped a major bomb and then run for the hills."

When she says it like that, it dawns on me how much of a jerk *I am*. She has a point. Without considering Jonas's feelings, I dropped a whopper of a bomb and then told him we would be better off apart. A knee-jerk reaction, but now I am slowly seeing the error of my ways.

Since my pregnancy with Clementine, all I wanted was to do what was right for my daughter. Give her a good home. Shower her in love and smiles and laughter. And have good people around her. Her father and my family may have severed ties with us, but she has never felt unloved or unwanted a day in her life.

"How do I fix this?" I whisper-ask as fresh tears spill from my eyes.

"Give him a little time. And then, reach out to him again. Spill your heart out to him. Let him know you're sorry. Grovel, if necessary." I laugh at the last bit. "Just don't wait too long, Auti. Because men like Jonas only come around once."

Shit, shit, shit.

Did I royally screw myself by jumping the gun? I made a decision in the heat of the moment without really thinking things through. I made a decision based on the people of my past and how they hurt me and, by proxy, Clementine. But Jonas isn't like Clementine's father. Nor is he like my own mother and father, who disowned me.

Jonas is this sweet and wholesome guy. One who holds your hand and sets your body on fire at the same time. Who kisses me breathless as if I hold the key to a life he never thought he would possess. Who looked at me as if no one else existed.

What have I done?

Penny rises from the couch and kisses the top of my head. "I'm headed to bed. Try to get some sleep. It'll all work out, Auti. Just believe it will and it will."

"Thanks, Pen. Love you."

"Love you too. Night."

"Night," I whisper as she walks to her room.

I turn off the television and the light before heading to the bathroom. When I flip on the bathroom light and see my reflection in the mirror, I immediately flick the light off.

Looks as if I have been at a funeral for ten days straight. My eyes are veiny and angry, red and puffy. My cheeks and throat blotchy. And the mascara streaks down my face could double as clown makeup.

After I finish my nighttime routine in the dark, I slip into bed and kiss Clementine on the forehead. Turning so I face away from her, I cry silently into my pillow.

Cry for the loss of a good man. Cry for the mistake I made in assuming he would no longer want me once he found out I am a single mom. And cry for myself. For the throbbing ache in the center of my chest. The ache which only grows stronger with each passing second. The ache I deserve after what I did tonight.

But I will make this right. I have to. Not just for selfish reasons. Also because I need Jonas. More than I thought possible after such a short period.

I only hope he still wants me when I crawl back and beg for forgiveness.

SIXTEEN

JONAS

The entire day at work sucks.

I slept for shit last night. No matter which way I had lain in bed, sleep was impossible. I tried counting backward from one hundred. That only lasted to eighty-five, when my brain sidetracked and I had to start all over again. Tried listening to calming music, but it only fired me up more. Even tried a meditation app I downloaded at three this morning. Nothing.

Dad knows something is wrong. He sees the complete one-eighty in my demeanor. But he won't ask what has me on edge. When I feel ready to tell him, he knows I will. Our entire lives, that's how he and I operated.

So, he will wait patiently for me to explain why I can't focus on one goddamn thing. Why I have yelled and cursed more times today than I have in the last decade. Why I slam the tools down instead of carefully put them in their place. Why I have stormed out of the garage and into the office more than a dozen times in the last three hours.

It might be a while before I mention anything to Dad, though. My ego is littered with bruises while my heart lies scattered in bits.

She didn't even give me a chance. Not having a chance stings the worst.

Last night's conversation in the parking lot cycles through my mind for the thousandth time. Each time I recall what she told me, a new wave of emotion rolls through me. Anywhere from anger to frustration to agony to understanding. And then it starts all over again.

Autumn broke things off with me for one reason. Well, maybe two. To protect herself. And to protect her *daughter*.

Still blows my mind Autumn is a mother. Not because it was inconceivable to picture her with a small bundle in her arms. Picturing her that way is actually quite believable. But because she thought hiding a major piece of herself was the right choice. She once told me she hadn't dated in years. Is her lack of dating because she is a single mother?

Another stab to the heart.

I only got a small glimpse at life with Autumn on my arm. With her lips on mine. And I miss every second of it.

The hurt on her face last night flashes in my memory. She didn't want our evening to end the way it did. She didn't want *us* to end. But she did it anyway. To protect the only life she has known. To shelter her heart and the heart of her daughter.

How do I fix this? Fix us?

Because I refuse to believe there isn't still an us. I refuse to believe what we have is beyond repair. All I have to do is figure out how to go about it.

Minor relief washes over me when the Harley-Davidson clock in the garage reads five and I can call it quits for the day. But the day is far from over. Because today is Wednesday. Family dinner night. And family dinner night equals several sets of eyes and ears homed in on me. No doubt Dad will go home and tell Mom something is up. If my sisters arrive before me, the *what's-wrong-with-Jonas* gang will be in full effect upon my arrival.

Might be a good night to hang on the back patio with Anton.

When I get home from work and let Spartan out of his kennel, he mauls me as if I have been gone days and not hours. He licks my face and jumps excitedly around the living room.

"Well, I'm glad to see someone is happy to have me around," I tell him as I rough up the fur on his head. "You ready to see Grandma tonight."

Woof, woof.

I love how Spartan answers me as if we are having a genuine conversation. He has always been this way. Makes me laugh at times. Who knows, maybe he does actually understand what I say. Never underestimate the intelligence of your fur-child.

We go out in the back yard for a little bit. Spartan trots along the fence line and sniffs every possible tuft of grass to make sure no one else has marked his territory. I sit on the small outdoor couch set up on a paver patio I laid months ago. The L-shaped couch can easily seat five and has a matching lounger and two chairs. A canopy spans the entire patio and shades the seating while protecting the gas fire table set up in the middle.

Occasionally, I will sit out here and get lost in a book or the flicker of the fire. Being out here is a great place to unwind after a long day. Plus, Spartan gets extra outside time when I hang out here.

After Spartan alleviates a tenth of his energy, we hop into the Jeep and drive over to Mom and Dad's. I watch Spartan as he finds happiness in the little things—such as riding in the car or biting the wind or barking at a passing car—and do my best to soak up some happiness of my own.

The moment we walk in the door, Spartan runs off and Mom is on me as if I am three years old and fell from the treehouse again.

"How's my baby?" She frames my face and twists it left and right as she examines me.

"Fine, Mom," I say as she hauls me against her for a hug. I wrap my arms around her, close my eyes, and soak up her hug more than normal. Mom has always been a great hugger. Warm and giving and soothing.

"Don't you lie to me. Your father says you've been in a sour mood all day."

She releases me from the hug and holds me at arm's length. Her scrutiny is somewhat unsettling, but I know it comes from a heartfelt place. Even when I felt sad about all that happened with Cora, my parents never reacted this way. They checked in more often, but otherwise let me be.

"Well, he wouldn't be wrong. But I don't want to talk about it right now."

Her eyes scan every fine line and detail of my face. Judge my eyes and lack of smile. "Just don't keep it bottled up. Okay? Never solves a thing if you keep it to yourself."

I raise my right hand and press it over my heart. "Promise."

In a flash, she grabs my hand and drags me into the kitchen. "Now that that's out of the way, let's make dinner." And just like that, Mom makes me laugh.

Joining Jasmine and Jillian in the kitchen, Mom and I chop potatoes for cooking and mashing, and vegetables for salad. Garlic, garden-fresh rosemary and lemon waft through the kitchen, and it isn't hard to guess we are having Jillian's favorite—lemon and herb roasted chicken. We all work in synchronicity until dinner is ready.

As much as I wanted to seclude myself to the back patio earlier, it was better being in the kitchen with my sisters and mom. We worked as a unit and nothing needed to be said as we went about our individual tasks. Without a word, the women in my life helped lift me up. And I love them more for it.

Dinner went on much like it normally did. Lex flung bits of salad at my dad as he tickled the bottoms of his feet. Jasmine scolded Dad and told him to quit teaching

Lex food was a toy instead of something you eat. Anton laughed with Dad and egged him on. Mom asked Jillian about work and when the next batch of new fashions would hit the racks.

The only exception to the usual conversation was me. I sat quiet and shuffled the cut pieces of chicken around my plate. Stirred the mashed potatoes more than ate them.

As plates emptied, Mom went into the kitchen and grabbed dessert. Apple cobbler and vanilla bean ice cream. My favorite.

Dad must have called her during the day and forewarned her of my mood. Because the cobbler would've had to be in the oven long before the chicken. Plus, she would've had to shop for the missing ingredients I know weren't always in the house.

Jasmine scoops out a helping of cobbler. "What's the special occasion, Mom?"

She glances at me briefly before peering at my sister. "No special occasion. Just thought it'd be nice to have. Been a while." Shock must register on my face when Mom looks back at me because her eyes widen. All I do is smile in return.

Neither Mom nor Dad told Jasmine or Jillian about today. About my adult-sized temper tantrum. They really do love me. If my sisters don't know the nitty-gritty details, my parents get how bothered and upset I am.

After we all have our fair share of cobbler, my sisters and I go out on the back patio while Anton and my parents stay inside with Lex. We sit on the poolside loungers in silence for a few minutes and enjoy the soft glow from the twinkling lights around the yard. A breeze kicks up and Jillian shivers in the lounger on my right.

"Want my jacket?"

"Nah, big brother. But thanks."

"So, what's up with you?" Jasmine asks a moment later. I know she isn't asking Jillian, but I play coy anyway.

"Me?"

"Yes, you. You've been acting *off* all night."

Jillian sits up and spins to face both of us. "You do seem more bummed than usual."

Great. Mom and Dad may not have said anything to my sisters, but they are more intuitive than I give them credit for.

Maybe talking with them—two women I trust, and from different ages—will help. Fingers crossed.

"I recently started dating someone…" I trail off, trying to figure out what else to say.

"And?" Jillian drawls out the single-worded question.

"Jesus. Give me a minute." I pause and stare up at the stars. "Last night, she told me she has a daughter." To my left, Jasmine gasps. "Then she said we need to take a break."

"What? Why?" Jasmine asks.

As I continue to stare at the stars, I secretly hope I get the opportunity to sit under a starry sky with Autumn in my arms. Somewhere far from the city, where there is less light pollution and only the stars brighten the night sky.

Where we can point out different clusters and tell each other what we see.

"Not really sure. I think she's just scared to let anyone in. She's a single mom. And from what I know, it's been that way for a while. She told me I was the first person she's dated in years."

Now Jasmine sits up and faces me. It feels as if I am stuck in a sisterly vise. Except they won't squeeze the life out of me. They will just pump me full of advice. But their words of wisdom may be exactly what I need.

"Brother, if you're the first person she's dated in years —possibly the only person she's dated since her daughter was born—she had to have broken it off because she's scared. Letting someone in is probably huge for her."

I lift my head from the lounger and turn to my left. "Yeah, I get it, Jas. But why would she let me in to drop me five seconds later?"

"Easy," Jillian says, and I turn to face her. "She wants to see if you're worthy."

"If I'm worthy? What does that mean?"

"It means" —I turn back to Jasmine, almost dizzy sitting between my sisters— "she wants to see if you'll just let her go. Or if you'll step up and fight for her."

Okay. If I thought women were complicated before, now the ideal has been solidified. Women are the most complex and confusing creatures on the planet. They say one thing and want something completely opposite. How is any man supposed to grasp this concept? Or know when they are doing something right or wrong?

"And how am I supposed to do that? How do I fight?"

"Little things," Jillian says. "Leave notes where you know she'll find them. Send her flowers. Nothing major, just small tokens to let her know you're still thinking about her. As complex as we seem, big bro, we are simple creatures. Those little things add up over time. Women are more sentimental. Sure, we all love gifts. But when it comes down to it, we want the reason behind the gift, not just the trinket."

At the word trinket, I run my fingers over the Eisenhower dollar in my pocket. A token I have carried with me for years. Something Grandpa John gave me just before I started kindergarten. *"Keep this close by and it'll always give you luck."* Since he slipped the large coin into my small palm, I never left home without it. It was either in my pocket or my wallet or somewhere close by. It wasn't only special because Grandpa said it was a good luck charm, but also because it was a gift from him.

"So, if you were in my position, what would you do?" I ask them both.

"This all went south last night?" Jasmine asks and I nod. "Give her a couple days to breathe. Give her time to process everything. She asked for a break so she could think clearly about how you fit into her world. And her daughter's world, too. If you don't give her the time she needs, she'll push harder."

"Okay, I get that. But how much time is enough?"

"Maybe wait until the weekend. I like Jillian's idea with the notes," Jasmine states.

"Thank you." Jillian tips her head in gratitude.

"Write her a note. Tell her how you're feeling. It's easier to say things when you're not face to face. Then leave it somewhere she'll find it."

This is something I can get on board with. Writing her notes. Love letters. Something short and sweet which lets her know she is still on my mind. But for how long?

"How long would you suggest I do this?"

"Forever," Jillian says at the same time Jasmine says, "Until your hand falls off." We all laugh.

"Seriously, big bro. If things pan out with her, keep doing it. She'll love it."

Good to know. But it still doesn't answer my initial question. Maybe I need to rephrase.

"Okay. When do I take the next step? When do I move from letters to something more?"

Jasmine shrugs. "Whenever it feels right to you. If you leave her the first note and she reaches out to you, angry, back off. Otherwise, use your best judgment. Women like to be wooed. All of us. Woo her."

Woo her. Notes and flowers and standing on her front porch singing old love ballads. I got this. Maybe.

My sisters pile on top and hug the hell out of me. For a moment, I fake cough as their weight presses down. But as they lift off me, I wrap my arms around them and hug them tighter.

"Thank you both. I love you."

"Love you, big brother."

"Me too. Now make things right. Cause I want to meet her."

I laugh and sit up. "On it."

We all wander inside the house and exchange hugs before heading out for the night. Although I was hesitant to be here tonight. To deal with my family as they breathed advice down my neck. Being here was exactly what I needed. To be reset back to what matters. To get clarity only my family delivers.

As I head out the door with Spartan on my heels, Mom hands me a container of leftovers. "Extra cobbler." A gentle smile lifts the corners of her lips.

"Thanks, Mom. Love you." I hug her again.

"Love you too. See you next week."

The ride home has me thinking nonstop. Of what messages I want to write Autumn. Of what else I want to do to show her how much I care. A small list fills out in my head and I am excited to begin.

Once home, I get to work. Writing notes. Whipping out my sketchpad and my pencils, I draw for hours. Get lost in the notion of wooing Autumn. Of getting her to see I still want her, even if I have to share her.

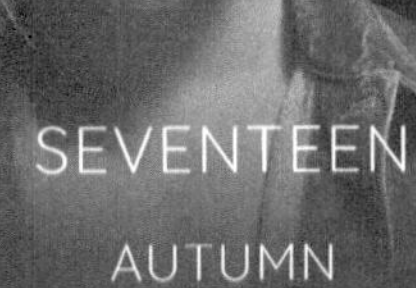

SEVENTEEN

AUTUMN

The last week has been miserable. Well, not completely miserable, but not really good either.

I miss Jonas. A lot. How the hell do you miss someone you barely know? But how do you not miss someone who walked off with a chunk of your heart? Because Jonas definitely took a piece of me with him on the back of his motorcycle. Hopefully bits of my heart aren't strewn all over the highway.

Although I have a feeling he would never do such a thing.

Clementine asked to set up the Christmas tree and decorate the apartment. The temporary distraction was needed, but only lasted for a few hours. In no time, the tree was up and littered with a mix of homemade and store-bought ornaments. Stockings hung from the far side of the breakfast bar we never sit at. Sporadic glittery

Santa's and elves and snowflakes were spread throughout the living space.

Everywhere you look, there is a splash of holiday cheer. The apartment oozed festive and fun.

Difficult as it has been, I kept a smile plastered on my face. The last thing I want or need is Clementine wondering why or what has me upset. To ask questions I don't know how to answer. The timing isn't right. Not yet.

Over the last five days, when I left the shop, I discovered a folded piece of paper under my driver's side windshield wiper. At first, I was leery. I'd heard stories about criminals who place things on cars to distract the owner before attacking them. With Reznor and Rex close enough to hear my screams, I scanned the lot, took a breath, and plucked each paper from the wiper blade. Then, I unfolded the page and saw who it was from. Warmth instantly spread through my limbs to my chest when I read it.

The first note, on Thursday, was short.

Autumn,

I'm sorry. I miss you.

Jonas

The note said so much with only a few words. Not just

an apology. Not just to say he missed me. But to remind me he was still there. And he was thinking about me after everything that happened.

On Friday, the paper on my windshield was bigger, the stock heavier. When I unfolded it, I gasped. Jonas had drawn what I assume was the two of us, curled up on a blanket in the park, watching a movie on the makeshift theater screen. His arm around my waist and body snug against mine. When I showed it to Penny, all she said was *"He's got it bad."*

Saturday, Sunday, and yesterday each ended with another note. Typically, I had two days off during the week. Plus, the shop closed on Sunday. But with everything that happened last Tuesday between me and Jonas, I came into work on my days off. Worked some. Hung out mostly. Even brought Clementine with me on Sunday while I worked on two desperate clients. Although the shop was closed, it was better than sitting at home. Chores only distracted so much of my time.

The other notes were much the same, but each got a little longer. Sweeter. Made me miss him more.

Autumn,

No matter what it takes. No matter how long it takes. I will fix us.

Jonas

Autumn,

The first time I saw you, I forgot how to breathe. How to speak. How to function. But then you smiled and the world righted itself again. Because you make the world, my world, a better place.

Jonas

Autumn,

On our first date, I constantly wanted to hold your hand. Touch your skin. Kiss your lips. But I was raised a gentleman. Raised to respect women and wait until they're ready.

When I kissed your lips for the first time... I never want to kiss another woman. Never want to taste anyone other than you. Because you're the perfect mix of everything I have ever wanted. Breathtaking and genuine and funny.

Jonas

I may not have seen Jonas in a week, but he still held my heart in his clutches. Don't think he will ever let it go. Not that I want him to. If anything, I want him to hold it closer. Longer. More tenderly. I want to hear him whisper the words on these pages—the ones secured in my purse, that go everywhere I go—in my ear. To say all these sweet words with his warm breath on my skin.

With each note I receive, Penny cradles her heart and coos. Begs me to call or text him. Give him another chance. And I want to. God, do I want to. I want his arms around me again. Want his lips on mine again.

But after how I behaved last week, I'm terrified to show my face again. How do I begin to fix this? Fix us. I harbor most of the blame with why we aren't together. Past insecurities gnaw at my happiness. Tell me romantic relationships aren't in the cards. So, how do I let Jonas in? How do I introduce Clementine into the mix? This is all so new to me—dating as a grown woman and single parent. The idea of us not working out, of Clementine getting hurt, terrifies me to no end.

Twenty minutes in with my current client—an eigh-teen-year-old getting her first tattoo—the front door jingles. Automatically, I peek up to see who walks in. The blonde from the bowling alley—Shelly, I think—ambles in with a cheery smile on her face. She glances over at me and her smile glows lumens brighter.

But it isn't her or her smile that surprises me. No, it would be the bouquet in her hands which has me stunned. Because I know who the arrangement is for and who sent it. Shelly delivers the bouquet to Penny and hangs out at the front desk until I finish the small script tattoo.

After I clean up the girl's tattoo and give her instructions for aftercare, she pays and leaves.

Now I have to deal with Penny *and* Shelly. Yay me — insert sarcasm.

"What's this?" I ask, feigning ignorance.

Penny rests a hand on her hip, pops it out, and cocks her head. "Really, Auti. Gonna play stupid?"

"You know what they say about assuming." I laugh and both of them stare at me as if they don't know. "It makes an ass out of you and me. Please tell me you both have heard that saying before."

Penny rolls her eyes and Shelly laughs. "Yes, dippy. I've heard the saying. And you know what I meant."

I ignore Penny and look up at Shelly. "Jonas?"

She nods slowly. "He's a mess, Autumn. I've never seen him like this. *Ever.* Not sure what happened last week, and I don't expect you to tell me. But please talk to him. Give him a chance. Give your relationship a chance." I subtly nod. "You make him smile. Like really smile. And I miss seeing his smile."

I miss seeing his smile, too.

I take in the arrangement. Unique and beautiful. A handful of soft pink roses. A vine of pale pink and white orchids. Small white flowers at the base. Light green and lavender succulent buds. Pulled together with curly willow and blue thistle. A blend of rustic and opulent.

Not too flashy. Not a typical floral arrangement. Perfect.

"Thank you, Shelly," I whisper.

Out of nowhere, Shelly hugs me. "See you soon," she says so only I hear her. Then, she releases me, pivots away, and walks out the door.

Penny tips her head toward the front door. "One of his friends?"

"Yeah. She was at the bowling alley last week."

I pick up the arrangement, turn on my heel, and head back to my booth. Attached to the bouquet is another note, and I would prefer to read it without Penny hovering over my shoulder. Not like I won't show it to her later, but I want to read it on my own first.

Leaning forward, I inhale the subtle perfume from the flowers. Understated and delicate, yet exemplary. I pluck the note from the plastic tong in the center and unfold it. Taking a deep breath, I scan the page and absorb each of his words.

Autumn,

There is something so classic about your beauty. You ravish me. Without doing anything extraordinary, you shine. Brighten the darkest night sky. Ignite a fire inside me. And without you, the fire has extinguished. My true north has vanished, and I'm wandering alone in the dark.

If you can find a place for me in your heart, I would love another chance. A chance to show you more than one person can love you. And when you're ready, I would be honored to meet the little girl who holds your heart captive. Because if she is anything like her mom, I already know how I will feel about her.

Please give me—us—another chance. I will do whatever, give whatever, you need. Time. Patience. As long as you are in my life. All I ask is that you call me. Talk to me. Let me back in.

Yours always,
Jonas

I read the letter again. And again. Then crush it against my chest and start crying. Reznor glances over the wall separating our booths, then over at Penny. Seconds later, Penny is in my booth and trying to snatch the letter from my arms. I fight her tooth and nail.

"If you won't let me see the letter, then you better start talking. I've seen enough tears from you over the last week to last a lifetime," Penny says, frustration lacing her tone.

"Pen, it isn't bad. Quite the opposite, actually. So, stop mothering me."

She extends her hand between us, flexing her fingers in a *give-me* motion. "If it isn't bad, let me see it."

"Can I have just this one to myself? Please."

Tilting her head to the side, she gives me a sad smile. "I guess. But if he makes you cry again, I'm cutting his balls off."

"Ouch," Reznor says. "Little extreme, don't you think, Pen?"

She shrugs. "Just telling it like it is." Reznor shakes his head and continues working on the guy face down in his booth.

I fold the letter up and tuck it away in my shirt—close to my heart and where Penny can't reach it easily. She harrumphs and leaves my booth. In a slight fog, I clean my workstation up and prep for the next person on my schedule.

Two more clients and then I am done for the day. Two more clients and I can leave work and call Jonas. Hear his voice again for the first time in a week. Although, with every note he has left me, I have read them with his voice in my head. Heard each and every word in his low baritone. Felt comfort with each letter. With the fact he was still nearby. Seeking me out.

The next three hours go by slower than any other time in my life. It didn't help that both my clients had no idea what they wanted inked in their skin. But it didn't shock me to find out they came in together. Eventually, the first decided on a rose. And although the second could have figured out her tattoo while number one was getting hers, it took her fifteen minutes past her session start time to realize she wanted the exact same thing. And it wasn't as if they had never gotten a tattoo before. Hell, they had them everywhere.

Finally, I finish up the night. Clean my workspace faster than any previous shift. Shoulder my purse, cradle the bouquet in my arms, and bolt for the back door. Once alone in the confines of my car, I inhale the gentle bouquet perfume one more time before setting it on the passenger seat. Then I dig my phone from my purse and open up Jonas's contact info.

The screen illuminates my face in the dark as my finger hovers over the call button. I suck in a deep breath and tap the screen.

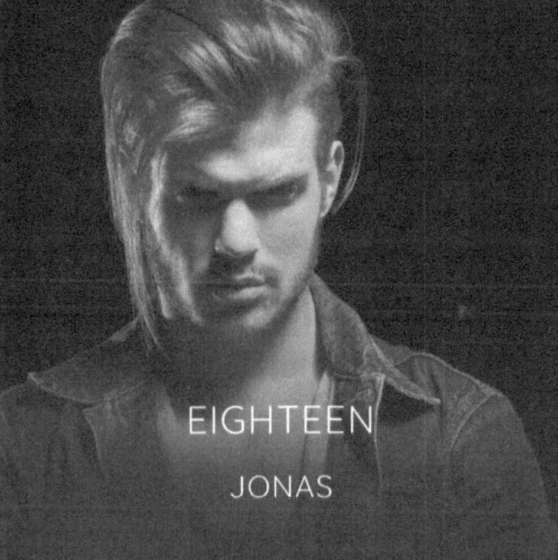

EIGHTEEN

JONAS

Shelly called me hours ago and said she delivered the flower arrangement and note to Autumn. I have been on pins and needles since. Yes, I realize she was working when the delivery arrived. But I really hoped I would have heard from her already.

Either Autumn has been crazy busy with work. Or she is avoiding me. Hopefully, it is the former.

Spartan noses my elbow and whimpers before running to the door which leads to the back yard. I ignore him the first two times. When he noses my elbow a third and barks at me for good measure, I rise from the couch, grab my phone off the coffee table, and head for the door.

As soon as I open the back door, Spartan bolts down the three short steps and races through the grass toward the back fence. His energy is off the charts and I wish I had a fraction of it.

"Ya freaking whacko," I call after him.

Sitting on the lounger on the patio, I light the fire bowl and lean back. Eyes closed and head against the cushion, I absorb the world around me. The still night air —cool and crisp. Perfect for the second official day of winter. The soft hum of an airplane as it flies overhead toward Tampa. The flames flicker in the rock-filled fire bowl, a faint smell of propane floats through the air. Spartan trots nearby, his coat brushing against my elbow as he passes me to scavenge in another section of the yard.

I love this small slice of heaven I created. But it isn't quite perfect. Not yet. And only one thing could make it perfect.

Autumn. And the echoes of young laughter and pitter-patter of small feet.

A wad of cotton clogs my throat and strips it dry as I daydream—well, night dream—of a future I hope happens. So strange, but I never imagined the future so in depth until Autumn. Sure, I wanted to land the woman of my dreams and build a life with her. But until Autumn, I never had vivid pictures in my head of the end result. Small Kodak moments captured in time, printed on matte photo paper, and wedged between glass and wood.

But I see it all so clearly now. See her beside me, for years to come.

My cell phone rings in my pocket and startles me from my fantasy. I bolt upright, fumble to get it out of my pocket and answer it just before it goes to voice mail.

A half second glance at the screen has me smiling from ear to ear. "Autumn?"

"Hi." Her voice wispy and muted. I melt back into the lounger and close my eyes.

Just the soft resonance of her voice settles every anxiety I have endured over the last week. Every questionable minute where I wondered if she would give us another chance.

"Hi," I say back. "How are you?"

As much as I don't wish Autumn to feel any sort of anguish, I secretly hope the last week has been as equally challenging for her as it has been for me. Although I only flaunted my emotions the day after, they ate away at me the entire week. With each note I wrote, I took pause. Stared at the paper for hours with pen in hand. How do you express yourself with so few words? How do you not slip up and say the words you feel will scare someone away?

I loved writing her the notes and letters, but they weren't so simple.

The drawing, on the other hand, was easy. Like extracting a strip of movie reel from my memory and scrawling it across paper with pencil. I could have drawn us together with my eyes closed. The subtle curves of Autumn's body as she lay on the blanket, her back to my front. My arm around her waist. Her warmth heating every inch of me.

I swallow and shake off the real-life fantasy floating in my thoughts.

"Okay, I guess." She says the words, tries to believe them, but the slight crack in her voice tells me she doesn't. Pain pierces my chest and I pinch my eyes tightly as she continues. "Thank you. For the notes and the d-drawing" —she sniffles— "and the flowers. They're all so beautiful."

Her heartache bounces through the air and smacks me like a bullseye in the chest. Settles deep. Liquifies and sheathes the rapid pulsing organ between my lungs. I clench my hand into a fist and press it over the sensation robbing me of breath.

"You're welcome," I croak out. "Meant every word. Every line and smudge."

On the other end, Autumn goes silent. The only indication the call hasn't dropped is her occasional sniffle in my ear.

What is going through her head? Why is she so quiet? Is she battling what to do next? Where we go from here?

God, I hope she wants to try us again. Give us another chance. With her biggest skeleton out in the open, and me still fighting for her, she has to know where I stand. That I still want her. Want more with her. Want more of us.

She has been silently sniffling on the other end for minutes now. But I don't break the silence. As many questions as I want to ask her, as much as I want to pour my heart out, I stay tight-lipped and give her however much time she needs. Time to formulate whatever it is she wants to say to me. Because I will wait as long as she needs me to.

"I miss you," she whispers. Three simple words. But how they swallow me whole and hug me fiercely. "A lot."

I inhale deeply, hold the air in my lungs for one, two, three before exhaling. Opening my eyes, I stare up at the inky night sky and land on the brightest star. Hold it in my sight and watch it brighten and dim as if pulsing.

"Me too. So damn much."

During the last week, Spartan has even grown frustrated with my temperament. Since he sees every side of me, he has sat grumpy beside me on the couch. Curled up with me at night. Groaned when I didn't want to throw his ball in the back yard. And licked my face when I spent too much time in bed or on the couch.

"Jonas…" My name leaves her lips as a plea.

My pulse kicks into fifth gear. "Yes?"

"I…" she starts, then pauses briefly. I don't dare interrupt her silence. Don't push her to say the words waiting in limbo. When she speaks again, it's not what I expect. "I'm sorry."

Why is she apologizing? If anyone should be apologizing, it should be me. I was the one who misconstrued things. Got frustrated with her evasion and lost my cool. I was in the wrong. She was merely protecting her daughter. She has every right to protect her daughter.

"Autumn, please don't apologize. It should be me saying sorry, not you."

"Maybe we were both in the wrong. I could have been more honest about the call when you asked. But I was scared. It still scares me."

"Will you tell me why? Help me understand."

She remains silent for a beat, then sniffles again. "Jonas, I haven't dated anyone since Clementine's father."

Clementine. How charming and sweet and totally Autumn. I wonder if Clementine is anything like her mother? Beautiful, charming, and someone I always want close. If so, consider me double screwed.

"How old is Clementine?" Not that it matters in my eyes, but I am curious how long Autumn has deprived herself of happiness. How long she has dedicated herself solely to this little girl. Not that I assume her daughter doesn't bring her joy.

"Seven."

To be honest, I am glad we aren't having this conversation face to face right now. Because seven was not what I expected to hear. Maybe a number closer to three. Not seven. Seven years is a *really* long time to not have any sort of romantic relationship. I understand her desire to be dedicated to her daughter, but as a woman—hell, as a grown human being—she has needs. Not necessarily sexual, but basic human desires. Companionship. Love. Having an intimate relationship—sexual or not—is basic human nature.

"Wow," I whisper. She starts to speak, but I cut her off. "Autumn, seven years is a really long time to rob yourself of love. Love other than the one you share with Clementine."

"Well," she starts. I picture her tucking her lips between her teeth a moment. "Her father and I separated before she was born. Being a parent wasn't in the cards for him."

In the blink of an eye, red pricks the backs of my eyes as I close them and grind my jaw. *Piece of shit. Fucking asshole.* I take a minute to simmer my boiling blood. Not only did this douchebag leave her, he left her high and dry when she needed someone most. Not to mention the prick abandoned his child. No wonder she has steered away from a relationship.

Breathing deep, I exhale and speak as calmly as possible. "Autumn, I'm so sorry. Can't imagine what that must've been like for you."

"Everything happens for a reason, right?" She says it with such nonchalance.

"Guess so." She has a point, though. Because if she was still with him, we might not have met. Might not be having this conversation. Might not have the possibility of getting to know one another and growing close.

"Can we save this topic for another time?"

"Of course."

"Jonas, will you forgive me?"

Her request renders me speechless for a moment. She is asking *me* to forgive *her*. The concept seems backward. Wrong. Just because Autumn had yet to tell me about her daughter, she wasn't the one out of turn. Protecting your child is never wrong.

"Only if you'll do the same. I shouldn't have been so harsh. Shouldn't have lost my temper. Should have let you tell me when you were ready. It was wrong of me to be upset over something so private."

"It's done then. All is forgiven." For the first time during this conversation, Autumn has a sliver of happiness in her voice. "Jonas?"

"Yeah?"

"I want to see you."

I sit up on the lounger and Spartan glances up at me from his spot on the patio. *She wants to see me?*

This is good. Really good. Because, fuck, I miss her. Her sweet smile and laughter that settle in the left chamber of my heart. Her fiery cognac irises which have me drunk in seconds. The warmth of her touch that fevers every molecule in my veins.

"Yes," I answer, too dumbstruck to form a proper response. "Would love to see you. More than anything."

She giggles and my chest swells in delight. "Glad to hear. Wasn't sure you would."

"Autumn, do you know how difficult it was to slip notes under your windshield wiper and not walk in the shop to see you? To sneak a peek at you through the windows? Walking away each night got more and more punishing. A couple times, I wanted to wait by your car and hand the note to you personally. But I knew it wouldn't be received the same. So, I left. As difficult as it was, I walked away and gave you time to think."

The first three nights I left notes and the drawing for Autumn, I stood next to her car for at least ten minutes. Stared at the driver's seat and pictured her behind the wheel. Imagined opening the door and her stepping out. Dreamed of her in my arms again. Of my lips on hers.

"Thank you," she whispers. "For giving me time to sort this out. To sort us out."

Us. Hope soars in my chest. "I got some sisterly advice," I confess.

"Well, your sisters are wise women." She giggles again. Each musical note of it lightens the weight I have felt over the last week. "Jonas, if you're open to it, I'd like you to meet Clementine."

Wow. This shocks me more than anything. Only because she has protected her daughter so fiercely over the last seven-plus years. Because she has forfeited her own happiness to make sure her daughter doesn't get hurt. Has dedicated her life to her daughter so she doesn't feel any less loved because her father abandoned her long before she took her first breath.

"Autumn…" My voice is barely audible. "I would like that very much. But only if you're comfortable with it."

"Wouldn't suggest it if I wasn't. But Jonas?"

"Yeah?"

"This is a really big deal for me. Me introducing you to Clementine… this has never happened before. I wasn't kidding when I told you I haven't dated."

The gravity of her repeated confession strikes me in the solar plexus. The words engulf me. Tell me how much I mean to her without actually expressing them in the terms most do. This is Autumn's way of saying she wants me more than a fling. Wants permanence. A life.

"Don't know what to say. I feel like an idiot."

"You're not an idiot. Just let me know you grasp how big this is for me."

"I do. Honestly, it's a big deal for me too. Just for a different reason."

For a moment, neither of us says anything. We sit in comfortable silence as the magnitude of what is happening between us evolves. Autumn wants to introduce me to her daughter. Wants me to meet her. And for her to know me. This isn't a baby step. It's a leap. A headfirst dive into uncharted waters. It invigorates me and scares the hell out of me in equal measure.

"Is Thursday okay?" she asks. "Or do you have plans with your family?"

I want to remind her Wednesday is when I have family dinners. But then it hits me. This is Christmas week. And Thursday is Christmas Eve. A day when most families gather and celebrate traditions other than exchanging gifts. Now that my sisters and I are grown, we don't get together until Christmas evening. So my oldest sister can celebrate with her husband and son however they choose.

"Thursday is perfect."

"How do you feel about pizza and a G-rated movie?"

I laugh. Never has greasy cheese-coated dough and animation sounded so wonderful. "Well, I've never met a pizza I didn't like. And I watch G-rated movies with my nephew now and again, so I'm up for it."

"Awesome," she says with enthusiasm. "If it's okay

with you, I'll figure out the where and when and what to see then text you."

In this aspect of her life, Autumn needs full control. And I will happily give it all to her. Give her whatever she needs so long as I get to be by her side.

"Sounds great. Can't wait to see you. And to meet Clementine. Thank you."

"Why are you thanking me?"

How in depth do I go? How do I tell her I am just thankful for another chance with her? The answer has so many layers, and tonight isn't the time to unravel them all. "Because you deserve it. Because you didn't completely dismiss me or my silly notes."

"They're not silly," she whispers.

"No, they aren't. But I've never written notes to anyone, and I felt like a teenager again. Felt like I was asking the girl stuck in my head if she likes me or not."

"Well, this girl likes you very much."

"Good to know." My cheeks sting from smiling. Only Autumn makes me this way. Happy like this.

"I should go. Been sitting in the parking lot behind the shop this whole time. Kind of need to head home."

"Head home. Sorry I kept you so long."

"No worries. I'll text you. See you Thursday."

"Thursday. Good night, Autumn."

"'Night, Jonas."

The call disconnects and I fall back against the lounger again. Spartan pops up on all fours and nudges my elbow.

But I ignore him for a minute as I stare up at the night sky. As the stars stare back at me with more twinkle.

I get to see her again. Hold her. And meet the little lady who is the most precious part of her existence. Hopefully that little girl approves of me too.

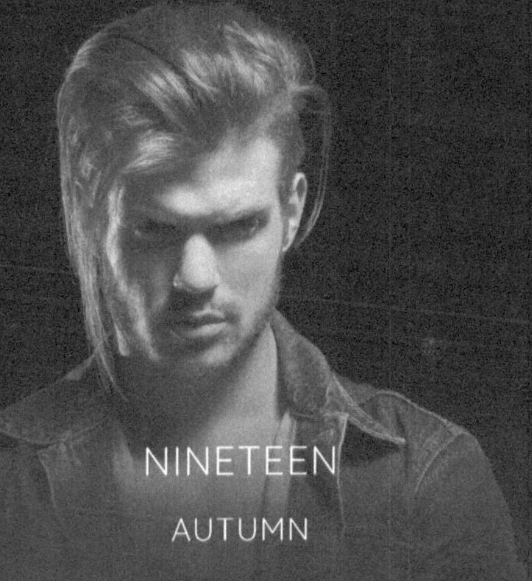

NINETEEN

AUTUMN

"Ready, pumpkin?"

"Yeah, Mama." Clementine picks up her small red purse and tosses the strap over her shoulder like any other day. Like any other night out for pizza and milkshakes.

Yesterday morning, while we sat down for breakfast, I told Clementine about Jonas. About the man who was a friend, but who I like more than a friend. The whole conversation with my seven-year-old daughter was awkward to say the least. Honestly, it felt like I was the child and she was the adult. I only imagine how weird and uncomfortable it will be to have the birds and bees conversation with her.

Although Clementine acts older than her age at times, she still holds so much innocence inside. And I take the blame as well as pride. Nowadays, too many kids grow up too soon. At every turn, I try to give my daughter a chance to remain a kid. To be spirited and not worry about things children shouldn't be burdened by—including my love life. Past or present. Most girls her age go out and do things I didn't until my preteen/early teen years. But I have done well at preserving her innocence as long as possible. Every once in a while, her sassy, trying to be older side comes out. Most of the time, though, she acts like seven-year-olds did before tablets, computers, cell phones, and online games stole their attention—and I am grateful.

We only get eighteen years to be a child. Adulting lasts three or more times longer.

When I asked Clementine if it was okay to share pizza and watch a movie with Jonas, her excitement shocked me. She jumped off the couch and started dancing. I bet it was a happy dance for pizza and a movie, but at least she wasn't perturbed by meeting Jonas.

"Let's go." We shuffle out the front door and soon buckle up in the Bel Air.

Part of me is happy Penny is at work, while part of me wishes she was home. Her constant attention would be both annoying and desirable. Her dating words of wisdom. Her constant nagging and mothering. Asking if I have my lipstick in my purse. If I put on deodorant. Reminding me to spritz perfume on my clothes and not my skin, in case Jonas kisses me. The little things which drive me crazy on a normal day, but would love tonight.

I back out of the space and drive toward the Italian restaurant we agreed to meet at. It butts up against the movie theater and makes pizza-movie night easy whenever I take Clementine.

In the passenger seat, Clementine bops to the song on the radio. Singing the lyrics she knows and humming the ones she doesn't. As on edge as I am about Jonas meeting Clementine, seeing her so at ease with the whole evening tapers the anxiety a smidge. I bask in her carefree existence. Her lack of fear or worry. Use that spirit to calm my nerves with each passing minute.

A few songs later, I steer the car into the lot. For a Thursday evening, the lot is fuller than expected. Granted, school is on break right now and parents are probably trying to find ways to amuse their children, so the crowd isn't a shock.

As I search for a place to park, I spot Jonas on his motorcycle in the next row. I swallow and clamp down on my lips. Clementine continues to sing, completely oblivious to the sudden panic attack creeping through my veins.

I pull into a spot and throw the car in park, but leave the engine and heat running. Clementine unbuckles her belt, but doesn't go to open the door. She knows if the car is still on, she stays inside.

When I glance in the direction of where I saw Jonas on his bike, he is no longer there. Instead, he slowly walks toward the car. I close my eyes and take a deep breath. *You've got this. Don't chicken out now. Not yet.*

"Mama? Are you okay?" Clementine rests her hand on my forearm and I open my eyes.

"Yeah, pumpkin. Will you please stay in the car a minute? I want to speak with Jonas before you meet him."

She nods. "Can you leave the radio on?" I love how something as simple as leaving the radio on will keep her happy.

"You bet. Stay here. I'll be back in a second."

"Okay, Mama."

Now or never, Autumn.

I open the door and step out. Jonas is a few cars away. I step around the front of the car and meet him at the rear of the car parked in front of me. Clementine still within sight, but far enough away she doesn't hear anything. Just want to gauge Jonas's mood before I open the floodgates.

God, he steals every practiced word from my lips and renders me speechless every time he is near. We haven't seen each other in nine days, but those days feel like months. Years. How is it possible he looks a hundred times more appealing? Taller. Broader. More handsome.

Two more strides and he stands inches from my touch. "Hey," he whispers. As if speaking too loudly will shatter our reunion.

"Hey." I lock on to his magnetic hazel eyes and swallow. Before I formulate what to say next, Jonas steps into me and wraps his arms around my center.

I melt into his embrace. Inhale deeply and pull in the scent of him—a distinct blend of sunscreen, gasoline, and the smell of Thompson's Garage. Bask in the warmth and strength of his arms snug around my waist. I would stay in Jonas's arms forever if given the opportunity.

Far too soon, he slips his hands to my hips and breaks the hug. But before I can pout, he dips down and presses his lips to mine. Shock registers for a split second, then slips away as my lips move with his.

Every anxiety-ridden minute I have suffered since we last saw each other vanishes. His lips brush against mine, slow and measured. Each move calculated and perfect. He swipes the tip of his tongue against my lower lip and I open up for him. His hands snake up the sides of my torso and frame my face as we memorize each other again. Memorize our individual tastes. The way our bodies curve in exactly the right places against each other. And the way we cannot get enough of the other.

Lost in the feel of Jonas pressed against me, in his taste, I audibly pout when he breaks the kiss. He chuckles and presses a chaste kiss to my lips again. "You have no idea how much I love it when you pout."

I fist his shirt, tug him closer, and rest my forehead in the crook of his neck. "Well, I missed you."

"Missed you too." Jonas slips his arms back around my waist and holds me close. His embrace is the most at home I have felt in a long time. He kisses the crown of my head. "Are you nervous?"

I nod into the collar of his leather jacket. "Definitely."

"Me too," he whispers. "But also thrilled."

I lean away, tip my head back, and take in his expression. He smiles, but his dimple I love so much doesn't pop up. His eyes are as soft and brilliant as always, but his pupils are dilated. And every few seconds, he looks toward my car. Where Clementine sits patiently, singing songs.

Taking a step back, I slip my hand down to his and lace my fingers between his. I lock eyes with him and smile. "You ready?" He nods but doesn't say anything.

Slowly, we walk hand in hand toward my car. Jonas's fingers squeeze mine slightly every other step forward. I weave us over to the driver's side. When we stop, I give him another kiss before opening the door and ducking my head inside. "Hey, pumpkin. Thank you for waiting."

"You're welcome, Mama."

Behind me, Jonas's fingers tighten around mine. I give him a gentle squeeze of reassurance. I reach in, cut the engine, and pull the keys from the ignition. "Grab your purse and crawl across the seat. Let's go get some pizza."

"Yay, pizza!" She slides her purse on her shoulder, locks her door, and crawls across the seat to exit through my door.

As Clementine steps out of the car, Jonas inches away from me. Not in fear. More like he doesn't want to give Clementine the wrong impression. But Jonas doesn't realize Clementine doesn't have any set impressions of anyone or relationships. Unfortunately, she hasn't witnessed many. Penny never brings dates home per my request. Just so Clementine doesn't feel uncomfortable with a stranger in her home.

"Pumpkin, this is Jonas." I glance up from my daughter to look into Jonas's eyes. "Mommy's boyfriend." Jonas tightens his grip on mine as a cute smile pops up on

Clementine's face. "Jonas, this is my daughter, Clementine."

He squats down to her height and smiles so bright. "Hi, Clementine." Jonas extends his hand to her. "It's nice to meet you."

She looks at his hand as her brows bunch together. Jonas meets my gaze and I shrug. And then Clementine launches forward and hugs him. When he loosens his grip from mine, I let him. I let him hug her back as I smile like a fool. I forgot to warn him Clementine is a hugger.

When she lets him go, she smiles at him. "Nice to meet ya." She glances up at me. "Can we get pizza now? I'm hungry."

And just like that, the awkward stage of the evening ends.

Jonas walks on my right, Clementine on my left. All of us connected. We stroll through the lot toward the pizza shop, Clementine swinging our connected hands and talking animatedly about all the holiday décor on the buildings. The sparkling reindeer and glowing lights and shimmering tinsel.

She asks Jonas if he has a Christmas tree up at his house. If he has cookies and milk for Santa and the special sparkly oats for the reindeer. I shrug and let him answer on his own. Clementine knows not everyone celebrates Christmas, but can't help her own enthusiasm for her favorite holiday.

"I don't have a tree up at home. Spartan would knock it down and eat the ornaments," he answers.

We arrive at the entrance of the packed restaurant. Jonas gives his name and our party info. A high school-age boy hands him a buzzer and lets him know it will be a ten-to-fifteen-minute wait.

The three of us sit on a bench just outside and bundle up close. "Who is Spartan?" Clementine asks.

"Spartan is my dog."

Clementine bolts up from the bench and stares at Jonas with wide eyes. "You have a dog?" Jonas nods and chuckles. Clementine turns her attention in my direction. "Mama, can we meet Spartan sometime?"

One thing you learn about children, especially younger children, is they speak their mind. It isn't until we grow older—somewhere around puberty—that we learn to taper our reactions and the words we say. Hopefully, I can continue to teach Clementine to voice her thoughts, but just be mindful of how she says things so as not to hurt anyone's feelings.

"We'll see, pumpkin."

Jonas leans closer to me, his breath hot on my ear. "He's good with kids. Licks my nephew to death." I hear what he says, but my brain won't react. Can't with his lips so close to my skin. As if he senses my debacle, he kisses the soft skin beneath my ear and sits up. "So, Clementine, what's your favorite part of Christmas?"

I shake my head and snigger. "You asked for it," I mumble.

Until the buzzer goes off, Clementine prattles on about her favorite parts of Christmas. All with hand gestures and full exaggeration. About her love of decorating trees and hanging the stockings. Squishing her fingers in the sugar cookie dough, licking the extras off the spoon, and frosting them after they cool. But most of all, she loves Christmas movies. *The Polar Express* and *The Nightmare Before Christmas*.

Jonas play-argues with her for a bit. Debating whether or not *The Nightmare Before Christmas* is a Halloween or Christmas movie. Clementine cocks her head as her brows pinch at the middle, settling the debate with a resounding "both."

As we walk to the table and sit in the booth—Jonas and I on one side, Clementine across from us—I can't help how *normal* this feels. How wonderful it all is. How jovial my daughter is in the company of Jonas. More so than I expected. But it warms my heart. Fills me more than I ever thought it could. To have my daughter happy in the company of someone I am growing more and more fond of with each passing day.

How could life possibly get any better? I don't see how it can.

TWENTY

JONAS

Mini-Autumn—aka Clementine—is the cutest little girl I have ever laid eyes on.

Not only is she a spitting image of Autumn—hair, eyes, ensemble—but she has an addictive personality. With her little hands flailing in the air as she tells me about the sparkly snowflakes her class made before the holiday break. And that she has never seen real snow before.

Part of me itched to tell her I would take her and Autumn to see snow one day. But I bit my tongue and listened to all her stories. Tales about her schoolmates—and the one boy who seems sad all the time, but who she makes laugh.

The more she says, the more I fall for Autumn and her mini, Clementine. God, even her name is fucking adorable.

We order pizza—a mini cheese for Clementine, while Autumn and I split a medium; ham and pineapple for

Autumn, and supreme on my half. Nothing about sitting in this pizza shop with Autumn and Clementine—surrounded by several other parents and children—feels wrong. If anything, nothing has ever felt so *right*.

Autumn rests her hand on my thigh and I set mine over hers. I haven't dated a lot of women. Most were one-night stands. Only there to fulfill a primal need while I pined for another woman. A woman whose heart belonged to someone else. Until Autumn, I didn't comprehend the connection Cora and Gavin share. Now, I get it.

When Gavin first flew in from Los Angeles to work, he had no clue he would see Cora. Actually, hoped he wouldn't because of how he left things with Cora. But the moment they saw each other again, it was like they never parted. That's how bonded they are. When Cora tried to explain it to me, I couldn't grasp how she still wanted him. How it was possible to be in love with him after so many years apart. After what he had done.

But now, I recognize the bond. Their constant need to be near each other. Because I feel the same thing with Autumn. Clementine is an added bonus. The little girl I never knew or saw coming, but has filled some gap in my heart in less than an hour.

Autumn rests her head on my shoulder and sighs. "How ya holding up?"

I turn and press a kiss to her forehead. "Fantastic. She's perfect, Autumn. You've done so good with her." She smiles into my neck. "Seriously. She is the cutest thing ever."

"Cuter than me?"

I chuckle and shake my head. "No. No one will ever be cuter than you." I kiss her forehead again and note the flush pinking her cheeks. "But since she is a mirror image of you, she takes second place."

The pizza arrives and we all go quiet as we scarf down our pieces. Clementine starts talking with pizza in her mouth, and I laugh when Autumn corrects her. Citing why it isn't ladylike to talk with her mouth full of food. Where most kids, including my nephew, would argue, she doesn't. She simply finishes chewing then picks up where she left off.

When we finish eating, I pay the bill and we head toward the movie theater. But stop short when we see the ticket line a mile long.

"How set are you on watching this movie?" I ask.

Autumn tucks her lips in her mouth a minute then releases them as she squats down in front of Clementine. "Hey, pumpkin. There's a really long line to get into the movie. Can we do something else instead?"

Clementine glances between the two of us. "Like what?"

"I have an idea," I say as Autumn stands up. "What about the arcade down near Park?"

"The Fun Center?" Autumn asks and I nod. "That might work. Pumpkin, what if we go to the arcade. We can play all kinds of games and win tickets for prizes."

Clementine claps rapidly. "Yay! Prizes. Let's go." She

grabs Autumn's hand and starts dragging her toward the parking lot. But Autumn digs her heels in.

"Hold on a minute, pumpkin." Autumn spins to face me. "Want to ride together?"

I shake my head. "Nah. I'd rather not leave my bike here. It's okay, we can meet there. Only five or so minutes up the road. Let me walk you to the car."

We all walk hand in hand back to Autumn's car. After Clementine gets in and her door is shut, I walk around to the driver's side with Autumn. Before she gets in, I draw her in close and kiss her. Deeper and slower than the kiss we shared earlier. She tastes sweet and salty and something distinctly Autumn. When she fists my jacket lapels and moans into my mouth, I reluctantly break the kiss.

"We're like horny teenagers," I say against her lips.

She giggles. "I really like kissing you. Will that be an issue?"

"Nope. Not at all."

"Good." She inches back. "We should get going if we want to get there before closing time."

"See you in a few." I kiss her again before jogging over to my bike.

I spark up the bike and put my helmet on. Glancing over my shoulder, I see Autumn back out of the space and drive away. Rolling the bike back, I fall in line behind her. We roll down the street and a sense of serenity fills me.

I may not be in the car with her, but I have never felt closer to her.

And Clementine… she is a hoot. I was so nervous to

meet this little girl. God, I don't ever remember being that nervous before. Where I was completely riddled with anxiety. Meeting Clementine felt more powerful than meeting parents. That little girl's approval could have possibly made or broken our relationship.

But from how everything went over dinner, I am positive Clementine approves of me and my relationship with Autumn. That little girl's approval means the world—not just to me, but also Autumn.

We pull into the parking lot at the Fun Center and I park the bike next to Autumn's car. When Clementine gets out of the car, she runs up to me and spreads her arms wide.

"You have a motorcycle?" she asks with wide eyes. "That's so cool!"

I laugh and squat down in front of her. "Maybe one day, you can sit on it with me." Autumn stares at me wide-eyed and mouth agape. "But only if it's okay with your mom." I stand back up and lean into Autumn, whispering so only she can hear. "The bike would be parked. No actual riding until adulthood."

"Thank god. I was freaking out for a minute there."

I want to tell her it was written all over her face, but I don't. "No need to panic." I kiss her temple. "Believe it or not, I know better."

She hums. "But I still want to ride on your bike."

In an instant, I picture Autumn snug behind me on the seat, her legs clamped around mine. Her arms wrapped around my waist. Hands under my shirt and grazing my abdomen. The trail of fire her touch would leave on my skin.

Fuck, I need to stop thinking about that right now. *Focus, Thompson.*

"Let's head inside and play some games. Clementine, have you played arcade games before?"

She shakes her little head. "Nope, just the games on Mama's phone. But not a lot."

"Well, you're in for a treat. Because arcade games are way more fun than games on the phone. Plus, you get tickets when you play. Then you turn in your tickets for a prize."

"What kind of prizes are there?"

We walk through the front door, music blares around us as kids run left and right to different games. Heading over to the check-in counter, I swap out twenty dollars for tokens. The girl behind the counter hands us each a small cup to carry our tokens and tickets in.

After we step back and organize our tokens, I show Clementine the various display cases and huge wall with prizes pinned to them. Anything from plastic vampire teeth to nail stickers to stuffed animals and everything in between. She oohs and awes over each item she sees.

She points to a small makeup set. "I want to win *that*."

"Okay, well let's go find what game we want to play so we can earn tickets."

Clementine bounces in place on her toes. "Let's do this," she announces and Autumn and I both laugh.

For the next hour, we play various video games, but

Pac-Man seems to be her favorite. Autumn and I try our hand at Skee-Ball and the basketball game. Both of us trying to find easy games for us to win as many tickets as possible.

When we tally up all of our tickets, we don't have enough for Clementine to get the makeup kit—which Autumn doesn't seem too upset over. But Autumn and I both still have tokens. So, we pass our tokens on to Clementine and follow her around as she tries different games.

By the time all the tokens run out, we have hundreds of tickets. I walk us over to the ticket feeder to redeem them in for a receipt. Clementine laughs when she feeds the long strip of tickets into the machine and it sounds as if it's chomping them up. Like a monster lives inside the ticket machine.

With her tickets, she chooses a stuffed animal. A rainbow unicorn with shimmering hair. She hugs it close to her chest and it warms my heart.

As we stroll out to Autumn's car and my bike, Clementine stops us in our tracks. "Mama, can we meet Mr. Jonas's doggy tonight?"

I smile, but keep my eyes straight ahead. Kids are the cutest creatures in the world. They say whatever pops in their head. Whether it be wanting to meet a dog or if they don't like someone's clothes or talking about body parts. They literally have no filter and I love it. I wish that little piece of humanity existed among all ages. But somewhere along the line, we are taught certain things are inappropriate to say in front of other people. Although, once you find your circle of people, that filter slips away.

"Not tonight, pumpkin. But I'm sure we can meet Jonas's doggy soon."

"Really?" she asks, hopeful.

"Promise, pumpkin."

We reach the car and Autumn unlocks it and starts it. I squat down in front of Clementine. "It was really nice to meet you, Miss Clementine. See you again soon."

She wraps her little arms around my neck and squeezes me as if I might run away. *Never*, I think to myself. "'Night, Mr. Jonas." I want to kiss her head, but don't. It's too soon.

Clementine hops in the car and slides over to her seat, buckling her seat belt without being asked.

"Thank you for tonight," Autumn says. "I had a really nice time."

"Me too." I step into her, rest my hands on her hips, and bring her flush to me. "Can't wait to see you again."

"Soon," she whispers a breath from my lips.

I close the space between us and press my lips to hers. Warm and sweet and inviting. She instantly opens up for me, and I brush my tongue against hers. When she moans against my mouth, I deepen the kiss. I could kiss her for hours and not tire from it.

Her lips on mine intoxicates me. Makes me drunker than her cognac eyes. The more I kiss her, the harder I fall. Fall for this astonishing woman. A woman I never saw coming. A woman I don't want a day without.

We kiss in the parking lot, against the side of her car, as if no one else exists. I frame her face in my palms. Draw her into me. Press my hips to her belly. Her hands slip beneath my jacket. Under my shirt. Graze the skin just above the waistband of my jeans.

I hiss and break the kiss. My lips still hovering a fraction above hers. "Autumn…" Her name a plea. A prayer. An urge for more. But I know there is nothing more we can do right now. Not in the middle of a parking lot, out in the open, with Clementine less than five feet from where we stand.

"Jonas," she moans. My name painful, but not in a bad way. More like she wants me just as badly as I want her, but knows this moment won't go much further than where it is now.

I lean my forehead against hers and breathe in her cherry vanilla scent. It inebriates and soothes me in equal measure. Settles every anxiety or fear I have experienced. Soothes me more than any other person ever has.

No doubt about it, Autumn is my balm. The remedy to any ailment I possess. As if made for me.

"Much as I want to stand in this parking lot all night and kiss the hell out of you, we should probably leave."

God, I don't want to let go of her. Don't want to stop kissing her. Or stop touching her. More than anything, I don't want her to stop touching me. Her fingertips on my skin elicits the most exhilarating sensation. Leaving a trail of sparks wherever she touches. Embers burning in their wake.

"Probably. But I don't want to," she confesses. "I wish I could invite you back to my place."

Me too. But even if Autumn offered for me to join her, I would be the gentleman. I would tell her it's too soon. All good things come to those who wait. At least that is what everyone says.

So why does that old adage feel like a line of crap right now?

All I want is to hold her in my arms all night. Sex would be great, but neither of us is ready for sex yet. Not mentally or emotionally, anyway.

"Yeah. But not tonight. Baby steps. Tonight was a big leap. For all of us. Let's ease into the rest of it. We have time."

She nods. "Lots of time." And I love the way the words leave her lips. Like more than a promise. A commitment.

I pocket her commitment and seal it away for safe-keeping. Hold it close to my heart. Let it warm my bones.

Taking a deep breath, I slowly inch away from her. Give us both room to breathe. To cool off in the chilled winter air.

I open her door for her, peek my head inside, and look over at a singing Clementine. "Night, Miss Clementine. Be good for your mom."

She waves at me. "Night. I will." She draws an X over her heart. "Promise."

Autumn slides into her car, but doesn't shut the door immediately. I lean down and kiss her innocently. With

Clementine's eyes on us both, I won't do more. A sense of inappropriateness washes over me like a cold shower.

"Night, Autumn. Text me when you get home so I know you made it okay."

The corner of her mouth kicks up. "I will. 'Night."

Reluctantly, I step back and close her door, tapping the roof. I walk over and straddle my bike, watching as she backs out. Clementine waves and I return the gesture with a smile.

As soon as they disappear from sight, I stare up at the night sky and smile at the brightly lit dark backdrop. Tonight, more stars appear in the skyline. Each moment with Autumn seems to add another star. Hopefully one day, the night sky will glow so bright, I won't need additional light.

The entire ride home goes by in a blur. A slideshow of memories of the evening. Memories I will never forget. And what I pray is the start of a million more memories. After I park the bike in the garage, I step into the house and tell Spartan all about Clementine. The little girl who will win his heart faster than she won mine.

TWENTY-ONE

AUTUMN

The past two weeks has been nothing short of bliss.

Jonas and I have seen each other several nights a week. Dinner at his house or my apartment. Although, Clementine prefers going to Jonas's. The second she laid eyes on Spartan; my daughter forgot I existed.

I didn't take offense to it. In fact, I found it downright adorable how the two of them hung out together. Clementine would hug or pet him. Talk with him—because yes, Spartan barked back when you spoke to him. They were like a dynamic duo.

Each time we had dinner at Jonas's house and had to leave, Clementine wrapped her small arms around Spartan and hugged him tight. Kissed his head and wished him a good night. Adorable didn't even begin to cover how they interacted together.

When dinner happens at the apartment, Clementine asks if Jonas will bring Spartan along. Bless his heart, he always finds a valid excuse as to why he can't come along. Tired. Grumpy. Had a bad day. As the list grows, it makes me laugh harder.

On a few occasions, Penny joined us for dinner. But for the most part, she goes and hangs with friends or chills in her room.

I told her it was cool if she hung with us, but she laughed it off and said, "It's pretty much a date, Auti. I will not be a third wheel." She makes a valid statement.

A couple nights ago, we watched a movie after dinner. Our nights together have been some of the best moments of my adult life, but they were also a strain. The more Jonas and I see each other, the less time I spent at the shop, and the more I considered it wise to shift my work schedule. Honestly, I don't know why I didn't do it sooner. It works better with Clementine's school schedule. Now, I work fewer hours in the evening and she spends less time with a sitter. It's a win win. More time with Clementine and Jonas.

And although we have been seeing each other almost nonstop for the last two weeks, we have yet to do anything beyond some serious kissing and light petting. Not that either of us doesn't want to do more. The perfect opportunity just hasn't presented itself yet. But it feels fast approaching.

Tonight, we are having dinner at Jonas's house. Clementine is bringing her favorite movie with her for us to watch afterward. This tends to be the trend with each dinner we share. The only night we don't see each other is when he goes to his parent's house for their weekly family dinner. It gives us both a night apart to do anything we want.

I park in Jonas's driveway and cut the engine. As soon as I do, Clementine unbuckles, grabs her purse with the movie tucked inside, and hops out of the car.

"Sparty," she hollers as she runs for the door. "I'm here, Sparty."

Her enthusiasm to see Spartan cracks me up. But what's even funnier is Spartan on the other side. Jonas has told me each time we pull up, after our first visit here, Spartan sits at the door and whimpers until Clementine walks in. Their instant connection is so freaking precious.

Clementine bolts up the three steps and turns the door handle, walking into Jonas's house as if she lives there. I laugh and shake my head.

As I step up to the front door, Jonas greets me with a chuckle. Both of us bewildered by his fur-child and my human one. "Hey, scarlet," he says, kissing the hell out of me as I shut the door.

Sometime over the last two weeks, Jonas started calling me scarlet. The first time he said it, I cocked my head in question. Wasn't sure if he was calling me someone else? Then, he explained between my lipstick, nail color, and my overall fashion sense, it fit. It didn't bother me. If anything, I loved it. Quite a bit. The term of endearment made my cheeks heat. Scarlet, of course. And since, he says it more often.

When he breaks the kiss—because let's be honest, I

will never break our kisses—I sigh and lean into him. "Hey. What's for dinner?"

We wander from the living room—where Clementine and Spartan sit on the couch and cuddle together as Clementine tells him about her day—to the kitchen. I could easily stare at the two of them for hours and not tire of how darling they are. Two peas in the cutest pod.

"Thought we'd have homemade chicken tenders with macaroni and cheese and corn on the cob."

"You really are domestic," I tease as I hug his middle and stare into the large pot of cheesy noodles. A girl could really get used to this. Her guy cooking dinner nightly. And if I get lucky, he will let me help with the dishes.

"My momma taught me right. Wanted to make sure we were all self-sufficient. Either that or so we could pull our weight in a relationship."

When I get the opportunity to meet Jonas's mom, I plan to thank her. She raised a wonderful man. No doubt his sisters are equally amazing. From what he has told me, during their weekly dinners, Jonas and his sisters usually make most of the meal. The only exception is when they have something which takes more time to cook.

"Look forward to meeting her," I say.

He stops stirring the pasta and I stop breathing. Did I go too far? Suggest meeting the parents a little too soon. Meeting Jonas's mom—since already meeting his dad—seems inevitable, but I don't expect it by any specific time.

Jonas sets the spoon on the rest and spins to face me. He clasps my hands and wraps them around his waist, drawing me near. My hips press to his upper thighs. He sweeps my long flowing hair off my cheek and tucks it behind my ear before cupping both my cheeks in his palms. Slowly, he closes the space between us and kisses me.

Fevered and intense. Lips smacking. Tongues tangling. Hips grinding. Moan emitting.

His fingers slip into my hair and curl in my locks. He draws me closer. Kisses me deeper. Kisses me as if I am his oxygen.

Over the last two weeks, I learned to wear my hair down more with Jonas. Otherwise, it ended up looking like a hot mess in less than an hour. At least with my hair down, I didn't spend every five minutes trying to fix it. And Jonas really loved my hair down. A lot. Oftentimes, his fingers toyed with the strands. While we cooked dinner. During movie time, while we spooned on the couch. Every possible chance he got.

When he breaks the kiss, I gasp and work to catch my breath. He rests his forehead against mine, eyes closed. We stand absolutely still for a moment, absorbing our exchange.

"Can't wait for you to meet her, and my sisters, too. Think they'll love you and Clementine. Plus, Clementine can play with Lex and Spartan. Whenever you're ready, of course."

I nod. "We should talk about it. Everything you've told me about them, it feels as if I already know them."

An angry beeping fills the room as the timer on the

stove interrupts our little moment. In the living room, I hear Clementine tell Spartan dinner is ready. And just like every other time she says this to him, he yips and bounces around the house. Because Spartan is trained to know the word dinner equals food. Same goes for breakfast. Clementine giggles every time she says it and Spartan flips out.

Jonas presses the buzzer and shuts it off. Then removes the lightly breaded chicken strips from the oven and sets the tray on trivets. After they cool a minute, we portion our plates then feed Spartan.

Just like we have several times over the last two weeks, we sit at the breakfast bar and eat our meal. When we finish, we settle on the couch and watch Clementine's movie. She lies on the end of the couch with a chaise—Spartan sprawled at her feet and facing the television. Jonas and I lay on the longer section of the sofa. Him behind me, his front to my back. Hand on my abdomen, toying with the hemline of my shirt. Knuckles brushing back and forth across my skin just beneath my navel. His breath hot on my neck below my ear. On occasion, he lightly kisses the sensitive skin there.

And every time he does, I groan as quietly as possible while grinding back against him.

As big a fan of foreplay as I am, this level of teasing may soon be my demise. Weeks of titillating torture. I love it and hate it at the same time. All I know is, is when we eventually have sex, it will be mind blowing.

Slowly, I turn around so Jonas and I lie face-to-face. I

brush his fallen hair off his forehead and lean into him. As I weave my upper leg between his, he draws me closer and throws his leg over my hip.

Weeks ago, it would have freaked me out to do this with Clementine in the room. But now, things have become more comfortable with all of us. One, her eyes are on the movie as she combs her fingers through Spartan's fur. Two, she has seen Jonas and I kiss so many times now, it is normal. Natural. Nothing to bat an eye at.

I brush my lips over his then retreat. "God, I want you," I confess. His hand on my lower back holds me in place as he slowly rocks his hips forward. My eyes roll back then close.

"Right there with you, scarlet. Not tonight, though," he whispers. "But soon."

I nod and bring my lips back to his. For the remainder of the movie, we make out like teenagers. Jonas tucks his hand between us and explores my skin beneath my shirt. He doesn't dip beneath my bra or push it to the side. And hell if I don't have lady blue balls by the time the movie ends.

As the credits scroll up the screen, neither of us moves. Clementine doesn't say a word about the movie being over, which means she recently fell asleep. But the moment we move, she will wake. It happens every time.

So, we stay right where we are. Cuddled in each other's arms. Lips locked and tongues a tangled mess. Hands traveling the others' body. Squeezing and groping. Taunting and teasing.

When Jonas's fingertips graze the elastic band of my panties, I gasp and tip my head back. He trails his lips and tongue down the column of my neck. I rock into him, needing to feel him against me. Even if we are both still completely clothed, I need the friction.

"Oh god," I whisper-moan.

Jonas's hands are in a frenzy—kneading my hips harder, driving us together over and over. He sucks at my skin, at the dip below my collarbone—from sternum to shoulder—nipping my skin when he reaches the end point. He rocks our hips together, again and again. The friction rubs me in all the right places. Sparks fire beneath my skin. A light sheen of sweat coats my skin. Energy swirls throughout my body, like a river from head to toe, and slowly converges beneath my navel.

His lips travel up my neck, across the line of my jaw, then return to mine. He devours me as if I am his last meal. Hips rocking in time together as his hand trails along my abdomen and lightly scrapes my flesh.

I moan against his lips, fist the fabric of his shirt, just before my body stutters and releases. He sucks on my lower lip as my orgasm consumes me. Swallows me whole.

"Fuck, that was sexy as hell," he whispers against my lips.

Clementine groans and I stop breathing. "Mama," she says, her voice thick with sleep.

"Yeah, pumpkin," I answer, hoping I don't sound too far off from normal. Jonas smiles wickedly in front of me and I resist the urge to slap him.

"Are we going home soon?"

"Soon, pumpkin."

She doesn't say anything else for a minute and I wonder if she dozed back off. When I lift up and glance over at her, her eyes are closed but her fingers are moving in Spartan's fur again.

"I feel bad," I tell Jonas.

He furrows his brow. "Why?"

Glancing down between us, I rock my hips against him and hear him groan. "Because I can't return the favor now."

He nods and kisses the tip of my nose. "Please don't worry about that. I'm a saint in the patience department."

"Still feel bad."

A wide, toothy smile spreads across his lips and his dimple makes an appearance. "Just remember it for when you *can* make it up to me."

I lean back in and kiss him, but he breaks his lips away far too soon and leaves me wanting. "Fine. Guess I better go. Not that I want to."

Jonas softly brushes his knuckles over my cheek. "More than anything, I want you to stay. But not tonight."

Pushing out my lip, I pout and laugh when Jonas drops his face in the crook of my neck and grunts. "Please stop pouting. You have no idea what that does to me."

"Oh really..." I kick the corner of my mouth up in a devilish smile. "Note to self. Pouting is my weapon."

"Yeah, that may be true. But I'm sure I have a few up my sleeve too."

I narrow my eyes at him and he laughs quietly. When he doesn't budge or say anything else, I shift to roll off the couch, but Jonas stops my momentum. Rolls me back to him and proceeds to tickle the sides of my abdomen. I shriek and twitch beneath his hands. Clementine wakes up more at the other end of the couch and sits up, watching as Jonas tickles me.

"Tickle Mama party!" she announces, way more awake than she was a minute ago.

And then Clementine crawls over and drops on top of us both. Her little fingers dig in near my belly and wiggle around. Jonas laughs as he and Clementine continue to torture me.

"Stop," I shriek. "P-please. Pr-pretty please." No matter how hard I try, I can't stop laughing.

Eventually, Jonas stops tickling me and suggests they *give Mama a break to breathe.* As much as the whole tickle fest made my abdomen sore and my throat dry, I wouldn't trade out this moment for anything. Jonas and my daughter tag-teaming me in the name of fun. Joining forces to make me laugh. Seeing Clementine jumping in the game with Jonas, it jolts something in the center of my chest.

My little girl has a father-type figure in her life. Someone she is fond of and loves spending time with. As this realization hits me, I stare at the man lying in front of me. Really look at him. Study the kindness in his gaze. The way he looks at me. And the way he looks at my little girl. How thoughtful and generous he is toward us both.

And at this exact moment in time, reality dawns brighter than ever. A truth I can no longer ignore. But a truth I am not ready to confess aloud.

I am in love with Jonas Thompson. Madly.

Leaning back in, my eyes open and locked on his, I kiss him tenderly. He closes his eyes briefly and exhilaration bleeds from his lips to mine. The surge amplifies and pulses through my veins. Wakes every nerve ending and lights me on fire. Spreads from my lips to limbs and comes back to center where it fuses together and forms a life all its own.

My pulse goes into overdrive and I breathe shallowly. When Jonas breaks the kiss, his eyes pop back open and he sees it. The intense emotion alive between us. What I feel. What I know he feels too. But we both stay quiet.

This is not the time or place. But soon, without a doubt, I will tell him.

"Mama, is it time to go home?"

My eyes don't leave Jonas's. "Why don't you pick up what you brought over. We'll go in a moment." But my eyes tell Jonas leaving is the last thing I want to do. A slow nod of his head, he then kisses the tip of my nose.

Reluctantly, I sit up and fetch my shoes. In less than five minutes, Clementine and I are ready to go. I wish for a valid excuse to stay longer, but it's late and Clementine is tired. And I should do what is best for her.

We walk out the front door. I unlock the car and start it up so the heat will warm the cabin. "Give me just a minute." Clementine rests her head against the door and nods. She will be out before we get home.

I close the door and turn to Jonas. We don't say a word. He holds my face in his palms and leans in closer. When his lips touch mine, he is so tender. More tender than I have ever felt before and I mold my body to his. Thread my fingers through the loops of his jeans and pull him against my waist. Hold him flush to me as we express all the emotions we aren't saying aloud.

Because Jonas feels it too—how deeply I have fallen—and matches the emotion.

When he breaks the kiss all too soon, he swipes both his thumbs over my cheeks and places one last kiss on my lips. "Drive safe, scarlet," he says, soft and gruffly.

"I will. And I'll text once we're home." The sentiment—those three words—almost slips from my lips, but I catch it. Catch it and remind myself now is not the time. Soon.

"If you really meant it when you said you'd like to meet my family, I can see if they have room for two more on Wednesday."

Placing one last kiss on his lips, I smile. "Yes, I would love to."

"I'll double-check. Not that I think it'll be an issue." He kisses my forehead. "'Night, scarlet. Get little C in bed."

"Night." I get in the car and back out of Jonas's driveway. On the drive home, with my baby girl in the passenger seat passed out, I recall my eureka moment.

The exact moment in time when I realized I am in love with Jonas.

Sure, we haven't been dating very long. Maybe a month altogether. But does love have rules? Is there some hidden decree which dictates how long you have to know someone before you can realize the depth of your affection for them? No. Because love has no rules. Never has. Never will.

Society may deem it odd to do or say or feel certain things in a relationship when it is still new. But societal rules were made by people who feared being vulnerable. And love is one of the most vulnerable emotions in existence.

Now, I just have to find the right time to tell Jonas of my revelation. And be ready to hear it in return. Because I see it in his eyes. Jonas Thompson loves me. Unconditionally.

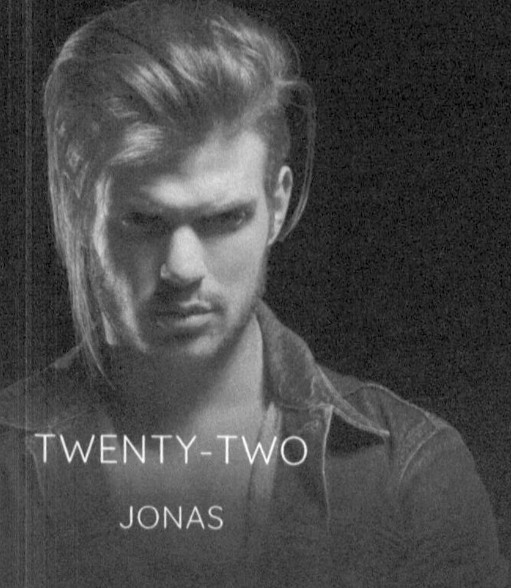

TWENTY-TWO

JONAS

After talking with Mom—who I knew would freak out in the best way—I open my text history with Autumn to let her know Wednesday is a go. I also mentally prepare her for the onslaught of questions she will get. Because as much as I love my mother and sisters, they are curious women. Especially since I have never brought a woman home. Ever.

The moment I get off the phone with my mom Saturday morning, I text Autumn.

Jonas: Mom is way too excited to meet you. Haven't said anything to my sisters yet, but I'm sure they know.

Autumn: Oh god. Should I be worried?

Jonas: Nah. They're harmless. But be ready.

Autumn: Don't think I've ever been this scared. lol

Jonas: I'll protect you.

Autumn: My hero.

Autumn and I chat a little longer. She and Clementine are going to the park with Penny and Rex, from the tattoo shop. From everything Autumn has shared with me so far, everyone in the shop is pretty close. More like family. When she first mentioned it to me, but didn't say anything about her actual family, I tucked that little tidbit away for the future. A conversation for down the road when Autumn is ready to tell me more about her past.

Reluctantly, I let her go so they can enjoy the park. Spartan and I head out to the back yard where I work on the flower beds more. Spartan lays in the grass and soaks up the sunshine for a while.

I add new fertilizer to the beds in the area I work on and plant the small shrubs and flowers I had Clementine help me choose. Last weekend, I told her I needed her help to make my back yard pretty. She stood tall, more than willing to assist.

We walked around the home improvement store for an hour and stared at rows and rows of options. We narrowed down her twenty choices to four, for now. When we got back to the house, she helped me plant the first flower plant. I told her I would do most of the rest and make the flower beds pretty for her to look at when we were outside.

In a matter of no time at all, this little girl abducted my heart. And honestly, I don't care if she never gives it back. She is the sweetest little human I have ever known. Mom, Jasmine, and Jillian will have a field day with her. And without a doubt, they will fall in love with her just as quickly. As well as with Autumn.

Halfway through planting, my phone rings in my pocket. When I pull it from my pants, I roll my eyes and answer. "Hey, Jas. What's up?"

"Mom says you're bringing your girlfriend and her daughter to dinner Wednesday."

Her words are a statement and leave it wide open for me to mess with her. "Do you have an actual question for me?"

"Don't be a jerk, Jonas. Anything you want to tell me before Wednesday?"

What? "Uh… I don't understand what you're asking. Is this a trick question?"

"Sorry, bro. Just didn't know if there's anything I shouldn't bring up. Never been in this situation before."

Alright, my sister is being dramatic. I roll my eyes and laugh. "Jas, she's not an outcast or something. She's a wonderful person. I really like her. She really likes me. And it just so happens she has a daughter. But you'll love her too. Both of them."

"Okay, brother. Just elbow me if I start acting weird."

I laugh. "Can I elbow you no matter what?"

"You're an ass."

"Love you too. See you Wednesday."

"Bye."

The call disconnects and I shake my head. Of my two sisters, I knew Jasmine would be the one to freak out more. Jillian has always been more laid back about life. Sure, she will ask questions, but it won't feel the same as when Mom and Jasmine do.

I finish putting the last of the plants in the soil and head back into the house. After washing up, I plop down on the couch and lay where Autumn and I do every time she visits. The fabric smells like her. Like vanilla and cherry and the distinct scent of Autumn.

Like a weirdo, I press my face into the cushions and inhale deeply. Only a few more hours and I will see her for dinner. I set an alarm on my phone and take a nap with my nose against the cushion where her scent is strongest. Fuck, I love her....

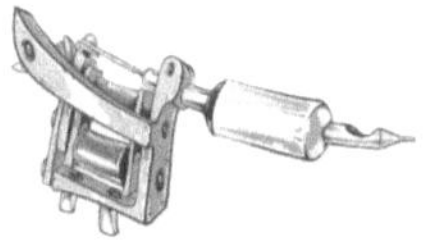

Autumn wanders around her apartment in search of a specific bandana she wants to wear in her hair. I offer to help, but stop after a minute when it seems I am only in the way. Clementine tries to tell her the last place she saw it, but steers clear of Autumn while she scours the apartment.

Five minutes later, the bandana is secure in her hair. But she fidgets more. Bites her lips frequently. Checks her hair. Questions what she wears. And I can't help but adore how nervous she is about meeting my family.

Her anxiety says more than any words. Says how much she cares—not just about me, but also wanting my family to like her. And Clementine.

I step up to her and rest my hands on her hips. "Autumn." She stops for a minute and stares up into my eyes. "It'll be okay." Her eyes dart between mine and don't calm down. At this rate, there is only one way she will calm down. So, I dip down and kiss her. Kiss her so deeply, I steal her breath.

When I break the kiss, she stares up at me as her body sags. "Thank you."

"Any time." I scan down the length of her. "You look great. Ready to head out?"

She stares down her front, then meets my gaze again with a sigh. "As ready as I'm going to be." Spinning away from me, she calls down the hallway. "Clementine, time to leave."

The cutest girl in the world comes barreling down the hallway with Spartan as her sidekick. I swear he has never been so loyal to a person before. Not even me. But any time Clementine is near, he switches to this whole new dog. Yes, he is still silly and wild, but he is also gentle and attentive with her. The two of them in the same room is the strangest and most interesting sight to witness.

When Clementine and Spartan stand a few feet away, I cock my head and take in the new accessory around his neck. A bright red bandana, folded into a triangle, and hanging proudly around his neck. And no joke, I swear Spartan smiles.

I bite the inside of my cheek. The last thing I want to do is laugh and let Clementine think it's about her. But I do want to laugh at Spartan's new attire. Especially since I tried to make him wear several similar items over the last three years and have failed. Put him in a room with Clementine for five-plus minutes and bam. Done.

"Spartan." He jerks his head my way. "Ready to go see Grandma?"

Woof, woof, woof.

"That is hilarious and cute as heck," Autumn says.

"Just wait, it'll get better when we get there."

The ride from Autumn's apartment to my parent's house passes quickly. Autumn bounces her knee in the passenger seat more often than not. Each time it bobs, I give her thigh a gentle squeeze to reassure her everything will be fine. Then again, can't say I have ever been in her shoes.

Sure, I have hung out with friends' families several times over the years. But meeting them was different. Cora is the only friend whose parents I met that made me semi-nervous. But they were hosting a Memorial Day BBQ and invited everyone. But she was the only person whom I ever had a romantic interest in as an adult where anxiety would apply.

It surprises me, though, how not nervous I am about tonight. Will my mom and sisters probably probe Autumn with a hundred awkward questions? I hope not, but wouldn't be shocked if they did. But I am driving the two most important people in my life right now to my parents' house—to our weekly family dinner—and I have never been calmer in my life.

Huh. No doubt this could be psychoanalyzed for days.

When I turn onto Mom and Dad's street, Autumn grips my forearm. And when I park the Jeep in the driveway, she practically digs her nails into my pulse point.

Spartan barks like the lunatic he is, dying to get out and run for the door. Clementine bounces in her seat with obvious excitement. While Autumn stares at my parent's four-bedroom house with lips tucked between her teeth and eyes scanning every flower and shrub along the exterior.

I lean over and kiss the soft spot beneath her ear. "Hey." Slowly, she rotates her head to face me. Our mouths a breath apart. "Breathe. There is absolutely nothing to be nervous about."

"Says you," she whispers.

"Promise I'll keep you safe. Just stick by my side." I close the space between us and kiss her sweetly. "Okay?"

She nods. "Yeah."

Both of us hop out of the Jeep. I fetch Spartan from the back, while Autumn helps Clementine down. As soon as we are close enough to the door, I let go of Spartan's leash and he bolts. Before he can bark for Mom to open up, the door flies open and he leaps into her waiting arms.

"Who's my favorite grandpup?" Mom asks Spartan. His responding bark makes me laugh per usual.

"Mom, he's your only grandpup," I say.

She rises back to her normal height and looks me square in the eyes. "True, but he doesn't know that."

I laugh as we step up onto the porch. "Mom, this is Autumn and her daughter, Clementine. Ladies, this is my mom, Irene."

"Autumn, it's wonderful to meet you." Mom lifts her hands and silently asks permission to hug. When Autumn leans in to reciprocate, I exhale.

"Nice to meet you, Irene." The hug lasts for two breaths, but Autumn relaxes the second Mom's arms wrap around her. "Clementine" —Autumn peers down at her daughter— "say hello to Miss Irene."

Clementine lifts her hand and waves. "Hi, Miss Irene." Then she leaps forward and hugs Mom's midsection. "Nice to meet you."

Mom laughs at Clementine's spunky nature before throwing a smile my way. A smile I have never seen before.

Once Clementine breaks her hold, Mom escorts us into the house. "Your sisters aren't here yet, but we can start prepping dinner now."

We step past the foyer and into the formal living room. The sofa, matching chairs, and table are like new, only because my parents hardly use the room. Usually, we sit in here during Christmas or other big gatherings. Otherwise, we sit in the family room.

I let Autumn know where she can set her purse and tell Mom I'm going to give her a tour before we start dinner. Mom agrees to keep an eye on Clementine, who is currently talking to Spartan. No doubt they will entertain each other most of the evening.

As we wander down the hall, I slip my hand around Autumn's and walk backward so I can face her. "Still nervous?" She has been silent—with the exception of introductions—since we left her apartment.

"Yeah," she says with a nod. "God, I've never been so anxious to impress people."

I lead us into the bedroom at the end of the hall on the right. My old bedroom, now a guest room. Shutting the door behind us, I steer us to the bed and sit us on the edge. "Hey, you don't need to impress anyone here. We don't operate that way."

"You know, I got that vibe from your mom right off the bat. But I think your sisters will be more critical."

Autumn may not know Jasmine and Jillian yet, so I get her concern. But if either of my sisters make Autumn uncomfortable or give her the third degree, I won't be the only person giving them a ration of shit. Mom and Dad would both jump in the ring and defend her too.

"They won't be. If either of them so much as says something off-putting, you'll have three people in your court." She smiles, but it doesn't reach her eyes and falls away as quickly as it appeared. "Hey." I pinch her chin in my thumb and forefinger, lifting her line of sight. "It'll be fine, scarlet. Promise."

She nods, eyes still swirling with apprehension. I hate how her nerves are eating her up. How they hinder the great night to come.

Leaning forward, I lower my mouth to hers. Kiss her slow and sweet. Part her lips with my tongue. Taste her distinct flavor, a flavor I cannot pinpoint but also cannot get enough of. Her hands trace my jawline. Nails scrape my scalp until they reach my longer strands and take hold. Drawing me closer. Deeper.

My hands drop to her hips and fist them as I step back, sit on the bed, and haul her onto my lap. Her legs straddle mine as if they have done it hundreds of times before. We kiss as if another opportunity won't arise. As if our lips won't have contact for days or weeks or months. Our passion is a firestorm. Unrelenting. Building. Flourishing into something primal yet unexplainable.

Autumn rocks her hips against me. Moans down my throat. The bulge beneath my zipper thick and swollen and starving for her. I break the kiss and trail my mouth over the soft line of her jaw, nipping and licking. Down the column of her throat as she throws her head back and gasps, fingers clutching my hair and locking me to her skin.

When I reach her shoulder, I stop and lay my forehead on her. Inhaling her delicious scent, I close my eyes and bask in her weight on my lap. If I keep this up much longer, every adult in the house will know what we are up to. Which will only serve to stir up more discomfort.

Our rapid breathing floats in the room as our pulses slowly settle. I lean back and trail my eyes up her neck until they lock on to her intoxicating irises. So many words pass through her eyes without a single word leaving her lips. And I feel it. Deep down in my bones, I feel all her unspoken thoughts. Because those same words trickle through my every vein and artery like DNA.

Neither of us has brought up the extent of how we feel for the other. But staring into her eyes right now, the way she refuses to look away, it is obvious she is in just as deep as I am.

Some men would be unsettled by this revelation — falling in love. Me? I indulge in it. Take it and tuck it safely inside the cage surrounding my heart.

I brush my fingers from her temple down to her lips. "As much as I'd like to stay in here the next several hours, we should finish the tour and help with dinner."

Autumn kisses my fingers before sliding off my lap. "Suppose you're right. Last thing I need is your family thinking we're in here having sex."

I laugh to cover my sudden choking. She pats my back a few times then laughs too. Rising off the bed, Autumn straightens her shirt and runs her hands down her thighs to smooth her jeans.

Once she finishes, Autumn steps between my legs and combs her fingers through my hair. "If we walk out with your hair like this, everyone will know what we were up to in here." She giggles as I roll my eyes closed and sit perfectly still.

Her touch is the cure to every ailment I will ever have. My remedy. Created for only me.

When she stops fixing my disheveled strands, I open my eyes. "Thanks," I whisper. "Let me show you the rest of the house. Oh" —I wave my hand around the room as I stand— "this was once my room."

"Fitting." She hums and nods.

Taking her hand in mine, I lead us back into the hall. I play tour guide through the rest of the house and finish up the circuit in the kitchen. Which is where my mom and sisters reside.

The moment we step into the room, all three of them look to us. Autumn's grip tightens and I kiss her temple. "Jasmine, Jillian, this is Autumn. Autumn, these are my sisters. Jasmine" —I point to my older sister, then to my baby sister— "and Jillian."

Jasmine picks up a hand towel and wipes her hands before extending one to Autumn. "Wonderful to finally meet you, Autumn. My son, Lex, is playing with Clementine in the family room. She's a doll."

"Nice to meet you. And thank you." Autumn smiles like a proud mom. A smile that warms me throughout.

Jillian steps forward and Autumn extends her hand. But Jillian takes us all by surprise when she hugs Autumn. Not that my family doesn't hug. We just don't generally hug new people. Especially Jillian.

"Wow, Jilli," I say when she releases Autumn. "Feeling extra affectionate today?"

She play-punches my bicep. "Ha ha, big brother. And so what if I am. Can't I be happy and want to hug people?"

"Forget I asked," I say, throwing my hands up in surrender. "Mom, what can we help with?"

Mom directs me to the cutting board to help with the salad. She frequently gives me the task and I wonder if my slicing and chopping skills supersede those of my sisters. While I slice carrots, Mom asks Autumn if she will help her with dessert—magic brookie bars. If there is one thing my mom is master of, it is dessert. And her magic brookie bars are to die for.

The kitchen fills with chatter as everyone catches up. Jasmine tells us how Lex heard someone say the word shit the other day and he won't stop saying it. I laugh, probably harder than I should, because my sister is adamant about raising Lex to be a proper young man. Mom chimes in and tells her about each occasion when we all said our first bad word. It only serves to make me laugh harder.

After Dad and Anton set the table, we all carry out dishes while Mom puts the magic brookies in the oven. We take our seats at the table and start passing around food from one to the next. Beside me, Autumn relaxes more. Clementine is the life of the party. And I spend the entire hour at the dinner table with a wide smile stretching my cheeks.

"Irene, I need this recipe," Autumn says as she chews her last bite of magic brookie bar.

Mom smiles at the other end of the table. "I'll jot it down before you go. Let's clean up and sit out back for a little bit before everyone goes."

And just like that, everyone rises from their seats and shuffles around to clean up. Then we all sit out back on the loungers near the pool while the kids watch a movie on television. Autumn sits between my legs and chats with everyone as if she has been here several times before. Her earlier nerves nowhere to be found.

When I check the time, I suggest we head out so Clementine can get a good night's sleep before school. We collect the goody bag Mom made us, give hug after hug, and say our goodbyes.

Once Clementine and Spartan are secure in the back seat, Spartan lays down and rests his head on Clementine's lap. Autumn and I hop in, and soon we head for Autumn's apartment.

Tonight went better than expected. Mom and my sisters didn't probe Autumn with questions. Thank god. The conversations in the kitchen and around the dinner table flowed naturally. And Autumn smiled often, as did I.

A few miles from the apartment, I stop at a red light and look in the rearview mirror to see Clementine asleep. I nudge my head toward the back seat. "She passed out."

Autumn glances back at Clementine briefly and smiles. "Was a busy night for her. But she had fun."

"Did you enjoy yourself?"

She nods before I face forward again and drive. "Yeah." She reaches across the console and rests her hand on my thigh. I swallow. "Your family is wonderful," she says wistfully.

"They are," I mumble as I envision her and Clementine as part of the family out of nowhere. Crazy how my mind jumps from point A to point Z before stopping at any of the other points in between. But I can't help how Autumn makes me feel. How she makes me long for more. To fall asleep with her in my arms and wake with her curled to my torso and tangled in my limbs.

A block from her apartment complex entrance, I strike up the nerve to propose an idea to her. After double-checking Clementine is still asleep in the back, I take a deep breath and swallow. I reach over the console and rest my hand on her leg.

"Autumn, I want to ask you something. But I don't want you to freak out."

She turns in the seat to face me better. In the process, my hand slides farther north and stops inches from the junction of her thighs. She doesn't lean back or shift it away.

"Okay," she drawls out.

"Keep an open mind and don't shoot me down right away." I glance over at her as I steer us into the complex. "Will you stay at my place?" I park the Jeep and take in Autumn's wide-eyed, frozen state. "Obviously not tonight, but one night soon."

Autumn looks to the back seat out of the corner of her eye. "Jonas, I don't know."

"Think about it. No rush. And Clementine can stay over too. The couch doubles as a bed too."

"Jonas…" I lean toward her, press a finger to her lips, and cut her off.

"All I ask is for you to think about it. No pressure. If you decide it isn't a good idea, I'll understand. But at least give it a day." She slowly nods, and I remove my finger from her lips.

I open and close my door quietly and meet Autumn on the passenger side. Before we open Clementine's door and I carry her in, I cage Autumn against the front passenger door. Her arms wrap around my waist, beneath my shirt. The heat between us wiping away the evening January chill.

Her nails softly dig into my skin as I lean down and press my lips to hers. The kiss starts off slow and steady, but heated. I paint her tongue with mine as soft moans echo in her throat. I deepen the kiss, shifting my hands to the back of her neck and the curve of her hip. My groin presses into her lower abdomen. Unhurried, her hands dance across my skin from back to front. Skimming up the length of my torso with purpose.

I hiss and our lips part for a second. In the darkness of the parking lot, Autumn kisses down the side of my neck. Claws down my chest. All but unmans me against the Jeep. *Sweet fucking Christ.* I drop my other hand to her hip, hold her steady, and rock mine forward.

"Fuck, scarlet," I whisper toward the heavens.

She kisses back up my neck until her lips reach mine again. We stand tongue-tangled like teenagers for I don't know how long. When I'm on the verge of ripping her clothes off in public, I tear my lips from hers. Her pouty lip makes an appearance and I laugh.

"We should stop, I know," she says.

Hesitantly, I step back from her and grunt. "Yeah, we should. Just consider what I said before. About staying over. Promise if you say no, I won't be upset."

"Swear I'll think about it."

After I give my body a moment to cool off, I open Clementine's door slowly, unbuckle her, signaling Spartan to stay while I carry her inside. Once I lay her in bed and slip off her shoes, Autumn walks me out. Kisses me again, but this time more tenderly. Every ounce of affection poured into the gesture before we say our good nights.

On the way home, one constant thought swirls through my mind. The possibility of soon not having to say good night to Autumn as one of us leaves. A man can only hope.

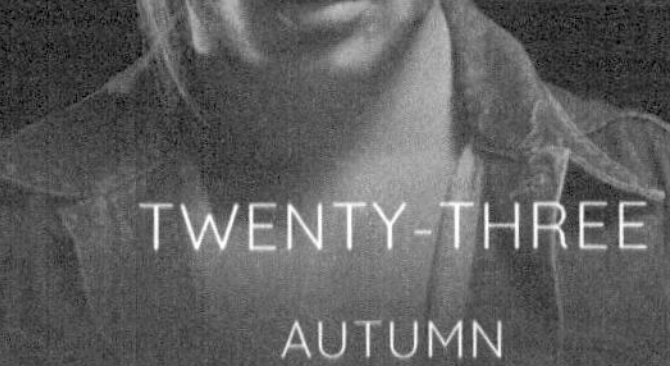

TWENTY-THREE

AUTUMN

"Earth to Autumn."

I snap my head up to find Penny staring me down, hand on her hip and brow cocked. "What?"

"Said your next appointment is here. I'll let them know you need a few more minutes to get ready." She scrutinizes my expression. "You alright? Haven't been yourself all day."

I sigh heavily and nod. "Yeah." Curling my finger, I beckon her closer. "Jonas asked me to stay the night. Clementine, too."

Penny steps back with the most wicked smile on her face. "And?"

"And nothing. He asked and told me to think about it." Now me spending the night with him is the only thing occupying my mind. My clients are lucky I haven't jacked up their art today.

She plops down on my client chair. "You are going to say yes, right?"

Herein lies the dilemma. Every atom in my body, every firing live wire zapping my skin, tells me to say yes. I *want* to say yes. But one thing still has me hesitant. Not Jonas. He is the best man to enter my life. The piece which has me mulling it over, to death, is Clementine. Not because I would bring her, but the possibility of her getting attached to Jonas.

What if our relationship is all smiles and laughter for a bit, but then something changes and it no longer is? What if Clementine falls in love with the idea of always having Jonas around, and then he isn't? These are the thoughts which have me uncertain. It's one thing for me to hurt, but I never want that for Clementine.

"Pen, I want to. Badly. But…"

"But what, Auti? Jonas is a good man. Everyone sees it. And I know you see it. So what has you second-guessing?"

I huff, hating that this conversation has to happen. Being put on the spot sucks, as does my uncertainty. "What if it doesn't work out with Jonas and Clementine gets close to him?"

Penny tilts her head to the side and pops her gum. "Honestly?" I nod and tuck my lips between my teeth. "Think you're more scared of you and Jonas staying together." My forehead scrunches and she holds up a hand to stop me from rebutting. "Auti, you haven't had the best relationships in the past. Clementine's birth father was the last person you were with, and he was an asshole. Any person who tucks their tail and runs when shit gets serious is a piece of shit. Especially after what went down with your parents."

Wiping down the counter and chair, I nod as Penny continues.

"Jonas is not Leo, Auti." I meet her eyes and she holds strong. "He isn't. And the way Jonas looks at you, the way he looks at Clementine... he wants so much more with you. Tell me you see it. Tell me you *feel* it. He flaunts his heart like a marquee sign."

I do sense the way Jonas cares about me. About both of us. Part of me is scared to take the next step. To get consumed by all that we feel. To open up, share my past, and let Jonas in all the way. Because if I open up, if I give him every little piece of my heart, and he crushes it... there is no coming back from such devastation. And if I fall that hard, that deep, and come out on the other side hurt, I can only imagine how my sweet, innocent little girl would handle it. Clementine should never have to experience such heartache. Not until she is strong enough, old enough, to deal with such anguish.

"Yeah, Pen, I see it." Probably because my heart reflects his. I pop up and glance at Rex and Reznor in the booths next to mine. "Boys?" They both perk up—eyes on their clients, ears on me. "Thoughts? Am I thinking too much into this whole scenario?"

Without a doubt, they have heard the entire conversation between me and Penny. Plus, they are family.

Between all of us—Rex, Penny, Reznor, Iliana, and me—there are no secrets. Granted, Penny is the only one who knows every sorted detail about my past, but no one is out of the loop. They know enough I don't have to skirt around topics. Penny and Iliana generally work opposite days or shifts, so Iliana and I aren't as close as me and Penny. But we are all tight.

"Think if you explain it to the little princess the right way—staying over—it shouldn't seem abnormal to her. And yes, I think you should do it." Reznor pauses to dip the needle in the ink cap. "You deserve happiness, A. I love seeing you smile. And he makes you smile. All the time."

As if on cue, a smile perks up the corners of my mouth.

"I'm with Rez," Rex adds. "He seems like a great guy; legit. And if he isn't, your brothers will make it right."

I laugh and shake my head. "Oh god." But Penny gives me a look that says *see, I'm right*. Yeah, yeah. "Alright, let me get back to work before the natives become restless."

The next few hours go by slower than desirable. With each line and dot and shading I etch into skin, I ponder over saying yes to Jonas. To his proposition of staying the night. A constant buzz courses through my body and it has nothing to do with the tattoo gun in my hand.

God, I cannot remember the last time I thought about spending the night with a man. Well, back then, they weren't men. Clementine's father and I had only been together six months when I found out I was pregnant. Pregnant at twenty. A single mother at twenty-one.

Sure, I had spent the night with other guys prior to Clementine's father, but during those days, most of us still lived at home with our parents. Spending the night wasn't so much an option, unless someone's parents were out of town. And that was almost never. At least, in the circle of people I knew then.

As an adult—a woman—this has never come up. That's what happens when you don't date. Seemed like the best decision at the time. Now, I wish maybe I would have given it a try once or twice. Just so I wasn't so inexperienced. Ugh.

When I wrap up with my final scheduled appointment, Penny skips over and watches me clean up. She doesn't speak a word. Just follows me with her eyes and pops her gum. But her gaze is loaded with questions. Questions I will answer, but not until she asks them. So, I continue to wipe everything down and dispose of my trash while she hovers like a grade A helicopter parent.

I laugh under my breath as she studies my every move out of the corner of my eye. Cracks me up how she waits —impatiently—for me to blurt out my decision. Penny has known me for years—I met her and the guys shortly before Clementine was born—and knows I won't freely hand out information. More often than not, someone has to ask for me to answer.

"You know, I thought maybe Jonas would've at least

gotten you to be more forward. But it would appear other-wise," she says, narrowing her eyes.

Now I laugh out loud. "Old habits die hard," I answer.

"Well, that's one habit I hope he influences." She gives me a snide smile. "So, did you figure out what to do?"

I nod. "Yep." Penny waits for me to say more, but I stay tight-lipped. It's too much fun dragging it out and torturing the hell out of her.

"And?" She waves her hand frantically as she pops another bubble. "You live to mess with me, don't you?"

Shrugging, I bite the inside of my cheek and try to taper my smile. "It's fun. What can I say?" Her chin juts forward and her eyes widen. "And I decided to say yes."

"Eep!" Penny squeals, a body piercing sound from her throat as she jumps up and down in place. "Oh my god! Oh my god!" She looks between Rex and Reznor. "You guys hear that? She's going to say yes."

Heat creeps up my neck and fills my cheeks. "Penny, shh." Reznor and Rex give me subtle smiles. They are happy for me, but I'm glad they don't shriek and draw all attention my way.

"Whatever," she says. "So, is he coming over for dinner tonight? Should I be the annoying roommate? Or do you want me to act ignorant to all these details? Not clap when you tell him."

Oh Jesus. "Penny, please just be normal. No clapping or screaming or teasing. Please," I beg.

"Fine," she huffs out. "I'll be good." Penny puts on her

cutest sulking face. "But when he leaves, I'm freaking out."

I snatch my purse and head for the exit. "I'm good with that. See you at home in a bit."

She waves. "Deuces."

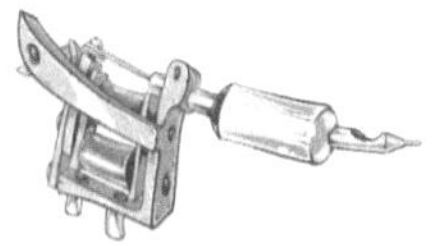

I put the salmon fillets in the oven just as there is a knock at the door.

Clementine barrels down the hallway. "Mama, Jonas is here. And Sparty." Her excitement makes me smile.

"Hang on, pumpkin." Although we know who is at the door, I still don't let Clementine answer the door without an adult.

She bounces in front of the door, eager to see Spartan. As soon as I unlock and open up the door, I don't know who is more excited—Clementine or Spartan. He bounds inside and she leads him to the couch. They plop down and she starts telling him all about her day. The project her class has been working on. The icky cafeteria food. Everything. And it is too damn cute.

"Hey," Jonas says as he steps inside and kisses my temple. "How was your day, scarlet?"

His lips on my skin always make me forget whatever I plan to say. The only thought invading my mind now is the heat from his lips spreading across my skin. When I remember how to use my voice again, I speak up. "Long."

He chuckles against my hair, wraps his arm around my waist, and pulls me into him. "Mine too. Glad to be here now, though."

I breathe him in and melt at the scent I classify as one-hundred-percent Jonas. "Me too." I lean back and look up at him. "Want to help me finish up dinner? Pretty much done. Just have to plate it."

We move around the kitchen in symmetry. Yin and yang. Dark and light. Moon and sun. Opposing forces balancing the other out. Ebbing and flowing.

Penny joins us for dinner when she gets home. We each take turns talking about our day, but we all give Clementine more time than the rest of us. She talks animatedly about the seeds the class planted and how they started sprouting today. All of us zero in on every word she says and ask more questions to hear her enthusiasm about growing herbs.

Plates cleared; we load up the dishwasher then head for the couch to watch an episode of *How I Met Your Mother*. Clementine and Spartan sprawl out on a blanket on the floor. I curl into Jonas's side at one end while Penny sits on the opposite end. Halfway through the episode, Penny rises off the couch and fake yawns.

"Gonna head to bed. Night everyone," she says then tosses a wink in my direction.

I roll my eyes. "'Night."

After her door clicks shut, Jonas shifts beside me and

finagles so we lay down. I scoot back and snuggle against his front as he splays a hand across my abdomen beneath my shirt. He kisses the spot beneath my ear and I close my eyes. Tingles ripple from his kiss on my neck to where his hand caresses my skin.

Jonas continues to explore my neck and ear with his lips, driving me wild. I lace my fingers with his. Tighten my hold with every other kiss. Breathe heavier with each press of his lips or nip of his teeth.

"Did you think about what I asked last night?" he whispers in my ear just before he takes my lobe between his teeth.

I clamp down on my lips and moan as quietly as possible. "Yes."

His lips pause at the curve of my neck. "Yes, you thought about it? Or yes, you'll stay?"

Chuckling, I spin around in his grip and face him. I lay my palm on his cheek and kiss him. "Both. Yes, I want to stay. For us to stay."

It takes a moment for my words to click into place, but as soon as they do, Jonas's eyes burn brighter. His hand skims up my spine beneath my shirt as he leans forward and presses his lips to mine. Consumes me. Gives me a piece of him.

When he breaks the kiss, I lift my gaze to meet his, and get lost in the intensity. In the volcanic eruption. Hot. Magnetic. Hypnotizing. It draws me closer and dampens my skin.

He glances over my shoulder to Clementine and Spartan on the floor. "Have you?"

I shake my head. "Wanted to tell you first. We can tell her together." He nods.

While the rest of the episode plays, Jonas and I lay facing each other, silent. And I have never been more comfortable in my life. Never more ready to share my life with another person. To let someone in and explore everything love has to offer.

And when we explain having a sleepover with Clementine, she seems nonchalant. Only excited she gets to spend the night with Spartan. It was all so easy. Simple. Perfect.

I hope our life stays exactly like this. Easy and blissful in our perfect little bubble.

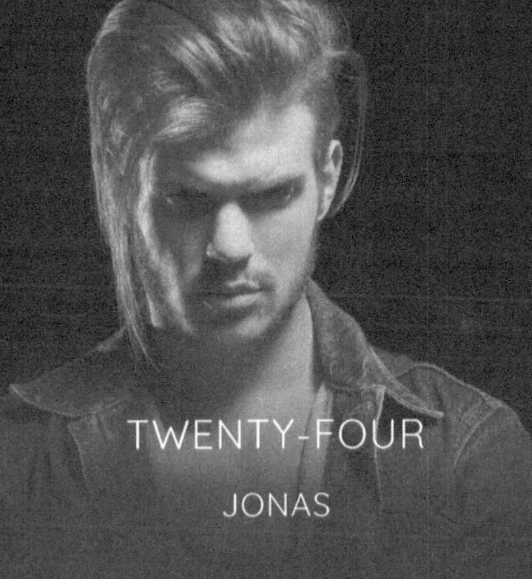

TWENTY-FOUR

JONAS

Autumn has been to my house before. Has seen every room. Traipsed her fingers on countertops and book-shelves and blankets. Stood at my stove and cooked along-side me. Cuddled with me on the couch and kissed me senseless.

But right now, I dash around the house as if none of that holds weight.

Tossing my clothes in the washer after moving the bedding to the dryer. Washing every cup, plate, and pan immediately after use. Wiping down the counters in the kitchen and bathroom. Scrubbing the toilet. And the shower. Dusting. Vacuuming. Mopping.

I woke before the sun came up. Made breakfast, then realized I needed to clean out the fridge. That very moment is when the manic cleaning marathon started. When I deep cleaned the entire interior of the house from top to bottom.

Spartan watches me with keen interest. Wondering what the hell is wrong with his dad. Tilts his head left then right as I dart from one end of the house to the other. But I don't have time to explain it all to him. Not like he would understand, anyway.

After making the bed and switching my clothes to the dryer around noon, I head outside and mow the yard. Thankfully, enough of my yard is landscaped that I only push the mower and thrust the weed whacker for an hour.

After a quick but thorough shower, I put away the last of the laundry and jot down some last-minute groceries. Out the door and at the store less than ten minutes later, I fill the cart with my normal weekly purchases plus some extras for tonight. During my last couple of grocery trips, I started picking up items specifically for Clementine. Little things such as her favorite juice and mini marshmallows, popcorn, and red licorice. The girl is fond of her movie snacks.

But today I plan to grab extras. Not just for Clementine, but all of us. Extra movie snacks and extra breakfast items.

Two nights ago, when Autumn agreed to stay over, my brain went frantic. I waited until yesterday to ask her what kinds of foods she and Clementine both liked for breakfast. Breakfast. A meal we haven't shared yet. A meal which could consist of hundreds of different options. Of all the meals, breakfast is generally the easiest. But only if you liked the standard breakfast foods.

With each day we spend together, I learn how much

Clementine resembles Autumn. Appearance. Personality. And their love for food. I honestly have no idea where they pack it all.

After I check out at the grocery store and head home, the first thing I notice when I walk in the door is the strong blend of multi-purpose cleaner and generic pine. Once I put all the groceries away, I sift through a few cabinets in the utility room and locate a small tote of candles I have collected over the years. Candles I rolled my eyes at during the holidays when my sisters gifted them. Now, I need to remember to thank them during family dinner next week.

I remove the lid from the black candle, bring it to my nose, and inhale. Masculine. A blend of leather and teak-wood. I light the wicks and place it as centrally as possible in the open floor plan of the house. Within minutes, the house smells less like a janitorial closet and closer to a men's clothing store.

A few minutes pass as I get lost in the flickering candle flames. Lost in the reality that Autumn and Clementine will be here in a couple hours' time. Since we have been officially seeing each other, shared dinners have happened almost nightly. But she or I always went home at the end of the night. And the thought of her not going home tonight has me unable to focus.

Tonight, Autumn will lay beside me. In my bed. Between my sheets. The heat of her skin pressed to mine.

Spartan barks and I snap out of my daydream.

"Thanks, buddy. Time to prep d-i-n-n-e-r and dessert." He barks again. "Mine, not yours."

I get to work in the kitchen and prep the muffin-sized personal pies. Assembled in the pan, I cover and set them in the fridge until it's time to put them in the oven. Then I get to work on the baked macaroni and cheese, coconut chicken bites, and parmesan zucchini fries.

I move around the kitchen with ease and send silent thanks to my mom for teaching me how to cook and bake. Whether it was only for me or me and others, learning how to cook is one of the most valuable gifts she has bestowed upon me.

As I slide the pan of coconut chicken in the oven, Spartan perks his head up from his spot on the couch and barks like a loon. Jumping down, he continues to bark while running in circles. When there is a knock at the door, he practically rips it off the hinges. I laugh as I walk from the kitchen to the front door.

When I open the door, Spartan launches forward and licks every square inch of Clementine's face. She giggles and wraps her little arms around his neck. "Sparty," she giggle-squeals.

"C'mon, buddy. Let them in."

Spartan scoots back. Autumn and Clementine step in and I take a deep breath. We have done this many times before, but it suddenly feels as if this is our first time. Anxiety surges in my belly like a summer storm rolling in off the coast. I step into Autumn and kiss her chastely.

And just as quickly as the storm rolled in, her warm lips against mine brings out the sun.

"Hey, scarlet," I croak.

She looks up at me from under her lashes, a shy smile on her lips. "Hey." Lifting the bag in her hand, she asks, "Where should I set this?" Her overnight bag.

This is really happening. Autumn and Clementine are here. And they are staying overnight. Not leaving until tomorrow.

"Let me." I take the bag from her and walk it back to my bedroom, setting it on the bed. When I spin around, Autumn stands in the doorway. Her eyes scan every inch of the room, stopping on me when she finishes.

Is she as nervous as I am? Maybe more. Neither of us has spent the night with another person in a long time. Not like this. Not with hearts out in the open and on the line.

In three short strides, I stand inches from her. Lower my mouth to hers and taste her again. Sweet and addictive. She grips the hem of my shirt and drags me closer. A soft moan spilling from her into me. My hands frame her face as I deepen the kiss. Consume her. Share one of the many ways I need her.

The timer on the stove beeps, letting us know a minute remains. Reluctantly, I break the kiss and inch back. "Help me finish dinner?" Autumn nods and presses her fingers to her lips.

"What're we having?" she asks as we stroll back into the kitchen.

The buzzer rings through the kitchen and I shut off the timer as I open the oven door. "Coconut chicken, baked macaroni and cheese, and zucchini fries," I tell her as I flip the chicken over and add the zucchini fries to the oven.

"Wow. Maybe I need to get cookies for your mom, too." I shake my head. "What? Not only are your parents generous, but your mom made you into every woman's dream man." She waves a hand toward the living room. "You clean. You cook. What other domestic duties do you fulfill?"

I cock a brow and smirk at her. "Hmm… I'll have to show you later." A blush I haven't seen on Autumn's skin in several days makes an appearance. And I love how her mind goes to exactly where I wanted it to.

She licks her lips and tucks them between her teeth a moment. "Later."

Soon, dinner is out of the oven and cool enough to serve. I pop in the muffin pan pies so they finish baking by the time we clear our plates. Autumn fills a plate for Clementine, then herself as I make mine. We sit at the breakfast bar and eat in silence for a few minutes. There is no unease. If anything, eating dinner with both of them feels like the most natural part of my day.

We all grab mini pies and ice cream after dinner and cozy up on the couch. Spartan tries and fails to eat Clementine's dessert, but she giggles each time his snout gets close. "What are we watching tonight?" I ask Clementine.

"Mama bought *The Secret Life of Pets 2* for tonight," she says, dancing in her seat as the movie starts.

I laugh alongside Autumn as we watch the silly animated kid's movie and finish our dessert. An hour later, Clementine softly snores on the chaise section of the couch with Spartan as her pillow. Quietly, I rise from the couch, collect our dishes, and take them to the kitchen.

As I rinse the bowls, Autumn wraps her arms around my waist and kisses over my spine. "She'll be out for the rest of the night," she whispers into my shirt.

Spinning to face her, I glance over her shoulder and take in the sight of Clementine and Spartan cuddling. "Should we leave the light over the stove on? In case she wakes," I ask and Autumn nods.

I take her hand in mine and weave our fingers together. Without a word, I flip the light over the stove on and steer us out of the kitchen. After we turn off the tele-vision and drape the throw blanket over Clementine, I lead Autumn down the hall and into the bedroom.

This is it. The moment that will change our relation-ship. Add more definition. Sharpen the edges. Bring us closer. Closer than I have ever been with any other person. Make us never want to be apart—at least for me.

Autumn closes the door behind us, and I have never heard the latch click so loudly. Facing Autumn, I walk us to the bed, my eyes tracing the curves of her silhouette as we move. The back of my knees hit the mattress and I draw her close. Wrap her in my arms. Feel the tremble of her hands as they snake around my waist and under my shirt.

I drop my chin, bring my lips within a breath of hers. "We don't have to do anything you're not ready for. If you only want to sleep, then I'll happily hold you in my arms all night. Okay?"

She nods and pushes up on her toes. Our lips connect and I roll my eyes closed. Heat swelters in my chest and blooms across every lick of my skin. And the second she paints her tongue across my lower lip, I open for her and deepen the kiss. Her heat matches mine and ignites the kindling simmering low in my groin.

I groan, slip my hands under her ass, lift her up and spin around to toss her on the bed. She thumps against the mattress and I crawl up her body, slamming my mouth back to hers. Our hands fevered. Lips irrational. Breaths erratic.

Autumn slowly peels my shirt up my torso and over my head, then discards it on the floor. She trails her fingers down my pecs, my abdomen, and along the waistband of my jeans. Reading every dip and line and ridge of my skin like braille. I suck in a sharp breath as she charts new territory and memorizes the landscape. Her fingertips sear my skin, leaving a tingling trail of sparks in their wake.

Her fingers wrap around the button above my fly and I stop her. "Slow. There's no rush." I dip down and kiss her sweet mouth. "I want us to savor this. To savor us."

I roll us over and relish the sight of her straddling me,

my palms cupping her hips. She strips her shirt off and tosses it in the same direction as mine. In the dim lighting, I make out the scalloped curves of her bra cups and sit up to get a closer look. The dark lace teases me. Taunts me. Sticks out its proverbial tongue and sneers.

I give her hips a quick squeeze before winding my hands to her backside and softly grazing them up the sides of her spine. She arches and presses her breasts closer to my face. And I can no longer resist the urge to taste her skin. Savor her uncharted territory.

Leaning in, I kiss the swell of her breast. Once. Twice. Lick along the lace edge of her bra cup. She rocks her hips against me, and I pin her in place as I grip her waist. Switch to the opposite breast and pay it equal attention. She threads her fingers in my hair, tips her head back, and moans at the ceiling.

As my tongue trails the swell of her breast, I unhook her bra and flatten my palms against her bare back as the lacy material falls between us. For the first time, the heat of her bare skin presses flush with mine. Fevered and damp and absolutely perfect. I stop breathing. Stop kissing her skin. Close my eyes and savor the moment. The heat, the longing, the absolute need for this connection.

After a beat, I roll Autumn to her back again. Kiss her lips. Kiss down the column of her throat. Along her midline to her navel. To her left hip, then her right.

She pants into the darkness as I unbutton her pants and drag the zipper down the teeth. As I peel the denim down her thighs, I spot her matching lace panties and smile. I pause to press my lips to the material. She groans and fists my hair.

I trace a finger along the waistband of her panties. "Did you wear matching bra and panties for me?" I rasp against her skin.

"Yes."

"You'll have to show them to me when the lights are on."

She moans. "Promise."

I kiss her hip and continue peeling away her jeans. Drop them to the floor, followed by my own. Pressing one knee, then the other, into the mattress, I crawl back up her body. Hover above and lock eyes with her. With exception of her panties and my boxer briefs, we are skin to skin. Her eyes swirl like the Great Red Spot of Jupiter. Call out to me. Seduce me.

"Are you sure?"

"Never been more sure," she answers and lifts her lips to mine. Sucks my lower lip. Then clutches the back of my neck and draws me low, low, lower until my weight presses into her.

Her kiss rages and amplifies and turns white hot. Has me sweltering and begging for more. Rocking forward and grinding my erection against the junction of her thighs. Her nails scrape along either side of my spine. I hiss as she tucks them beneath the elastic of my briefs and shoves them toward my ankles.

We fumble and laugh as we maneuver the last scraps

of our clothes to the floor. And when they drop away, all laughing stops. I kiss her gently. More tender than any time previous. Trace the curve of her jaw with my lips and pepper kisses down, down, down her body.

When I stop at the junction of her thighs, she sucks in a breath and holds it. I trace up the midline of her body with my eyes and revel in the sight of her. Fuck, she is perfect. "Is this okay?" I ask as it dawns on me that not all women enjoy oral sex.

"God, yes," she moans and I chuckle.

But it's the second she threads her fingers in my hair and thrusts my head between her thighs that I stop laughing. I clutch her hips, run my nose along the thin strip of hair, and inhale. *Fuck.*

As if a light flips on in my head and my primal nature surfaces, I lick up her center and taste her for the first time. Sweet and salty and one-hundred-percent Autumn. Addictive and crucial. God, I could exist solely with the taste of her on my tongue.

I take my time. Devour her. Flick her clit with my tongue and lick up her seam. Insert a finger. Then another. Watch her writhe as I bring her higher and higher. Inhale her pheromones as she edges closer to orgasm. Groan against her skin as her whimpers escalate. Suck and lick her flesh when her release spills around my fingers. *Holy Christ.*

"Jonas…" she whimpers. "I need you. Need to feel you inside me."

I crawl back up her body and kiss her as if I never will

again. She moans against my tongue as her hand dips between us and wraps around my erection. I break the kiss and gasp as her hand slides up and down my length.

Shifting closer to the bedside table, I open the drawer and grab a condom. I tear open the foil, slip out the condom and roll it on. Pressing my weight back over her, I line myself up with her entrance and wait.

In this monumental moment between us, there is one thing I want to say to her. Tell her. What this means to me. What *she* means to me. How much I cherish her. How I always will. But it might be too soon for her.

I lower my lips to hers. Kiss her tenderly. Tell her with my lips and not my voice. Sweep my knuckles lightly over her cheek as I slowly rock forward and push inside her. We both gasp into the silence. Lock eyes and hold. Don't flinch as her body adjusts to my invasion.

Her nails bite my upper glutes. "Please, Jonas," she pleas.

I rock back, then forward again. Her nails dig deeper and my eyes roll back. I drop my head into the crook of her neck and find my rhythm with her. Relish in her heat and the vice-like grip her body has on mine. I kiss and nip at the base of her throat. Stroke slowly in and out. Kiss my way back up to her lips and express how much she means to me with my body.

For the first time, Autumn breaks our kiss. Gasps and whimpers as her nails rake up my back. Her body hugs me like a glove. Squeezes. And Jesus fucking Christ... I bite my lip and restrain myself as I wait for her climax to peak. She pants sweet little whimpers into my ear as it hits. Takes her over.

White-hot heat snakes around my spine and fuses in my groin as her body milks mine and I lose all sense of reality. I slam my eyes closed as stars steal my vision. Blind me and help me see clearly for the first time in my life. I clamp down on her shoulder with my teeth and release inside her. My pulse throbs behind my ears. Pounds viciously and creates white noise.

I breathe her in as she strokes her fingers up and down my spine. *I love you.* The words are on the tip of my tongue, but I bite them back. Instead, I lift my head and lock onto her gaze. Drown in her fiery cognac irises. Get drunk in them.

A cluster of loose strands lay haphazardly on her face, and I sweep them away. Kiss her slow and sweet.

"Jonas, I…" She stares up at me with unsaid words on the tip of her tongue. Words I want to tell her too.

I brush my knuckles over her cheek and press another kiss to her lips. "I know. Me too," I whisper.

And without actually saying the words, we have both just said we love each other. The actual words may not have left either of our lips, but it's there. Pumping through the atriums and ventricles of our hearts. Ebbing and flowing with each breath we take. Rooted deep in the confines of our marrow. Consuming us.

After I dispose of the condom, I crawl back into the bed, curl up behind Autumn, and swathe her in my arms. She draws lines with her fingers over my forearms before rolling over to face me. Autumn inches as close as humanly possible and hugs me tight.

"Good night, Jonas." She presses her lips to the hollow point at the base of my throat.

I kiss the crown of her head and secure my arms around her. "'Night, scarlet."

TWENTY-FIVE

AUTUMN

I have no clue what time it is right now. Nor do I care. Only one thing, one person, matters right now. Jonas.

His still sleeping form lays peacefully beneath me. Chest rising and falling in a slow, rhythmic pattern. Disheveled hair I itch to comb my fingers through. Long lashes brushing softly against his sun-kissed skin. A peppering of stubble that makes my mouth water and has my thighs squeezing together.

Thin rays of sunlight dance across his bare chest as I lay with my chin on my hands just over his heart. *Tha-thump. Tha-thump. Tha-thump.* Steady and sure, I study the pattern of his heartbeat and lock it in my memory. A safe place. So any time we are apart, I can rest my hand over mine and imagine his is there with me.

And then the rhythm changes. Picks up speed. Wakes up.

His breathing becomes more noticeable. Not louder,

just deeper. His body stirring to life as he leaves the land of dreams.

When his arm shifts and his hand slowly trails up my spine, I hold my breath. Relish in the warmth of his skin skirting over mine. The trail of fire his touch leaves in its wake. Watch as his eyes slowly open and notice me ogling him. The way his incandescent irises swirl with love and hunger and bliss. I lose focus as a soft, radiant smile lifts the corners of his lips. The lips I want to kiss all day. Every day.

He tucks his hands under my arms and slides me up his body. Brings us face to face. And it strikes a match low in my core. Roars into a bonfire. A wildfire.

"'Morning, scarlet," he whispers against my lips. His fingertips dance up and down my spine. Create a buzz in my veins. A hum low in my belly.

I press my lips to his and kiss him as if he is my lifeblood. Breathe him in as our lips break apart. Revel in the flutter swelling in my chest. "'Morning."

He turns his head and glances at the clock on the bedside table. Just after seven. Feels I have been awake hours. "I haven't slept this late in a while."

"Did I wear you out?" I tease.

He groans and brings his lips back to mine. Slips a hand into my hair and presses the other against my lower back. Curls his fingers in my hair as the kiss morphs from wholesome to libidinous. Rolls me over and pins me to the mattress with my hands above my head as he peppers kisses down my throat, my breasts, my belly.

Freeing my hands, he nips and licks a path down to the apex of my thighs. Inhaling deeply before his tongue darts out and sweeps a line up my slit. I bow off the bed, rock my hips into him, and fist his hair.

"Fuck, I love the taste of you."

A moan bubbles in my throat and spills from my lips. With every flick of his tongue, a new flash of euphoria glows in my vision. With each pinch and roll of my nipples, white noise fizzles my hearing. Fever blazes inside me and slicks my skin. Builds. Expands. Then constricts and erupts and renders me senseless.

Slowly, the room comes back into focus.

Jonas is above me on his haunches. He rips open a condom wrapper and rolls it down his length. I lick my lips.

One day, I will taste him on my tongue. Feel his silky hardness against my lips and down my throat.

Without preamble, he lines himself up with my entrance and rocks his hips forward. I tip my head back and gasp. Solid and thick and perfect. When I open my eyes, his are locked on the line of my face. Watching me. Memorizing me.

He slips a hand under my neck and holds me in place as he pulls out to the tip and drives back forward to the hilt. The entire time, his mesmerizing gaze stays locked with mine. An inferno of heaven and earth.

Then he rocks his hips again. And again. Eyes never straying. Speaking volumes all on their own as we make love. As he places a chaste kiss here and there.

And when his lips part, when I know he is close, a new sensation floods my veins. Red and potent and fervent. It fills my vision and expands the thumping organ in my chest. Intensifies. Surmounts every doubt in my heart. I allow it to consume me and hold me captive as I bend to its will.

Then I let go. Release and give in to the glorious vibration swimming in my bloodstream. Savor the ardor dominating Jonas as his body tightens and reddens and empties inside me.

Damn, he is beautiful.

We don't move. Don't look away. Not until our pulses settle and our breathing regulates. And even then, we don't stray far from one another.

Reluctantly, we rise from the bed and dress. I slowly crack open the bedroom door and see Clementine is still curled up with Spartan. I tiptoe to the bathroom and go about my morning routine. Jonas comes in, shuts the door, and does the same. As if we have done this time and again. The way we move around each other feels natural.

When we slip out of the bathroom, Jonas kisses me on the forehead. "Any breakfast requests?"

I shake my head. "Whatever you make will be perfect."

As Jonas heads into the kitchen, I wander over to Clementine and gently wake her. Even though I would love more individual time with Jonas, I don't want to disrupt her routine too much.

Any other time in history I have woken Clementine,

she was a grump. But not this morning. And I don't know if it's due to her furry bedtime companion or she slept really well. Either way, I will gladly take the change.

"Can I watch cartoons?" she asks.

"Sure, pumpkin." I flip on the television and let her choose which show she wants to watch. And once Spartan comes back in from doing his morning business outside, he hops back on the couch and watches cartoons with Clementine.

Soon, we all sit on the couch—well, everyone except Spartan—and eat French toast, scrambled eggs, sausage, and hash browns. I peek over at Jonas and sigh. This all just feels so *normal*. Right. Perfect. As if everything in my life is finally falling into place.

In place with Jonas at my side.

Once Jonas loads the last of the dishes into the dishwasher, he suggests we go outdoors and enjoy the day. Although it's mid-January, the temperature hasn't dropped too much. And I packed options and jackets for me and Clementine.

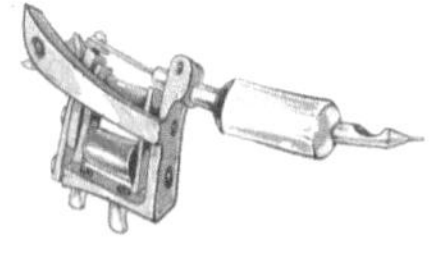

The beach in January is an odd place. Odd because there aren't thousands of bodies covering every possible grain of sand. No beach towels stretched out or umbrellas shading patrons. No permanent perfume of shea and coconut floating in the air.

In January, most walk the beach in jeans and sneakers and long sleeves. Couples huddle close to one another for warmth. People sit on collapsible chairs in the sand and listen to the small waves crash along the surf. Occasionally, you spot a snowbird in shorts and flip-flops. Some in swimwear. One or two dipping their toes in the Gulf.

I shiver at the prospect of getting in the water this time of year. Unless it's in a heated pool or hot tub.

Jonas, Clementine, and I wander hand in hand on the white sands in Sand Key Park. Every fifty feet, Clementine begs us to lift her off the ground and swing her between us. Her resounding fit of giggles each time we do has me hoping she will ask again. Because her giggles match the happiness swimming throughout my body. A happiness I haven't known until now. A happiness I want forever.

Not that I never felt happiness when it was only me and Clementine. My daughter fulfills me in a way I never knew possible. She fills gaps in my heart. Makes me smile when I have a bad day. Gives me purpose when I feel as if I have none. Keeps my feet on solid ground. Makes me see the world in a new light.

But with Jonas, happiness feels different.

Jonas blankets me in warmth. Stirs passion in my soul. Resuscitates me after years of not experiencing a connection with another person. Bonds me to him with his lips and words and skin on mine. Grounds me when life feels off kilter.

For years, I wondered why I never had the urge to date. To spend time with someone romantically. I always told myself it was because of Clementine. Because she needed me, and my attention was best spent focusing on her.

Then Jonas stepped into the picture. With his sad heart and soulful eyes, he stole my breath from the start.

I tried to fight our connection. Tried to deny anything was there. But I knew. Knew I was lying to myself to guard my heart again. Guard it from hurt and heartache and abandonment.

But Jonas will never leave my side. Never.

"Let's go to the playground before we leave," Jonas suggests.

Clementine bounces between us like a kid on a sugar high. "Yay! Jonas, will you push me on the swings?"

He looks down at her and smiles. The way he adores her has me melting into a messy puddle of emotions. "Of course, I will."

For the next twenty minutes, Clementine hauls Jonas around the playground like a rag doll. Asks him to push her on the swings. Join her on the teeter-totter. Spin her on the merry-go-round until she dizzies and can't walk straight. Go down the slide after her.

And he does it all. With a smile on his face and without an ounce of hesitation.

I sit on a bench and warm myself in the sunlight as I

watch my daughter and the man I *love* play together. I listen to their banter and laughter as she tries to outrun him and he chases her. Watch her squeal in delight as he catches her, swoops her off the ground, and tickles her into a fit of giggles.

Life couldn't be any more perfect.

All too soon, we hop in the Jeep and drive toward my apartment. The closer we get to my home, the less it feels as if I belong there. Penny and I have shared an apartment since the beginning. Turned housing into a home. But for the first time in my adult life, I don't feel as if I am headed home.

Jonas is home. Wherever he is, that is my home. And after spending the night in his house—in his bed—I don't know how I will sleep any other way.

As if he hears my thoughts, he lays a hand on my thigh and glances my way for a split second. "You okay?" he whisper-asks. "You've been awfully quiet."

I nod. "Yeah. Just thinking."

"About?"

I shift in my seat so I face him more. "How much your house feels like home," I mumble. Although Clementine is happily singing to the radio in the back seat, her little ears pick up so much. I don't need her partially hearing what I say and misinterpreting it.

A smile kicks up the corners of his mouth as he lightly squeezes my thigh. "Honestly, I've been trying to drag out the day. Didn't really want to make the drive back here." He lifts his hand from my leg, and I immediately miss his warmth. But I don't go without it for long as he cups my cheek. "As much as I'd love to drag you back to my house, I don't get to make that decision. My greed isn't what's important. What does matter is what you want for you and her." He nudges his head toward the back seat. "Whatever you decide, that's what I'll go along with."

He drops his hand to mine and lifts it to his lips, kissing my knuckles. Inhaling deeply, I ponder over his words. Smile at how lucky I am to have found such a wonderful man. Revel in the notion of how patient and kind he is, and how he will wait alongside me until I decide where we go from here.

How did I get so damn lucky?

Jonas steers the Jeep into the complex and winds around to my building. As my car comes into view, my heart bottoms out. I swipe at my eyes and squint as if I am not seeing things clearly. But I am. And I think I am going to throw up.

"Why is he here?" I mumble.

TWENTY-SIX

JONAS

Autumn tenses beneath my hand as I park the Jeep.

"Why is he here?" she asks no one in particular. Her eyes shoot daggers toward her car, where a man stands in a suit and tie with a cell phone glued to his ear.

I cut the engine and glance over at her. "Autumn, who is that?" Tears well in her eyes as she shakes her head. "Are you okay?"

She shakes her head again. "No," she whispers.

Leaning across the console, I frame her face in my palms. "Talk to me. You're scaring me."

"Mama, can we get out?" Clementine asks as she unbuckles her seat belt.

"Not yet, pumpkin. In just a minute." Autumn lifts her somber eyes to my concerned ones and I hold my breath. Fear and anguish and panic mar her features. She leans closer so her lips are at my ear. "That's Clementine's birth father," she whispers so only I hear her.

I lean back and stare at her wide-eyed. "What's he doing here?" At this point, Autumn and I talk in hushed tones. The only thing I know about Clementine's father is that he abandoned Autumn before Clementine was born. And that is more than enough to tell me what kind of human he is.

She shrugs. "Haven't seen or heard from him since he left years ago." Autumn shifts her eyes toward Clementine. "She doesn't even know who he is. Not his name or what he looks like. And I'd imagine the same in reverse."

Stroking a thumb over her cheek, I try to soothe away some of the worry Autumn must be experiencing. "Well, let's grab your stuff and go into the apartment. If he wants to talk, he can do it without her present." I nudge my head toward Clementine.

Autumn nods before we both open our doors and get out of the Jeep. She helps Clementine out while I grab their bag from the back seat.

As we meet at the front of the Jeep, the man starts walking toward us. I step in front of Autumn and Clementine and act as a barrier. The sight of him makes me sick, but I swallow it down and guard the two most important people in my world.

"Help you with something?" I ask as he approaches us.

The man does his best to look around me, but I tower over him and shield Autumn and Clementine from his view. "Who the fuck are you?" he bellows. "Autumn! A word. Now."

Who the fuck am I?

Well, asshole, I am about to become your worst fucking nightmare. Especially if you continue to talk to my girls like a dick. No man—or woman—disrespects my girls. No one.

I swing my face back in his line of sight. "Hey," I thunder and wave a hand in his face. "You need to step back. Now." I return his tone with a verbal punch. "Back. Up."

When he steps back, I look over my shoulder and signal Autumn to take Clementine inside. She complies without hesitation. Once Clementine is behind closed doors, once she is out of earshot and Autumn returns to my side, I get in this piece of shit's face.

"Who the *fuck* am I?" I belt out. "None of your damn business. And neither are they. Not since you jumped ship and left them to drown. What kind of man does that? What kind of man abandons his own child? You've got a lot of nerve coming here."

"You done, pretty boy?" He cocks an eyebrow at me. "Who I am and what I did have nothing to do with you. Matter of fact, you can be on your way. Seeing as this doesn't involve you."

I throw my head back and laugh. "Everything to do with them involves me. But you wouldn't understand such a concept. So get back in your car and drive off to wherever it is you came from."

Autumn grips my bicep and stands unified beside me. She hasn't said anything since we exited the car. Honestly, I think she is too afraid to speak. I don't know much about this guy, but from his demeanor I know he is a pompous prick. And if Autumn didn't want me to speak, she would have given me a sign or stopped me when I overstepped. She hasn't done either.

We stand five feet apart, glaring at each other. His clothes may scream money, but his expression yells piece of trash. As does his lack of human decency.

He takes a step back. Then another. Sizes me up with a snarl. Shifts his gaze to Autumn and his snarl turns mocking. As if he has a secret. As if he holds the key to her future.

"Sorry we couldn't have a civil conversation, Autumn. Seems lover boy does all the talking for you now."

"Say what you came here to say, Leo. Then leave and never come back."

The sneer returns to his lips. "Just thought I'd give you a heads-up. Being the nice guy I am."

A chill snakes down my spine that has absolutely nothing to do with the winter temperatures. I glare at this pathetic excuse of a man and try to read the hidden message in his words. But he holds his cards close. Waiting for the perfect moment to throw down.

I glance down at Autumn. She tilts her head as confusion mars her brow. "Quit being cryptic. Heads-up about what?"

My eyes dart back to him as he takes another two steps back. His sneer slithers into a smile that makes me uncomfortable. Autumn clamps on to my arm tighter and sucks in a breath. Both of us waiting for the other shoe to drop.

"I'm filing for sole custody of our daughter. Clementine, right? You should be served tomorrow."

And I can't breathe.

Continue Jonas & Autumn's story
in Love Buzz!

Jonas

When I woke this morning, I didn't expect this. For
Autumn's past to step in and rip away everything I love.
Autumn asks for patience, but with each passing day, she
slips farther from my grasp.

I refuse to lose Autumn or Clementine. Not to him. Not to
anyone.
They are my girls. Always.

As the picture perfect life I envision with them slowly
fades, the pain beneath my sternum grows more powerful.
Each passing day, my chest tightens at the loss of them.

I never imagined I would discover the love of my life, only
to lose her.

Autumn

When I woke this morning, I never saw this coming. My
ex storming back into my life and threatening to steal
everything I hold precious. Not just my daughter, but also
my livelihood. And I refuse to let him do either.

Until this ends, I must let go of my newfound selfishness and focus solely on Clementine.
Until this ends, I must forget about love. Temporarily.

When I memorized Jonas's heartbeat, I had no idea I would need to recall it in my lonely bed so soon.
I had no idea my heart would ache so profusely in his absence.

I have never known pain like this. And I have never been so torn.

...hopefully, our love will survive the storm.

Thank You!

Thank you so much for reading **Fine Line**, book one in the **Inked Duet**. If you would take a moment to leave a review on the retailer site where you made your purchase, Goodreads and/or BookBub, it would mean the world to me.

Reviews help other readers find and enjoy the book as well.

Much love,
 Persephone

More by Persephone Autumn

The Click Duet

High school sweethearts torn apart. When fate gives them a second chance, one doesn't trust they won't be hurt again. Through the Lens (Click Duet #1) and Time Exposure (Click Duet #2) is an angsty, second chance, friends to lovers romance with all the feels.

The Insomniac Duet

He was her high school bully. She was the outcast that secretly crushed on him. More than ten years later, he's her boss, completely oblivious to their shared past, and wants no one but her. More importantly, he doesn't understand her animosity toward him.

Transcendental

A musician in search of his muse and a woman grieving the loss of her husband. Two weeks at an exclusive retreat and their connection rivals all others. Until she leaves early without notice. But he refuses to give up until he finds her again.

Depths Awakened

A small town romance which captivates you from the

start. Two broken souls have sworn off love. Vowed to never lose anyone else. But their undeniable attraction brings them together and refuses to let go.

Distorted Devotion

Swept off her feet by love, life takes a dark, unexpected turn. Now the love of her life may be the cause of her death. Check out this gripping, romantic suspense.

Undying Devotion

A long-term couple with a secret life. Their friends envy the bond they share, but remain oblivious to their lifestyle and how deep the bond lies. A turn of events has her wanting to spill every secret.

Beloved Devotion

She asks the love of her life to marry her. When her girlfriend hesitates, then says yes, she is determined to learn why. As the pieces start to fall in place, she discovers she doesn't know her fiancée at all.

Ink Veins

Persephone Autumn's debut collection, Ink Veins, explores topics of depression, love, and self-discovery with a raw, unfiltered voice.

Broken Metronome

When the music of the heart dies…

Broken Metronome is an angsty poetry collection full of heartache and the possibility of what may have been.

Sweet Tooth

Two people with the same rule. No dating. What happens when they bend the rules? A steamy standalone romance with a trigger warning.

Inked Duet Playlist

Here are some of the songs from the ***Inked Duet*** playlist.
You can listen to the entire playlist on Spotify!

Robbers - The 1975
Let Me Down Slowly - Alec Benjamin
Say Hello 2 Heaven - Temple Of The Dog
Pain Told Love - Tribe Society, Kiesza
Nathalie - Pepita Slappers
Fallingforyou - The 1975
Anchor - Novo Amor
Wrong Direction - Hailee Steinfeld
I miss you, I'm sorry - Gracie Abrams
this is how you fall in love - Jeremy Zucker, Chelsea
Cutler

Acknowledgments

My family always gets the top spot in my acknowledgments, so here we go!

To my wife… the last year and a half has been crazy. For both of us. Thank you for rooting me on, for pimping me out to everyone you talk to, for spreading the word about my books whenever possible. You're the best cheerleader. And thank you for supporting my dream to publish all the voices in my head. Life hasn't been easy the past 18 months, but we've done pretty damn good.

To my daughter… you are always the light at the end of my tunnel. The one person who motivates me to do better, to be better, because you are beyond brilliant. You've accomplished so much and it challenges me to do the same. I love you forever!

To my dad… no one has championed for me the way you do. I am forever grateful and proud to be your daughter. Thank you for every ounce of love and support, for your pride in what I do. I love you so much.

To my kick ass editing team, Ellie and Rosa… you ladies rock! Thank you for dealing with all my punctuation frustration and spelling mishaps. Thank you for your amazing feedback and for calling out adjustments. You make my books so much better with your magic fingers.

To Kat… you make my covers so damn beautiful! Thanks for putting up with my craziness from time to time and letting me know when my cover ideas are meh lol. You're an awesome human and friend, and I'm so glad I found you.

To my early readers and promo peeps… thank you for reading my books! Thank you for wanting to read my future books! This author gig isn't the easiest, but you make it so much better. Much love!

To my author friends… I look forward to squeezing you all one day. Thank you for any and all support you give. For letting me share my covers and releases in your groups or on your pages. For sharing my books in your newsletters. For answering any questions whenever I bug you. We have to stick together through all this author madness, and I'm glad to have you in my corner.

To everyone who's read my previous books… THANK YOU! Thank you for loving my work enough to read more than just one. Thank you for not throwing my book away. Thank you for looking forward to the next book.

To every person new to my books.... THANK YOU! Thank you for taking a chance on me and reading my work. Writing is wonderful and crazy and frustrating. But for every person who reads my words, writing is worth it every single time.

About the Author

Persephone Autumn lives in Florida with her wife, crazy dog, and two lover-boy cats. A proud mom with a cuckoo grandpup. An ethnic food enthusiast who has fun discovering ways to veganize her favorite non-vegan foods. If given the opportunity, she would intentionally get lost in nature.

For years, Persephone did some form of writing; mostly journaling or poetry. After pairing her poetry with images and posting them online, she began the journey of writing her first novel.

She mainly writes romance, but on occasion dips her toes in other works. Look for her poetry publications and a psychological horror under P. Autumn.